W9-BEK-674

THE DOUBLE WEDDING RING

MARGARET SMITH

CLARE O'DONOHUE is a freelance television writer and producer. She has worked for a variety of documentary and informational shows on HGTV, Food Network, the History Channel, and truTV, among others. She is the author of the Someday Quilts series as well as the Kate Conway series.

Praise for *The Lover's Knot*

"Clare's first book is a fun read for those who love mysteries, romance, and, of course, quilting! Her twists and turns in the story line make this a delightful escape."

—Alex Anderson, cohost of
The Quilt Show, host of *Simply Quilts*

"A stitch above most craft cozies." —*Publishers Weekly*

"O'Donohue debuts her Someday Quilts Mystery series with a promising story about women's friendships and quilting. It is a pleasant, even a gentle read—except for the cheating boyfriend and the murder." —*Booklist*

"Fans and those who enjoy Monica Ferris's knitting mysteries will snap this up. Not to be missed." —*Library Journal*

Praise for *A Drunkard's Path*

"O'Donohue deftly weaves clever crime-solving with valuable quilting tips." —*Publishers Weekly*

"O'Donohue aims to make those who love quilts feel right at home." —*Kirkus Reviews*

"O'Donohue crafts a plot with all the twists and turns of the drunkard's path quilt. But fear not—if you don't quilt you will still enjoy this lighthearted mystery." —ILoveAMystery.com

"It's easy to get wrapped up in Nell's story. Charming." —ReviewingTheEvidence.com

"Clare O'Donohue's Someday Quilts mysteries are as intricate and magical as a real quilt. For anyone who loves a mystery or just a good story about art and quilting, *A Drunkard's Path* is the perfect read to snuggle up with." —BookLoons.com

"A captivating mystery, well told." —MysteriousReviews.com

Praise for *The Double Cross*

"A wealth of quilting information for readers so inclined. Like its predecessors, it's a fine piece of work." —*Richmond Times-Dispatch*

"A delightful cozy, a mystery to be sure, but also a study of relationships. Nell [Fitzgerald is] as interesting and unique a character as any quilt. The mystery is enjoyable, but it's the appealing characters—their friendships and romantic relationships—that set this series apart from its peers." —MysteriousReviews.com

"Interesting mix of characters. O'Donohue manages to keep all the threads interesting and the tension just high enough to keep you turning the pages. *The Double Cross* makes the point that cozy craft mysteries don't lack for high tension and an exciting conclusion."

—GumshoeReview.com

"I have greatly enjoyed Clare O'Donohue's first two Someday Quilts mysteries, but *The Double Cross* is by far my favorite. *The Double Cross* proves that old-fashioned mysteries are not dead."

—BookLoons.com

"A knotty new Nell Fitzgerald mystery in the series that's beguiling cozy fans and quilters alike. A fast, warm read best enjoyed while wrapped in a handmade quilt on a blustery fall day."

—MonstersAndCritics.com

Praise for *The Devil's Puzzle*

"A modern-day Jane Marple on steroids."   —*Suspense Magazine*

"Quilting details, a sharp picture of small-town life, likable characters, and two appealing romantic relationships add to the enjoyment of this mainstream cozy mystery."   —*Booklist*

"A haven for those who love a good mystery as well as the history and colorful ambiance involved in the craft of quilting. A good story with a dash of romance."   —*BookPage*

"A great cozy mystery."   —*Parkersburg News and Sentinel*

"A clever whodunit with a slew of suspects, amiable characters, a wealth of local color, and a generous helping of quilting."

—*Richmond Times-Dispatch*

ALSO BY CLARE O'DONOHUE

SOMEDAY QUILTS MYSTERY SERIES

The Lover's Knot

A Drunkard's Path

The Double Cross

The Devil's Puzzle

Cathedral Windows (A Penguin Special eBook)

Streak of Lightning (A Penguin Special eBook)

KATE CONWAY MYSTERY SERIES

Missing Persons

Life Without Parole

DISCARDED

The Double Wedding Ring

A SOMEDAY ✂ QUILTS MYSTERY

FEATURING NELL FITZGERALD

Clare O'Donohue

Dillsburg Area Public Library

17 South Baltimore St.
Dillsburg, PA 17019

℗

A PLUME BOOK

PLUME
Published by the Penguin Group
Penguin Group (USA), 375 Hudson Street,
New York, New York 10014, USA

USA | Canada | UK | Ireland | Australia | New Zealand | India | South Africa | China

Penguin Books Ltd, Registered Offices: 80 Strand, London WC2R 0RL, England
For more information about the Penguin Group visit penguin.com

First published by Plume, a member of Penguin Group (USA), 2013

P REGISTERED TRADEMARK—MARCA REGISTRADA

Copyright © Clare O'Donohue, 2013
All rights reserved. No part of this product may be reproduced, scanned, or distributed in any printed or electronic form without permission. Please do not participate in or encourage piracy of copyrighted materials in violation of the author's rights. Purchase only authorized editions.

LIBRARY OF CONGRESS CATALOGING-IN-PUBLICATION DATA

O'Donohue, Clare.
  The double wedding ring : a someday quilts mystery, featuring Nell Fitzgerald / Clare O'Donohue.
    pages cm.—(Someday quilts mystery)
    ISBN 978-0-452-29879-8
  1. Quiltmakers—Fiction.   2. Quilting—Fiction.
3. Wedding rings—Fiction.   4. Murder—Investigation—Fiction.   I Title.
    PS3615.D665D76 2013
    813'.6—dc23
    2013014197

Printed in the United States of America
10 9 8 7 6 5 4 3 2 1

Set in Granjon
Designed by Eve L. Kirch

This is a work of fiction. Names, characters, places, and incidents either are the product of the author's imagination or are used fictitiously, and any resemblance to actual persons, living or dead, businesses, companies, events, or locales is entirely coincidental.

ALWAYS LEARNING   PEARSON

To my niece Grace, a remarkable young lady who has given me the gift of teaching her to quilt

ACKNOWLEDGMENTS

Archers Rest may exist only in fiction, but it has become a real place to me—filled with the wonderful memories of Nell, Eleanor, Jesse, and the quilt group. Through this place, I've become friends with so many wonderful mystery writers and readers, and have had the fun of meeting quilters around the country. I am so grateful to this tiny (and dangerous) town. Those who've helped me bring Archers Rest to life include my agent, Sharon Bowers, my editor, Becky Cole, her assistant Kate Napolitano, and my publicist, Mary Pomponio, as well as all the folks at Plume. Thanks all of you for your support, hard work, and friendship. Thanks to Alex Anderson, who helped me navigate through the quilt world, and to the writers and friends at Mystery Writers of America for helping me navigate through the publishing world. And thanks, especially to Kevin, V, my family, and friends for putting up with my staring into space, random mumbling, and occasional bouts of crazy.

There are four corners to my bed,
on which I now this new quilt spread.
May I this night in trouble be,
and the one I love come rescue me.

—According to quilt superstitions, this poem should
be recited the first night using a new quilt

CHAPTER 1

It was dark. Whatever sliver there was of a moon had hidden behind the buildings along Main Street, leaving only the slightly open door to light my way. I grabbed the trash from the cutting table, bits and pieces of fabric so small that even seasoned quilters would find little use for them, and headed into the alley.

I threw the trash into the Dumpster, my last chore of a very long day, and turned toward the back door to the shop. The wind picked up—an icy January wind that made me glad I'd thrown on my coat before venturing outside. I heard a noise behind me, and just as I turned to see what it was, the wind slammed the shop door closed, locking it. I had my car keys in my pocket, but my purse, cell phone, and, most important, the keys to the shop, were still inside.

"Eleanor is going to kill me," I muttered, my breath forming icy circles in the night air. The question was would I call her, and let her kill me now, or leave it until tomorrow. It wasn't a hard decision. Jesse was waiting for me at his place with a hot meal and a tall glass of wine. Tomorrow would do.

I walked around to the front of the shop, checked the front door just to be sure. Also locked. I'd volunteered to stay behind and close up. We had post-Christmas markdowns out and everyone, especially my grandmother, had put in lots of additional hours. Eleanor

Cassidy owned the shop and said the extra work was her responsibility, but she was in her seventies and had a lot on her mind these days. I wanted to help, both as a granddaughter and an employee. And now I'd locked my set of keys in the shop.

Someday Quilts would be fine, I decided. The place was locked up tight and the only thing I hadn't done was put on the new alarm we'd had installed. It was Jesse's idea after a string of vandalisms hit the town during the summer. He'd had something similar installed at his house, and both alarms went directly to the police station in the event of a problem. Jesse, the town's chief of police, was still careful about setting his, but at the shop, once the culprit had been caught, we'd pretty much forgotten about the alarm.

Besides, Eleanor had made the bank deposit on her way home. There wasn't anything to steal except some fabric and the twenty dollars in my purse. Assuming someone would bother to try. Things had been pretty quiet in Archers Rest lately.

"It's fine," I said to no one.

But as I spoke I thought I saw something through the window. I clenched my jaw and kept looking. As the moon moved slightly I could see that a pile of small fabric pieces, known to quilters as fat quarters, had fallen over. Fat quarters I thought I'd stacked low enough to stay in place.

"When the door slammed shut they must have gotten knocked over," I said to myself. That made sense. One stack of fat quarters out of place was not a crisis. But my freezing in front of the shop was quickly becoming one. I headed to my car.

✂

The streetlight that normally lit the way to Jesse's driveway was burned out. No matter. My headlights worked just fine, and once I turned off the car, I was only a few feet from his front door.

I stepped out into the cold night and the silence that descends on

Archers Rest when the sun goes down. I glanced to my left, suddenly nervous. I couldn't tell what had attracted my attention. Maybe it was the smoke, small wisps of cigarette smoke escaping through the open window of a dark SUV parked just outside Jesse's house. I could barely make out a figure inside. A man; that was all I could tell.

"Good evening," I said, sounding cheery while letting him know I'd noticed him.

There was no answer.

I shrugged. It was cold and dark, and I wasn't much in the mood to chat anyway. The man I loved was inside waiting for me, and he was making me dinner.

After more than a year of uncertainty, difficulties, and dead bodies, my life in Archers Rest was finally filled with good news. And I wasn't going to let anything get in the way of just how happy it made me feel.

CHAPTER 2

"Snow."

I opened my eyes and blinked slowly. Jesse was holding the curtain open so I could see what had happened overnight. A blanket of beautiful white snow was covering our town.

"Finally," I said. "I thought we'd go the whole winter without it."

Getting out of bed is harder in the winter. My toes hit the hardwood floor, and my bare legs felt the cold. I was wearing a long T-shirt, enough to keep me warm when Jesse was beside me, but not nearly enough for a cold January morning with snow on the ground.

"You need a quilt," I said, as I joined him at the window.

"Make me one."

"I keep meaning to," I admitted, "but I can't figure out exactly what I want to do, and it has to be right."

I kissed him and immediately smiled. We were still in that stage, I realized, where we couldn't keep our hands off each other, couldn't stop smiling in each other's presence. We would be annoying to the rest of the world, so thankfully we were alone—a pretty rare situation lately.

"Happy anniversary," Jesse said. "One year today since our first date."

"Not technically. It's actually one year today since you stood me up for our first date."

"We went on it eventually."

"Obviously."

"Big plans for today?"

"The wedding," I said. "I have a lot to do."

He chuckled. "You do realize you're not the bride?"

"You wish."

He leaned against my ear and whispered, "Just name the day."

He stood behind me, wrapping his arms around me. I leaned into him, resting the back of my head on his shoulder.

"I have a lot to do," I said as he kissed my neck.

"I'm not stopping you."

"I have to go through the RSVPs and get some idea of how many people are coming to the wedding."

"The whole town is coming." He kissed my ear.

"It's not exactly the whole town," I pointed out. "Plus I still haven't heard from my parents or my uncle Henry, or a few of Gran's friends from quilt shops in the area." He wasn't listening, and I was losing my focus. "Did you lower the heat?"

"No."

"Where's that breeze coming from?"

He wrapped his arms tighter. "Maybe we should go back to bed. I still have two hours before I have to pick Allie up from my mother's house."

"That's weird."

"That I have to pick up my daughter?"

"No, Jesse, out the window. That car." I pointed toward a black SUV parked in front of Jesse's house. "It was there last night. There was a man sitting in it. I noticed him when I was pulling into your driveway. I think he's still there."

Though much of the car was covered in snow, I could see what looked like an arm, dressed in a dark coat, leaning out of an open window.

"You didn't say anything about it last night."

"It wasn't suspicious last night. I figured he was waiting for someone, or one of your neighbors was sneaking a cigarette." I stared at the SUV. "But what's he still doing there? Who sits in a car all night in thirty-degree weather with the window open?"

We watched for more than a minute and the arm didn't stir. Eventually Jesse moved away from me, grabbing his jeans and a sweater, dressing as he talked. "I'll go down and find out."

I quickly pulled on my clothes and ran downstairs after him. As I passed the kitchen I noticed the back door was open, but Jesse had gone out the front. I quickly closed it and grabbed my coat. I was still trying to get my boots on when I reached the front door. Jesse was already at the curb. I watched as he reached in the open window to unlock the driver's side door. As he did, the man sat motionless.

"What the hell?" Jesse took a step back.

"Is he okay?"

"He's . . ." He didn't finish the sentence. Instead, Jesse crouched in front of the man, first lightly tapping his face, then rubbing him harder on the chest with his knuckles. He didn't get a reaction.

"Roger!" Jesse yelled. "Roger. It's Jesse. Talk to me." He turned back to me. "He's a block of ice. Call 9-1-1. Get an ambulance here, and call the station. I might need detectives."

"You know him?" I didn't wait for an answer. Instead I rushed back inside, grabbed Jesse's phone, and made the calls. When I came back out, Jesse had moved the man from the car to the sidewalk, and was performing chest compressions on him. Though he was putting considerable effort into saving the man's life, I could see there was no point. The man's lips were blue; his eyes were open and blank.

The ambulance pulled up as we stood in the snow, and Jesse let the EMS workers take over. They quickly determined there was nothing they could do and we all stood helpless in a circle around the dead man.

He looked to be in his late thirties, maybe five nine, slim even in a leather jacket. He had sandy brown hair, cut short, and his clothes looked neat, though not expensive. There was something familiar about him, but I couldn't quite figure out why. Death changes a person's face, leaves it waxy and pale.

I wanted to look closer, but Jesse had my arm. It wasn't unusual that he wanted to keep me from a dead body. In our year together he'd tried to keep me from several of his investigations. What was unusual was that he wasn't examining the body. He was just standing, holding my arm, and looking down the street.

"Jesse . . ." I started. "Who's Roger?"

As I spoke, two squad cars from the Archers Rest Police Department pulled up, and four officers joined us.

"Everything okay, Chief?" Greg asked, as he stamped out a cigarette and gave me a quick "I'm going to quit" eyebrow raise. Greg had an innocence about him, but he also had great instincts. He was getting too good to be second in command in a small-town police force, and both men knew it. But sometimes Greg got a little ahead of himself, which irritated his boss. I could see that he was trying hard to do the right thing now without overstepping Jesse's authority, a difficult balance considering the situation. "Why don't you both go inside and I'll take it from here?"

Jesse bit his lip. I could see that he was shaken, but he wouldn't give in to his emotions nor would he walk away from a case. When a crime had to be investigated, Jesse was all business. He took a deep breath and looked at his detective.

"It's okay, Greg. I'm still the chief here. This man seems to have been parked out in front of the house all night. He must have died from exposure."

I pulled away from Jesse's grip and leaned closer. On the left, where his hair had been more exposed to the elements, there was a crusting of ice, but on the right side there was no ice. And yet I could see that the hair on the right side was clumped together as though it had gotten wet. I ignored Jesse's warning to move back and examined the hair. "I don't think he died from exposure, Jesse."

"He's frozen solid, Nell."

I pointed to a small hole on the side of his head, near the back. Jesse walked toward me and examined it. He seemed suddenly pale, as if he might faint. I took his hand. He squeezed it, then let go.

"How could I have missed that?" Jesse asked.

"You were trying to save his life."

He nodded but didn't look satisfied. Jesse prided himself on being a good cop, and that meant being unemotional and keenly observant. At the moment, he was struggling with both. "This is a crime scene, Greg."

Greg nodded and headed toward the body. "I'll check his pockets for ID."

"You don't need to." Jesse's voice was deep, solemn. "His name was Roger Leighton."

Greg looked at the dead man's face. "Was he from town? He doesn't look familiar."

Jesse shook his head. "No. He wasn't from here. I'm the only person in Archers Rest who would have known him."

CHAPTER 3

"I have to call Anna." Jesse was pacing in his kitchen; his hands were shaking.

We'd waited in the cold until the coroner's office came and removed the body and the car had been examined for evidence, then towed to the police parking lot. By the time we'd come in, I was freezing. And worried.

"You still haven't told me who he is."

Jesse sat at the kitchen table. I put a cup of hot coffee in front of him and he drank about half of it before looking up at me. "I met him right after I got out of the police academy. He'd been on the force for maybe ten months when I arrived, but he called me 'the rookie' whenever we saw each other." Jesse smiled at the memory. "Later, when I made detective, we became partners."

"You worked in vice."

Jesse didn't talk about his days working in the New York City Police Department very often. Unlike me, he'd grown up in Archers Rest. He attended college nearby and married Lizzie, his college sweetheart. His dream had always been to be a New York City police detective, so they moved to the city. Within a few years, Jesse had everything he'd wanted: a beautiful wife, a newborn daughter, and a detective's badge. Then Lizzie was diagnosed with cancer.

They returned to be near family and live a quieter life in Archers Rest. Months later, Jesse was a widower and the chief of police of a small upstate New York town.

"Did he say anything to you?" Jesse asked.

"Last night? No. Not a word."

"But you're sure he was alive."

I nodded. "He was smoking a cigarette. I couldn't see much, but I could definitely tell that."

"He said he'd given that up when Lizzie was diagnosed with breast cancer. Roger and Anna both. They said they didn't want to smoke around her, so they both stopped."

"I guess he started again. Unless . . . all I really saw was that it was a man. I didn't look that closely. I didn't know I'd need to. Besides it was freezing and you were waiting inside."

He nodded and then, more to himself than me, he asked. "Why didn't he just come to the door? Why didn't he call? It must have been important for him to drive all the way here. If he had just come to the door . . ."

Jesse was doing what we all do after a tragedy, torturing himself with the "what ifs" and the "whys" that never find satisfying answers. I had a theory about why Roger hadn't come to the door, but I hesitated to say it. Maybe he wanted to speak with Jesse alone about some problem, working up the courage with a cigarette. Then, when he saw me go into the house, he might have sat in the car and waited for me to leave. But I didn't leave, and whatever trouble he was running from caught up with him as he waited. That was my "what if"—what if I had left instead of spending the night, would Jesse's friend still be alive?

"Was he involved in anything that might . . ." I tried to say it gently, but it was a hard question to ask about a friend.

Jesse seemed to be thinking the same thing. "He was very straight and narrow when we worked together. Everything by the book," he said. "He was a good guy. He was the best cop I ever worked with."

"Maybe it didn't have anything to do with work. He might have driven up here looking for someone he could trust."

"Well, he obviously didn't come to the right person." Jesse leaned back in his chair. "I need to call my mom and tell her to keep Allie a little while longer. I don't want her coming back to crime scene tape."

"I already called," I assured him. "She's taking Allie to the movies. She said she can keep her another night if you like."

He sighed. It was just after nine a.m., and the day was already too long. Jesse looked ready to collapse into bed, and I wished he had the freedom to do that. But I also knew he wouldn't.

"When was the last time you spoke to Roger?" I asked.

"I don't know. A couple of years ago, maybe longer. We lost touch. We had . . ." There was a catch in his throat. "We had a falling out."

"About what?"

"It doesn't matter."

That hurt a little, his shutting me out, but I tried not to take it personally. "Is Anna his wife?"

"I think so. I mean I'd heard through friends that they were separated. I don't know if they got divorced, though. They were always breaking up and getting back together. Lizzie used to say she never knew whether to address the Christmas cards to Mr. and Mrs. Leighton, or just Current Occupant."

"And you don't know why he would be parked outside your house?"

"No idea. The last time he was in town was for Lizzie's funeral, and that was more than three years ago."

"But someone knew he would be here. Or else how would the killer have found him?"

"Why didn't he just call me?" As he said the words, Jesse

grimaced. It was as if he knew why but couldn't say the reason out loud.

Maybe a change of subject would help, I thought. "Did you open the back door this morning? Or forget to lock it last night?"

"No. Wasn't it locked?"

"It was wide open when I came downstairs."

"I'm sure it's nothing. Just a faulty lock and a good wind."

"But the alarm . . ."

"We were distracted." He smiled. "And when Allie's not here I'm less paranoid about safety." He got up and put his coffee cup in the sink. "I should go to the station and see if Greg has come up with anything."

I stood in the doorway. "Jesse, I know you're used to being strong and doing everything on your own. But we're together now. You don't have to go through this alone."

He stared at me, tears welling up in his eyes. For a moment, I couldn't tell what he was going to do, but he wrapped his arm around my waist and pulled me toward him. We held each other for a long time, saying nothing. I could feel his tears on my shoulder so I held on as tightly as I could.

✄

After he left, I stayed behind to clean up. We'd left the bed unmade and last night's dinner dishes in the sink. It was very little, but I wanted Jesse to come home to a clean house after what I knew would be a very tough day. But even after the house was sparkling, I still lingered. I found myself wandering into the living room, looking at the photos he kept there. There were two of Jesse and me together, at a carnival over the summer, and with Allie at Christmas just a few weeks ago.

And there were photos of Lizzie. She was very pretty. She was petite, maybe five foot three, with short blond hair and a bright, beaming smile. They'd made an interesting couple to look at. Jesse was over six feet, dark hair, glasses, and had the serious expression of a man much older than he was.

As I looked at a photo of the two of them on a beach vacation somewhere, I felt a little inadequate. I knew it was the natural thing to do after someone has died, but no one had ever said a bad word about Lizzie. All I ever heard was how friendly, how patient, how understanding . . . how everything she was. And how much in love Jesse had been with her.

I put the beach photo down when another caught my eye. I hadn't spent much time looking at it in the past. It was Jesse, Lizzie, and another couple at a party. The woman was a dark blond, very stylishly dressed. The man had his arm around her. He looked happy. This was where I'd seen Roger Leighton. Both couples were smiling, celebrating something. It had been taken maybe five years before and already two of the people in it were dead.

"Well, that's an unhappy thought," I said to myself.

I put the photo back where it was and looked around for my things. I had to go to work, and I had lots of calls to make about the wedding. The wedding—just the idea of it made me smile. My grandmother Eleanor, after decades of being a widow, had fallen in love. She was a nervous and excited bride, and I was the maid of honor. Not many women get to help plan their grandmother's wedding, but she was more than that to me. She was my friend, my employer, and my housemate. It was too happy an occasion to be ruined by anything. Even by this.

I grabbed my coat and got ready to leave for work, but there was something else I had to do. I walked to the back door and checked it once again. The lock certainly seemed sturdy to me, but that door was definitely open when I'd come downstairs a couple of hours ago. I knew it had been locked the night before. Jesse is the king of careful. But when I mentioned it, he hadn't been concerned. Maybe I shouldn't be either. Except I was. I looked for scratch marks around the key, or a sign of a break-in at the doorjamb. There was none, which should have reassured me. But I couldn't erase the nagging fear that someone had walked into the kitchen last night while Jesse and I were asleep upstairs. The alarm on the panel next to the door was switched off. Had we really forgotten to set the alarm when we went upstairs? Or had someone else done it? The code was Allie's birthday, not something an ordinary burglar would know. But nothing was taken, so ordinary or not, Jesse hadn't been robbed. Another thought crept in. Could it have been Roger's killer? What did he want? And would be come back? A chill went down my back.

As I left Jesse's house, triple-checking that the door was locked behind me, I looked around. The car was gone; the street was quiet. I walked over to the burned-out streetlamp that prevented me from seeing into the car. I couldn't get a great view of it, but I could tell one thing: the bulb under the large glass cover wasn't burned out. It was missing.

CHAPTER 4

I'd only been quilting for a little over a year and I'd already tried my hand at most techniques—from hand appliqué to longarm quilting. I'd carefully re-created quilts from patterns as old as the Civil War, done more than a few traditional pieced and appliquéd quilts, and had even started dying my own fabrics for mixed media art quilts, with photographs and painted touches.

And while I loved both the traditional designs and the innovative patterns that we stocked for sale, lately I'd been coming up with ideas of my own. I'd made several quilts that hung around the shop, all my own design, though they borrowed from previous traditions. I liked building on what had come before—seeing what was old in a new light, and paying homage to the women, and the men, who had been creating quilts for centuries.

At the moment, I was playing with a new idea, a quilt that combined the clean, geometric lines of the modern quilt movement with William Morris–inspired appliqué. When I was playing around with the design on paper I was worried it would be a mishmash of styles, but as I cut the fabric I could already tell it would work. I'd cut squares out of several shades of solid gray in sizes from four inches to twelve. I'd arranged the pieces on a design board to make a top that seemed like randomly placed squares of varying

Dillsburg Area Public Library

**17 South Baltimore St.
Dillsburg, PA 17019**

sizes, but was in fact a carefully planned puzzle. Then I cut large flowers from solid purples, blues, and greens that I intended to appliqué over the squares. What was a very simple, very modern quilt top would soon be something entirely of my imagination.

Twenty-four hours earlier I imagined I would spend the day behind the counter happily hand-appliquéing my flowers, helping customers, and passing the day quietly. But I'd already given up on that plan. I knew word of Jesse's friend's death would get out, and Someday Quilts would be the go-to place for everyone who wanted to be the first to know.

All the information I could provide was what I had seen—cigarette smoke last night and a dead man this morning. Beyond that, I wasn't going to be much help to the curious. Jesse's years in New York and his marriage to Lizzie were big blanks in our relationship. I knew about his childhood and about his life now, but that period—the time in New York City with Lizzie—he glossed over as if it were too painful to discuss. I didn't ask him about it. I guess I'd always been afraid of his admitting that his life now paled in comparison to those years.

I stopped by the house to change clothes and get the keys. Eleanor had been distracted by the news, so thankfully she didn't give me a hard time about letting the shop door lock behind me. She just handed the keys over and told me that she'd be at Someday later, once she'd done some shopping. She was doing a lot of shopping these days, but who could blame her? It was nice to see her so happy.

I drove to Main Street, parked, and got out, but somehow I wasn't ready to walk the few feet to the shop. Instead I stood quietly, breathing in the cold, crisp air and readying myself for the day. I felt overwhelmed, unprepared for Jesse's grief, and maybe even a little uncertain of the memories it would bring back for him. At twenty-seven, I was only a few years younger than Jesse, but I was definitely out of my league in life experience. A broken engagement, a move

Dillsburg Area Public Library

17 South Baltimore St.
Dillsburg, PA 17019

from New York City to Archers Rest, and a reboot of my career from magazines to art school was big for me, but it could hardly compare to his responsibilities and the sudden, irrevocable changes he'd been forced to endure.

I wanted to help him. And while I could do my usual snooping, being the town's Miss Marple wasn't going to be enough this time. What would be enough, I wasn't sure.

After a minute I forced myself to move toward the shop. I was being overly dramatic, I decided. Jesse and I were fine; nothing had changed between us, or would. Whatever part of his past had come looking for him last night, it wouldn't get in the way of his future, and that was with me.

The certainty felt good for a moment, the day seemed a little brighter. I was in charge of my life again. But that didn't last. I put the key into the lock of the shop's door, and pushed the door open. I assumed everything would be just as I had left it except for the one pile of easily righted, overturned fat quarters from the night before.

But it was a mess.

"What happened?" Natalie was suddenly behind me as I opened the door. Natalie was my age but had already been married for six years and had two kids. And the tone in her voice was the same one she had whenever her kids got into trouble.

"I didn't do anything," I protested. "I left the shop neat and tidy, like always."

"And then a hurricane went through it?"

She was right. Just yesterday Natalie and I had spent several hours making fat quarters, an oddly soothing and repetitive job. Once a fabric got low on the bolt, we'd cut the remainder into half yards of fabric, then cut that piece into half vertically, making pieces that were eighteen inches by twenty-four, instead of the normal quarter yard of nine by forty-four. The yardage is the same, but for many quilt projects the rectangle works better than a long, narrow strip.

But all the fat quarters we'd made, all three hundred of them, were now scattered on the floor. The decorative yarns that had been arranged in a basket by the back wall were thrown about as well. Even a freestanding pattern rack had been toppled.

"It wasn't like this when I left," I said. "The wind closed the door behind me. . . ."

"The wind didn't do this much damage."

"I was the only one here."

As the words came out of my mouth, both of us saw something dash by. Natalie jumped. In only seconds she had lifted herself up and was now on the cutting table.

"We've got mice," Natalie said.

"It was black and white. I don't think there are multicolored mice," I told her. "Are there?"

"How would I know?"

I took a deep breath and headed toward whatever it was. I grabbed a yardstick as my weapon, suddenly realizing that a quilt shop has a lot of sharp instruments—we had forty scissors and rotary cutters lining a wall—but none of them are useful unless you want to get up close and cause a lot of damage. I didn't plan on doing either. If it was a mouse, and I was very much hoping it wasn't, then I intended to persuade it to leave by whatever means would allow me to keep my distance.

Behind me I heard, "Don't come in here."

I turned around and saw Natalie call out a warning to Eleanor. Barney, her faithful and now deaf golden retriever, beside her.

"Don't listen to her." I gestured toward the pair. "Barney go in there and sniff out the mouse."

I yielded my yardstick to his doggy senses. He might be quite old and gray, nearly fourteen now, but he could still smell.

"What are you talking about—and what happened?" Eleanor dropped a shopping bag on the floor and came toward me. Although she was seventy-four, my grandmother didn't need a yardstick to get rid of mice. She had authority even vermin would understand.

As she got to my side, Barney ran past us and into the classroom. We held quilt meetings there every Friday and dozens of classes in every kind of quilting we could think of—from beginner nine-patches to elaborate art quilts. And now it was infested. Where there was one mouse . . . I shuddered to think.

From the classroom we heard Barney bark. A low, excited bark. It wasn't loud or full of warning. It almost seemed like he wanted to play. He barked again. And then there was a weird, long growl. Very angry, and definitely not coming from the dog.

Eleanor went first. I followed. Natalie stayed on the cutting table and yelled after us, "Tell me what you find."

In the classroom, Barney was barking into a basket of one-and-a-half-inch strips, leftovers from a class Eleanor had taught on scrap quilting. Something in the pile was moving.

"What is it, Barney?" Eleanor approached slowly.

Barney looked up at her, excited, happy. Whatever it was, he wasn't afraid.

Eleanor got closer and I moved closer, too. Suddenly, a paw came out of the scraps. I jumped back.

"What was . . ."

Then, a head. A furry little head that was white with black spots, as if a cow had been turned into . . . a kitten.

"Oh, how cute. . . ." I reached out and got a scratch. The head disappeared into the basket of fabric scraps, letting out a small hiss as a warning.

"Leave her alone. She's scared." Eleanor grabbed Barney's collar and brought him to the office, shutting the door behind him.

Natalie was suddenly behind me.

"It's a kitten, by the looks of it," I told her.

"Let me see." She practically ran into the classroom. Now she was brave.

✂

For an hour, three grown women and a dog waited patiently for the kitten to come out of her hiding place in the basket. I ran to the store for cat food, Natalie went across the street to the coffee shop for milk, and Eleanor sat quietly on the floor near the cat, speaking softly. Barney whimpered in the office, feeling—justifiably—shut out, when all he wanted was to make friends.

Finally, after we'd given up and gone back to work, helping customers and cutting fabric and explaining to the dozen or so people who asked that, yes, there had been a death at Jesse's but there was no news on that front, a little meow came from the classroom.

I moved as quietly as I could. The little thing was gobbling up the cat food as if it hadn't eaten in days. Make that weeks. Once I was able to see it, it was clear it couldn't be more than a few months old. And it was so thin I worried that the poor little thing might not live through the day.

"What do we call it?" I asked.

"Her." Eleanor was the only one the kitten would let near her, and we had to trust that she had determined the gender correctly.

"Scraps," Natalie suggested.

"Calico?" I offered.

Eleanor shook her head. "The black spots on her head look like a four patch to me. Let's call her Patch."

At that the kitten meowed, which we assumed was approval.

CHAPTER 5

After she ate, Patch found a folded quilt on a back table. It was a good choice; a brightly colored churn dash that Eleanor had made as a sample of the new batik fabrics. I'd meant to hang it, but that would have to wait. Patch plopped herself in the middle of it and promptly fell asleep.

Despite the crazy introduction, she had made it a happy morning, and I'd almost forgotten about my unfinished quilt, my to-do list for the wedding, and the death at Jesse's. Until the phone rang.

"It's me." Jesse sounded tired and it was only one o'clock. "Lunch?"

"Jitters?"

"I'll be there in five." He hung up. A nine-word conversation that told me what I needed to know. Jesse was overwhelmed and sad. Although I obviously didn't want him to be feeling the way he was, I was happy that he'd reached out to me for comfort.

I walked across the street to Jitters, my favorite hangout in town, and not just for the coffee. The owner, Carrie Brown, was a member of the shop's Friday quilt group and a close friend. Both Carrie and I were transplants. She'd arrived in Archers Rest just a few years before I had. She was more settled, two kids and a business, but we bonded over the Archers Rest quirks we didn't always understand. The one thing we both got used to quickly was how fast news spread in town, and Jitters was gossip central.

She poured me my favorite blend before I'd even ordered, handed me a chocolate cupcake, and sighed. "I've been hearing the news all morning and I don't know which I want to ask about more, the kitten or the body. Do you have a name?"

"Patch."

"Patch? Was he a pirate?"

"A pirate?" It took me a second to catch on. "No, the *kitten's* name is Patch, short for Four Patch, I think. The man at Jesse's was named Roger Leighton. Jesse's police partner from his days in New York."

"How is Jesse?"

"Sad. Feeling like he let Roger down somehow," I said. "I don't know what he could have done differently. Roger only came into town last night."

"Last night?" Carrie stared off into space for a moment, thinking. "What did Roger look like?"

"Ordinary, I guess. He was average height, late thirties, light brown hair . . ."

"Black leather jacket and jeans?"

"Yes. How did you know?"

He was in here last night," Carrie said. "He had green tea and a gluten-free cookie. He asked if it was organic, which it is."

"What time?"

"Seven, seven-fifteen. It was weird. He wanted his tea in a to-go cup, but then he sat at that table. . . ." She pointed toward a table near the window. "I saw him watching across the street, right at Someday Quilts, like he was, you know, casing the joint."

"You watch too many movies."

"What would you call a man who sits and stares at a business, watching people come and go?"

I shrugged. "Casing the joint, I guess."

"Okay then." She sounded victorious. All the members of my grandmother's quilt group, myself and Carrie included, had turned ourselves into amateur sleuths. Or busybodies, depending on who was doing the describing. In either case, we prided ourselves on our growing knowledge of crime and crime terminology.

"Did he do anything other than stare?"

"No. But I did mention that the chief of police's girlfriend worked at the shop. Just to make it clear there was no point in trying to rob it," she said. "And he had the funniest answer."

Carrie poured another coffee and plated another cupcake. She nodded to someone behind me, and I saw that it was Jesse. "On the house," she said. "I'm sorry about your friend."

Jesse took a long drink from his coffee. "Thanks, Carrie," he said. "Nell, you want to sit on the couch?" He posed it like a question, but he was already walking toward it.

"In a second," I called after him. "What did Roger say, Carrie?"

She leaned in and whispered, "He said, 'I hope she likes heartache.'"

✂

Jesse and I settled into the big purple couch by the window. I was watching him, but he was staring past me at a mural I'd painted on the wall when Carrie first opened the place.

"You're very talented," he said. "You could be a painter, if that's what you want to do."

I'd often wondered what career I'd pursue when I finished art school in the spring, and I was happy to talk about it with Jesse. But not now. Not when I could see he was using it to avoid discussing what was really on his mind.

"Have you learned anything since this morning?" I asked.

"No. I talked to Anna. She was heartbroken. They were separated, but that didn't necessarily mean . . ." He seemed to lose his train of thought. He kept staring at the mural, a depiction of a big city skyline being poured from a coffeepot.

"It didn't mean . . ." I prompted after a few minutes.

"Lizzie used to say that when you really love someone, you always love them. No matter what comes between you. Even death."

"She was right," I said.

Jesse kept staring at the mural.

"Do you want something to eat?"

"I have that." He pointed toward his uneaten chocolate cupcake.

"I meant food; a sandwich, a salad, something like that."

"I was thinking that maybe Roger came up to talk to me about Anna," he said.

"But you said you hadn't seen him in three years."

"I kept in touch with Anna. Kind of. She sent Christmas cards and presents for Allie. And we'd e-mail once in a while."

"Did she ever say anything about their marriage?"

"No. She'd just ask what Allie was up to; how my mom was doing; questions about you." He smiled. "And she talked about the business she'd started. It was really haphazard. Maybe once every couple of months or so."

"So why would Roger want to talk to you about her?"

He shrugged. We were sitting next to each other, but there was a distance between us. I wanted to comfort him, to share his grief, but I could feel him closing me out.

"You haven't been in touch in several years," I said, "so maybe Roger wanted to talk to you about something from your days in New York. Maybe an old case or a friend you had in common. Has there been anyone from that time that you've talked to lately? Did you get an unexpected Christmas card, or maybe a phone call? Something you might not have placed any importance on?"

Jesse sat there staring out the window. I waited in silence until it was clear he didn't intend to answer me.

"Carrie said Roger was here last night," I told him, "looking out this window across the street at Someday Quilts."

Jesse looked at me. It was the first indication I had that he'd been listening. "Why?"

"I don't know. Carrie told him your girlfriend worked at the shop."

"That was a mistake," he said. Then he got up. "I should go."

"Jesse, I want to help you."

"I know. I just don't think you can."

I sat there and watched Jesse walk out of the shop. As he reached the street, a police car pulled up. I could see that it was Greg who was driving. Jesse leaned in the window and the two chatted for a moment, then Jesse hit the door of the car and shouted something. Greg got out of the car, and Jesse got behind the wheel. He sped away nearly knocking down his best officer in the process.

Greg walked toward the coffee shop and I willed him to come inside. Greg was very loyal to his boss, and my going into the street to ask what had happened would make him uncomfortable. And it would definitely be something he'd feel obligated to tell Jesse. I needed any conversation we had to seem casual, something Greg would see as two friends talking and therefore wouldn't bother to relay. I hated manipulating Greg, but Jesse was keeping something from me. As much as I didn't want to drive him further away by pushing too hard, I wasn't going to sit around and do nothing while he was in need of help.

When Greg walked into Jitters, I started to get up, ready to head to the counter for a refill on my coffee so I could bump into him. But just as I heard Greg give Carrie his order, someone hit me on the back of the head.

CHAPTER 6

"Nell Fitzgerald. What are you doing sitting there?" Maggie Sweeney's gray hair was piled high on her head, her Laura Ashley–style dress peeked out from a heavy brown wool coat. She was my grandmother's age, and her match in personality and practicality. She was also one of my dearest friends.

"Where am I supposed to be sitting?" I asked. Greg took his coffee to go and walked out of the shop. He glanced my way, looking nervous. Maybe he'd hoped to accidently bump into me, too. "Why did you hit me?"

Maggie plopped down next to me on the couch. "It's a bag of fabric. You'll recover. Besides I called your name and you ignored me. Awful morning. How is Jesse holding up?"

I shrugged, repeating the same line to Maggie I'd given to Carrie. Just thinking about it made me feel helpless.

"Well, we'll all do what we can," she said. "I'm bringing a lasagna over to his house this afternoon, as well as my banana bread."

"I love your banana bread."

"Then I'll bring you some, too." She patted my hand. "Poor Jesse. So much loss for such a young man. This was a good friend?"

"I think so. He's never talked about him before, but they were partners on the police force when Jesse lived in the city."

"Curious that he came up to see Jesse. This Roger Leighton didn't call, didn't e-mail. He came in person with no warning."

"He must not have wanted to risk anyone else finding out that he was coming up here."

Maggie nodded. "He was just waiting in his car outside Jesse's house, poor man, like a duck in an arcade booth."

I felt a knot tighten in my stomach. "I think I may be partially to blame," I confessed. "I think Roger might have been waiting for me to leave."

Maggie narrowed her eyes. "But you're assuming that Roger was coming to Jesse for help. It's also possible he was coming to harm him," she said. "Your being there might have prevented Jesse from being killed." I hadn't considered that. "Jesse is a strong man with good people who love him. You'll be there for him, and we'll all . . ." She hesitated until she found the right way to say it, "we'll all help in the way we like to help."

"Can you check into him? Roger Leighton, I mean. Maybe there's a newspaper article or something that'll give us a clue."

Maggie nodded. "I'll start looking this afternoon. And Carrie still has her friends from her days in the banking industry. Maybe there's something in his financials," she said. "We'll all do what we can, but you can't neglect your duties as maid of honor."

"Most of it is under control. I have to check on the order for the flowers and make sure that I have the decorations. There are lots of little details that need to be dealt with. I want the wedding to be perfect."

"Well, it won't be. Nor should it be. It will be lovely though. God knows we've all worked our thimbles off trying to get this ready."

We had. It was Eleanor's quilt group, but the rest of us—Natalie, Carrie, Maggie, Natalie's mother, Susanne, the local pharmacist, Bernie, and I—had formed our own sub–quilt group for the purpose of making Eleanor and her fiancé, Oliver, a wedding quilt.

Oliver was a well-known painter, and he saw in my grandmother a fellow artist and soul mate. Their love story was unexpected, but it was inspiring and joyful.

Our secret sub—quilt group was making its wedding quilt of twelve-inch square blocks. Most of the blocks were appliquéd with roses, but each of us had taken two to decorate as we pleased. Mine had appliqués of Barney in one, and Oliver's easel in another, as symbols of things that each loved nearly as much as they loved each other. The blocks were assembled, but the quilt needed to be quilted, the binding sewn on, and a label made, signed, and attached. Each task had been assigned to a person, so I didn't worry that it would be done on time. Besides, not getting a quilt done on time was something of a tradition. There were women I knew still working on baby quilts for kids entering high school.

We were also making small pillows for each of the fifty guests, with appliquéd roses on them, and we'd decided to sew tablecloths for each of the five small tables that we would have to fit into Eleanor's living room for the reception. All of the work was going on behind Eleanor's back, but she'd have to be a fool to not know what we were up to. And my grandmother was no fool.

"If it can't be perfect," I said, "it will be close."

"I'm sure the ceremony will go off without a hitch," Maggie agreed, "but we have to focus our energies on the bachelorette party."

I laughed, my first of the day. It felt good. "I don't really think Grandma would want strippers and lingerie. And if she does, I don't want to know about it."

"I wasn't talking about that sort of thing. I was talking about getting all the women together to celebrate our dear friend and this exciting new adventure she's embarking on. We may not see much of her once the wedding is behind us and they've left town."

"What are you talking about?"

"Oliver's bought that big house in South Carolina."

I sat up. "When? Eleanor didn't say anything to me about it."

"I suppose she's waiting to tell you, dear," Maggie said. "It will be good for her to retire and enjoy Oliver for as long as they've left."

"Retire?" That was another piece of news I hadn't heard. "But even if Eleanor would retire, why couldn't she do that here?"

"This has already been a long hard winter and we have a long way to go. If you think it's cold for you, wait until your bones creak. I imagine they're both looking for a little sunshine and mild weather. Oliver said the house is near the ocean, so can you imagine how lovely it must be? We'll all have to go visit, of course, but it won't be the same. Which is why we need a party to celebrate dear Eleanor."

Maggie kept talking. Something about having people to her house for the bachelorette party, or maybe doing it at the shop would be better. A big dinner, lots of wine . . . I wasn't listening. My grandmother was telling people she planned to retire and move hundreds of miles away, and I was the last to know. A day that had started off badly was now getting worse.

$\mathscr{C}$HAPTER 7

When I got back to Someday Quilts, I immediately went to Eleanor's office, but she was gone. Natalie had little Patch curled up on her lap and didn't seem to notice me at all. She was too busy stroking the kitten's fur while Patch slept contentedly.

"She's so precious I just want to eat her."

"Why do people say that?" I asked. "People are always saying that to babies and puppies and anything cute. Are we cannibals at heart or something?"

"What put you in a bad mood?"

"Eleanor's retiring." I told her everything Maggie had told me, and I could tell by the shocked look on her face that she hadn't known anything about it either.

"She's closing Someday?" Natalie looked on the verge of tears. She sunk back in her chair and sighed heavily. That woke Patch, who meowed at her, concerned that her new friend was unhappy.

I shrugged. "Why tell us if she is? We only work here."

"Don't get overly excited by it, Nell. Maybe Maggie is jumping to conclusions."

Aside from being a mother of eleven, grandmother of twenty-five, and great-grandmother of two, Maggie was a retired librarian and the researcher of our little amateur detective agency. Maggie didn't jump to conclusions, and Natalie knew it as well as I did.

"Well, maybe Eleanor's waiting to tell us," Natalie tried again. "Maybe it will be a surprise. Maybe she's giving the shop to you!" She jumped up to hug me, grabbing poor Patch and squeezing her between us. I expected the kitten to yelp but instead we got a long, satisfied purr.

Was that Eleanor's plan—to give me Someday Quilts? And if it was, did I want it?

I would have liked a moment to consider the idea, but suddenly the shop got busy. A month before, we'd been featured in a national quilt magazine as one of the best shops in the country because of our eclectic mix of both modern and traditional fabrics and the wide range of classes we taught. Plus the article had a photo of us with Barney front and center, his goofy doggy grin making the quilt shop a must-stop destination. Lots of out-of-town quilters had begun making a special trip just to see the place, meet Barney, and feed their insatiable need for all things quilt.

For more than an hour, I stood behind the desk ringing up sales while Natalie was busy at the cutting table. At the first sign of customers Patch had retreated to the office. I envied her the peace and quiet. I wanted a moment to think everything through, to put a needle in my hand and quietly appliqué while my mind settled on an answer to what seemed to be dozens of new questions. But there was no letup of customers.

When I saw Jesse walk by the shop, I nearly left the customers to run out and see how he was, but instead I watched him. He didn't look in the window as he usually did. In fact, he didn't seem to be looking at anything in particular. He was just walking in a sort of daydream. Jesse was always alert, always on duty, so seeing him like that was unsettling, even a little frightening. But then I'd never seen Jesse suffer a loss before.

I debated whether he'd want me to say hi—if it would be a welcome part of his day or just disturb his daydream. But my decision was made for me when a woman in a bright pink coat put a pile of about twenty different fabrics on the counter, along with several patterns, two rulers, and a rotary cutter.

"Did you find everything you needed?" It was my standard line, though with this woman buying up half the store, it was impossible to imagine she hadn't found *more* than what she needed.

"No, actually," she said. "Where's the pattern for that?"

I turned to where she was pointing and saw one of my own quilts. The pattern was Amish inspired, with long bars of alternating grayish blue and taupe. Where I went my own way was in the colorful pink, orange, and purple flowers I'd appliquéd along the edges, set off with deep green leaves and twirling vines.

"There is no pattern for that," I told her. "It's just something I made."

"When is it coming out?"

"It's not," I explained. "It's just . . . mine. To decorate the shop."

She sighed and looked at her abundant pile. "Well, I guess this is all then. But when you do make a pattern for it, let me know. I'll sign up for your newsletter."

I almost told her we didn't have a newsletter, but I didn't want to disappoint her again. Instead I took her e-mail address and started a list. Maybe we should have a newsletter. Something to talk to Eleanor about . . . one of many things to talk to her about.

Bernie Avallone came into the shop, waved at me, and headed for the wall where we kept mostly tone-on-tone fabrics. She went straight for the blues. The good thing about having one of the quilt group members shopping was, in a pinch she could also help out with the customers. Like everyone in the quilt group, Bernie was as familiar with the inventory as I was.

"What's the name of the woman who runs things?" the woman in the pink coat asked me.

"Eleanor Cassidy. She's not here right now."

"Well then, tell her for me that if she hangs quilts in her shop the quilts should be available as patterns."

"I will," I said.

As she left, weighed down by her purchases, I wondered how many unfinished quilts that woman had at home, along with patterns, books, fabrics, kits, and magazines. More quilts in her imagination than she could make in a lifetime, and yet she was annoyed that somehow one quilt pattern had slipped through her fingers. I knew exactly how she felt.

"She's right you know," Bernie said as she dropped a group of fabrics on the cutting table.

"She is," Natalie agreed. "You should make a pattern of that quilt. And the others."

"I don't know how."

Bernie rolled her eyes. "You made a pattern to make those quilts in the first place, didn't you?"

"Yes, but I wasn't worried about being exact. I was just playing."

"Well, now that you've played, let the rest of us in on the fun."

"Especially now that it will be your shop," Natalie added.

Bernie looked from Natalie to me. "Your shop? Are you planning a coup?"

"Natalie is just—" I said, unable to finish. Natalie had jumped in with the story I'd heard this morning. Bernie almost didn't believe it. Apparently no one knew what Maggie had told me. Maybe it wasn't true after all. That was a hopeful thought. Enough was changing. I wanted Someday to stay the same.

I walked to the cutting table and petted the fabrics Bernie had chosen. Non-quilters don't understand that a lot of the enjoyment we get from quilting is running our fingers over the soft cottons, feeling the cool, smooth fibers underneath our hands. It's calming, and I needed a little calm at the moment.

"These are great fabrics," I told Bernie, ignoring her questions about Eleanor, "but they're mostly medium tones. Have you thought about adding some lights and darks to give it more depth?"

Bernie examined her fabrics. "Well, how did I fall into such a beginner's trap?" She laughed to herself. She went back to the blue fabrics and pulled another ten bolts. What she brought back to the table was a dizzying array of shades, from baby blues, to teals, to navy.

"Much better," I said. "Quarter yards?"

"Better give me a half yard of each. What I don't use will go in my stash."

"You have more fabric in your stash than we have at the shop."

She smiled. "You never know when there will be a blight on the cotton crop, and we'll run out of fabric."

"Don't even think it." I laughed. "What would we do at quilt group if we didn't have quilts to show?"

"Aside from gossip and eat?"

"Exactly. The quilts provide cover for the real activities."

Bernie sighed. "I won't be able to make the meeting Friday. I'm going to Boston Tuesday for a pharmaceutical convention and I thought I'd stay for the weekend and visit some sites."

"I can't make it either," Natalie said. "My in-laws are coming for dinner."

It had been like this a lot lately. When I first joined, nothing short of a funeral kept the entire group from meeting every Friday, but things had gotten busier for everyone. It wasn't unusual to have only half in attendance. With Eleanor moving, and the shop's future in question, it could get to the point where we just disbanded.

As Natalie cut, Bernie examined a sketch I'd made of a quilt I was thinking of doing. It was a medallion quilt. It featured an appliqué of flowers in the center, surrounded by row after row of borders, some pieced, and some appliqués of animals and flowers.

"This is stunning, Nell."

I blushed. "Thanks. I did it in art class when I was supposed to be doing a still life of a vase full of roses. I just kept thinking how much better I would like it in fabric. I was also thinking . . ." I grabbed my sketch pad and flipped a few pages forward, "that this sketch of the gazebo in the park would make a nice quilt. I could simplify it a little so it would be easier to appliqué."

"This blue . . ." she held up one of the bolts of blue fabric, "would make an excellent choice for the sky."

"I was thinking maybe several layers of different blues." I grabbed the fabrics I had planned to use. I was getting excited now, as talking about a new quilt always made me.

"You should make it for Eleanor and Oliver. What an amazing wedding gift."

That stopped me. "Do you think there's time? We already have the quilt we're making as a group. I was assuming I'd buy them something. I just hadn't figured out what it would be."

"Buy something?" Bernie looked horrified. "But you paint and quilt. You have to make them something. It's so much more special."

"There's nothing I could make them that would be nicer than what they could do themselves," I said. "Oliver's paintings hang in museums and Eleanor . . ." I waved my hand around the shop, and the many beautiful quilts that decorated the place. "Eleanor's quilts are stunning."

"Which is why they will both appreciate your considerable talents turned into a one-of-a-kind wedding gift," she said. "Buy something?" She shook her head in disbelief. "I'm surprised at you. Of course, if you do make this for Eleanor, don't start it on a Friday. Friday quilts are ill-fated."

"Why?" Natalie asked.

"If you start a quilt on a Friday you won't live to see it finished."

"If that were true, quilters would be dropping like flies," I pointed out.

"Fine, don't believe in quilt superstitions," Bernie said. "Even though they've been around for generations and have served us all well." She tried to look annoyed, but she smiled at herself. Bernie was still true to her sixties hippie youth, and she loved breaking with tradition more than anyone. But some traditions even Bernie believed in. "At least embroider a spider on it for good luck. I don't see smooth sailing for this wedding, so we need all the luck we can get."

She wasn't just a pharmacist, Bernie was our group psychic despite being wrong as often as she was right. But it was better to take her seriously, just in case.

"Then a spider it is," I said, as I drew a small spider in the corner of the gazebo sketch.

"And hearts," she told me. "Lots of hearts. All the quilt traditions call for lots of hearts on a bridal quilt."

"Is this Nell's quilt or yours?" Natalie asked.

Bernie raised an eyebrow. "It's Eleanor's, so it should be as lovely as she is."

As Bernie spoke, I saw Greg out the window. He was standing at the corner, writing out a parking ticket to a car too close to the corner. I grabbed my coat without a second thought. "Bernie, take over for me at the register."

"But I need to pay for my—"

"Ring up your own purchases."

While Natalie cut for another customer, Bernie brought her fabric to the counter, and I ran out the door.

CHAPTER 8

"Lousy job for cold weather," I said as I approached Greg, who was writing the license plate onto the ticket.

"Sure is." The annoyance in his voice was obvious. "It's not my idea."

"You know Jesse is just upset about his friend," I said. "I saw that he was a little rough on you. . . ."

Greg leaned his lanky frame against the hood of the car. "I get that." His tone softened, more hurt and concern than annoyance. "I wish I could help. I've been taking a couple of criminology classes in Peekskill. I've learned a lot about forensics, profiling, even how to run my own sheriff's department. I don't think Jesse realizes what I can do."

"He does, Greg. He knows you're the town's best detective."

He smiled a little and rolled his eyes. He was the town's only detective, but that didn't diminish his talents. "Lot of good it does me. I barely got a chance to look at the body, let alone investigate."

"Well, you know that he died from a bullet to the head." I tried to sound encouraging.

"That's all we have," Greg said, "plus the fact that he was driving a rental car he picked up in Tarrytown yesterday morning."

"Tarrytown? I thought he lived in New York City."

"He did. Queens to be specific. And he owned a car. And yet he went to Grand Central Terminal, bought a ticket to Tarrytown on the nine forty-five a.m. train, and then when he got there, he walked to a car rental place, rented that SUV, and drove the rest of the way up here."

"If he was going to take the train, why not take it all the way to Archers Rest?" It took more than three hours from the city, but there were two trains a day that stopped at our little station.

Greg shrugged. "Wish I knew. If Roger was hiding from someone, he didn't exactly try very hard. He used his own credit card to buy the ticket and rent the car."

"It sounds like you're making progress. So why are you giving out parking tickets instead of working on the murder?"

"Ask the chief. He told me to ticket this car."

"This car specifically?"

"Yeah, he said it was a danger to anyone turning the corner."

The car was a late-model dark blue sedan, the sort of car I'd drive if I didn't want anyone to notice me. I didn't recognize it from anyone in town, but Archers Rest was just large enough that it was impossible to know everyone. "Why didn't he write the ticket himself?"

Greg rolled his eyes. "Nell, you're dating the guy. If you haven't figured him out yet, then I can't help you."

I knew what he meant. When Jesse was upset and didn't want to talk about it, he tended to focus on the smallest of details. I guess because that was all he felt he could control.

"But there are other officers on the force. . . ." I started.

"I somehow got on his bad side. I don't know how. All I tried to do was explain a little about a new technique to re-create crime timelines." Greg put the ticket under the windshield wiper blade of the offending car, and flipped his ticket book closed. "He's been weird since it happened. I found a card in the dead guy's pocket and was putting it into evidence and Jesse told me not to. But that's procedure. I told him, and he got mad at me about it."

"Maybe it wasn't relevant."

"Everything's relevant this early in the investigation. That was one of the first things Jesse taught me after I became a detective."

"Do you remember what the card said?"

"It was a business card. C. G. Something. New York City," he said. "Look, Nell, I know you help with stuff that comes up at the sheriff's office. I know you're really good at it, but it's up to Jesse to tell you. . . ."

I'd overstepped. One minute we were sharing, and now I was in danger of this entire conversation being reported back.

"I'm sorry," I said. "Sometimes my curiosity gets the better of me. And Jesse is so sad. I don't want to make things worse. I just don't know how to help."

"We should be turning this whole investigation over to the state police, you know, because of Jesse's connection to the victim. But he won't hear of it. His town, his case. And I guess I get that. If my friend were dead in front of my house, I'd feel the same way," he said. "You know I'd do anything to help the chief."

I liked Greg so much. He was sweet and helpful. I could feel his frustration and I shared it. Jesse was a stickler for procedure, so why wasn't he following it?

"Maybe he just wanted to bag it himself," I said. "I mean, he's so particular, and that man was his friend. . . ."

"He put the card in his pocket, unbagged. Chain of evidence is broken. It's useless now. I mean, if it leads to the killer and it goes to trial, a defense attorney could say we made the whole thing up. It's just not how things work."

"You'll catch the guy who did this, Greg. I know Jesse wants that more than anything. There has to have been other evidence."

He nodded. "Just the notebook he had on him. At least we got that into evidence."

"What was in the notebook?"

"No idea. Jesse took the evidence bags."

"And there was nothing else in the rest of the car? Maybe he had an address, a piece of paper . . ."

"Nothing. The rest of the car was spotless."

As he spoke I saw Jesse drive by in the squad car. He drove past us, so I wasn't sure he saw me talking with Greg, but then he stopped the car a few feet away. Greg looked like he'd been caught doing something wrong, so I decided to take the hit. "I'll talk to him," I said.

I could see Greg was relieved. "Tell him I'm heading back to the station."

As I walked toward the squad car, I turned briefly to look at the blue sedan. To my eye it didn't seem parked too close to the corner, so I made a note of the license plate. Just in case.

CHAPTER 9

"Hi." It wasn't an inspiring start, but it was something. I opened the passenger door and got in.

Jesse looked at me as if he didn't know me, then something roused in him and he smiled. "How's your day going?"

I wanted to tell him about Eleanor and the shop, and Patch, and about the woman wanting to buy a pattern of my quilt. I wanted to do what I always did, share the tiniest details of my day and hear the tiniest details of his. But this wasn't the time for it. I could tell that much by the worn look and the tiredness in his eyes.

"How are you doing?" I asked instead.

"I don't know. I still can't believe it. I can't understand what he would want up here."

"Okay, so let's concentrate on what you do know and work from there. Maybe something will stick out."

He smiled slightly. "You've become a real pro at this," he said. "The coroner confirmed what you saw, the bullet to the back of his head killed him, probably in a matter of seconds. There was pooling of blood in the lower extremities, which meant he hadn't been moved. So he died in the driver's seat of that car while I was in the house, only thirty yards away, having dinner."

I let the comment go. It was unfair for Jesse to feel guilty about

Roger's death, especially since I was the one who could have seen something, could have said something to Jesse that might have prevented it. I almost said as much, but getting into a competition with Jesse over who was more to blame was not only pointless, it was the surest way to push us apart. Instead, I took a deep breath and concentrated my focus on the investigation. "Could the coroner say when?"

"Impossible to say exactly because of the cold. But we know he was alive at nine-twenty," he said.

"Because that's when I saw him."

"Exactly."

"But I told you, I don't know that it was him."

"It had to have been Roger. He died in that seat, so unless the killer was in the front seat of Roger's rental car, got out and let Roger in after you passed by, and then shot him . . ."

"Which doesn't seem plausible . . ."

"Exactly," he agreed. "It's much more likely that someone got in the car while he was waiting outside my house to talk to me, or . . ."

"Or forced him at gunpoint to your house," I said, finishing his awful thought. "Jesse, someone might be trying to hurt you. You need police protection."

"I am the police."

"Maybe Greg . . ."

"I don't need a babysitter."

"Well, for Allie's sake . . ."

"I can protect my own daughter," he snapped at me.

He was scared, sad, confused. I placed my hand in his and held it. I had a lot of questions, but they could wait, so I said the only thing I could think of that really mattered. "I love you, Jesse Dewalt."

I could feel his shoulder soften slightly. He leaned his head against mine. "I love you, too, Nell Fitzgerald."

We sat for a minute, then Jesse let go of my hand. "I have to get back to work."

"Come over tonight for dinner. Eleanor asked me to invite you."
It was a lie, but a small one. Eleanor would have invited him if she'd
thought of it. And chicken that I was, I assumed an invitation from
her would carry more weight than one from me. "I would feel better if you and Allie were close by."

Jesse hesitated then gave me a half smile. "Yeah, okay. I know
Allie wants to rehearse her big moment as flower girl."

"And Oliver probably wants to know your plans for a bachelor
party." Jesse was, after all, the best man.

"Do you throw a bachelor party for a senior citizen?" he asked.

"We're throwing a bachelorette party for Eleanor."

Jesse laughed. "I really didn't want to know that. Okay, dinner
tonight."

"Seven o'clock."

I got out of the car and watched him slowly pull away. I was glad
our conversation had ended on a light note, but as the car turned the
corner and out of view, I felt a heaviness in my chest, and a sudden
chill that had nothing to do with the January winds.

CHAPTER 10

As I knew she would be, Eleanor was delighted to have Jesse and Allie for dinner. "I should have thought of it myself," she said when I asked her. "After all that poor man's been through."

I was chopping vegetables for the salad as Eleanor checked on the peach cobbler she was making for dessert. The roast was resting on the counter, the potatoes were mashed, and the broccoli was chopped and ready to be steamed. Eleanor had made an amazing dinner, as always, and was in last-minute fussing mode.

I finished the cucumber and moved on to chopping tomatoes. I steeled myself and asked something I'd been meaning to ask for a long time. "What was he like then?"

"When Lizzie passed away, you mean? He collapsed into himself. You could feel the grief coming off him like heat from an oven. It was painful just to see him, to see him trying to smile for Allie. Without her to take care of, he would have just joined Lizzie in the grave I think."

"What was she like?"

"I didn't know her well. Her people are farther south on the Hudson. When I met her, she was already sick, and, of course, that changes a person. She knew she didn't have much time and every minute she could spend with her husband and daughter was precious to her."

"It seems like she was perfect."

"No one is perfect. She was very nice." My grandmother studied me a minute. "You're very nice, too, Nell. And Jesse loves you very much. Don't get insecure about this. It will do you no good, and, frankly, it's not a very attractive quality in a young lady. Focus yourself on the future, not the past."

"Speaking of the future," I started. I'd been debating how to begin this topic since I got home, but now that I had my courage I decided to go for it. I wanted Eleanor to tell me. I didn't want to have to jump on her with rumors. But she hadn't said a word about it, and I couldn't wait any longer. "Maggie told me something interesting."

"Maggie is an interesting woman," Eleanor said as she turned away from me and began examining the wineglasses. "I'm going to miss her when Oliver and I move south."

And then the doorbell rang.

✄

Oliver stood at the door with flowers and wine. I waited as he kissed Eleanor's cheek, hung up his coat, and put his gifts down on the hallway table. Then he greeted Barney like the old friend he was, and finally he looked up at me.

"Hello, my dear. How is art school these days?" Oliver asked in his clipped British accent. Tall, lean, with a neat white beard and a full head of white hair, he made an imposing, but equally charming, impression. Oliver was a world-renowned artist who, a year ago, had offered a special seminar to aspiring artists in the area. When Oliver met my grandmother at a reception of his work, he'd been smitten. And somehow, against all odds, my fiercely independent grandmother found herself in love.

"We're still on winter break," I said. "We go back for my final set of courses at the end of the month."

Dillsburg Area Public Library

17 South Baltimore St.
Dillsburg, PA 17019

"So amazing to think where you were as an artist a year ago, and where you are now," he said.

"It's amazing where we all are in our lives," Eleanor added. "So much has changed in so short a time and I could never have imagined any of it."

"You're leaving Archers Rest," I said in a rush. It came out wrong. Whiny, hurt. I tried again. "Maggie mentioned you guys are thinking of—"

"Just winters." Oliver leaned toward me, put a protective arm around my shoulder, and walked with me to the kitchen. "I can't take the cold anymore. It's a sacrifice for Eleanor and I feel like hell about it. Leaving Archers Rest and the shop for months at a time. I wasn't sure she'd say yes."

"But she did say yes?"

"I have no idea," he said. "She told me she would think about it. I'm awaiting my lady's pleasure."

Eleanor let out a loud cough. "I am still here, you two. So you can stop talking about me as if I'm in the other room."

"Okay," I said, "then you've decided to say yes?"

She looked from me to Oliver and back to me. "I have. Just now, talking about how you have to move forward in life, I decided I would."

"But Maggie knew about it this afternoon."

"I talked to her first to get her thoughts on it. She's my dearest friend." She reached out and softly brushed my cheek. "Well, maybe not my dearest anymore, but she's my oldest friend."

I wasn't sure how I felt, but I knew that whatever loss I was experiencing was more about me than about her. Eleanor and Oliver were starting a new life together and that was a wonderful thing. "I'm happy for you, Grandma, for both of you, if that's what you want."

The doorbell rang again. Oliver went to answer, escaping, he said, before we turned to tears in front of him. But there were no

Dillsburg Area Public Library

17 South Baltimore St.
Dillsburg, PA 17019

tears, at least not sad ones. I was happy for my grandmother. Happy she was marrying Oliver, and she was going to relax and enjoy herself. She had certainly earned it, raising two kids alone, running a business for forty years, and taking me in more than a year ago when my life was complicated and unhappy. My fears were selfish, and, worse, I felt like a child for wishing she would stay.

✂

We all ate too much, but a dinner at my grandmother's house is like that. The roast was tender, the broccoli had the right amount of bite, and the potatoes were creamy without losing their flavor to butter and milk. By the time we'd finished the second bottle of wine and moved on to coffee and peach cobbler, I was stuffed. But I managed a sliver. And then another.

While the rest of us were eating, Allie kept the conversation moving with all the important questions.

"Do I walk down the aisle first?" Allie asked Eleanor.

"Yes, the flower girl always goes first. And you'll be so lovely in your dress."

"But I won't be the prettiest. You'll be the prettiest," Allie said, "because you're the bride. And when Nell marries Daddy, she'll be the prettiest. Isn't that true, Daddy?"

Jesse blushed a little. "Yes, Allie. The bride is always the prettiest."

"And the groom the handsomest," Oliver added. Then he winked at Allie, who burst out laughing in the way only a seven-year-old can. It must be wonderful to feel there's an answer for everything.

"When Nell and Daddy get married, you'll be my great-grandpa," she said to him.

Oliver reached across the table and touched her hand. "It will be my honor."

I got up from the table to clear the dishes. All the Jesse and Nell wedding talk was making me a little uneasy. I couldn't say why, exactly. I wanted to marry Jesse. Someday. I just didn't want to talk about it constantly.

Eleanor saw I was uncomfortable and jumped in to help. She turned to Allie. "Did your dad tell you about our kitten?"

Jesse looked at me. "You have a kitten?"

I nodded. "I meant to tell you this afternoon, but it kind of got lost with everything . . ." I let the sentence trail off.

"Where's the kitten?" Allie demanded.

"Upstairs in my room," I told her. "I brought her home with me, but she's still not used to Barney so I'm keeping her in there during the night and I guess we'll bring her to the shop during the day." I looked to Eleanor.

"I suppose. I hadn't really thought about it," she admitted. "I didn't even decide whether we should keep her. She might already belong to someone. We should post signs or something."

"I'll put something up at the shop," I agreed. "And Jitters. And maybe the library."

"I can put an all-points bulletin out on her and see if anyone's filed a missing kitten report." Jesse smiled.

Eleanor turned to him and winked. "When it comes to getting the word out, I'll match the gossip line that runs through my shop against your police force any day."

"Can I meet her?" Allie didn't wait for an answer. She ran from the table and up the stairs. Barney, never to be left out of anything, chased after her.

Jesse took my hand. "Thank you for today."

"I didn't do anything."

"You were there."

I looked over at Oliver, who was drinking his coffee and trying not to interfere with my moment with Jesse. "I guess you'll be my grandpa after the wedding," I said.

"Why do you think I'm marrying Eleanor? I want to be related to you."

I rolled my eyes but laughed. "You guys are supposed to be planning your bachelor party."

"Under the circumstances . . ." Oliver said, "I think Jesse's energies would be better spent elsewhere."

"Roger was my best man," Jesse told us. "The night before my wedding, he took me out for a drink. Lizzie was mad. She thought we'd go out and get drunk at a strip club and I'd show up late to the church or, worse, not at all." Jesse laughed at the memory. "But Roger and I just sat at an Irish place down the block and talked."

Jesse let go of my hand, so I sat next to him, and watched as he lost himself in the past. "He said I was crazy lucky to have conned Lizzie into marrying me. He said she was way out of my league. And she was. And he said that if I ever needed him for anything, he'd be there for me. A best man isn't just for the wedding. A best man is for life, he said. Vigiles keep vigil."

"What does that mean?" I asked.

"It was just something he said to me a lot. 'Vigiles keep vigil.' He said it was our code. It means police keep watch, or something," he said. "And Roger did. He always had my back. Always. And I didn't have his when it mattered most."

I opened my mouth to speak without any idea what to say. "We'll find out what happened—" I started before a commotion broke out above our heads.

"Daddy!" Allie yelled from upstairs.

Oliver and I followed Jesse up the stairs and into my room, where Eleanor and Allie stood in the doorway and pointed toward the area rug at the foot of my bed.

Barney had his nose pressed against the floor, his paws flat on either side, and had made his whole body as little as possible. No small feat for a golden retriever. It was clear he was trying to convey that he was not a threat to Patch, who was inches away from him. When we peeked in the room, the kitten hissed in our direction and arched her tiny back.

"Maybe we should get Barney out of there," I suggested.

"Wait," Allie said. "It's cute."

So we waited. Within a minute, Patch forgot about us and turned her attention back to the dog. She reached a hesitant paw out and touched Barney's snout. Barney didn't move. Then the kitten moved even closer. She sniffed at the poor dog, who was doing his best imitation of a statue. Then she moved toward his eye. She stared at him, and he blinked back. I could see his tail moving a little, wagging with the excitement of a new friend.

Then, for no reason at all, she moved away, ran under the bed, and hissed.

Eleanor came into the room and petted her old friend. "That was a lovely first date," she told him. "Give her time and she'll be madly in love."

Barney was almost totally deaf so he may not have heard her, but he certainly understood. He leapt up and licked Eleanor's cheek, and we all went in to congratulate the old dog on his patience.

Allie looked under the bed and saw Patch. "She's scared."

"We should rehearse for the wedding." Eleanor grabbed Allie's hand. "Why don't you come with me to the living room. We'll practice there."

Allie took my hand. "You too, Nell."

"Coming with us?" I asked the men.

Jesse shook his head. "Oliver and I have bachelor party plans to discuss."

"A trip to Vegas, I assume," Oliver agreed. "Something that requires bail money."

We all retreated downstairs. Allie, Eleanor, Barney, and I went off to the living room while the men returned to the dining room talking about scotch and cigars.

I sat on the couch and watched Allie walk down the aisle we'd formed between the couch and the two chairs that sat opposite. Allie took each step carefully, pretending to hold a basket of flower petals that she tossed onto the floor. She was followed by Barney as ring bearer, then Eleanor. I smiled and applauded each time, trying to look as if I were completely immersed in the proceedings, but all I could think of was what Roger had said to Jesse years before. "Vigiles keep vigil."

Was Roger coming to Jesse for protection, or did he spend the last night of this life watching Jesse's back one last time?

CHAPTER 11

I choose three different blues, all tone-on-tones so the pattern wouldn't distract. They were my background sky colors. The blues were close in tone so they almost melted together, but still they were three distinct fabrics. I cut a five-and-a-half-inch by twenty-two-and-a-half-inch strip of each and sewed them together so I had a piece that was fifteen by twenty-two. Then I sewed that to two green strips that I'd cut at the same size as the blue. Five strips sewn together to make the background for my gazebo quilt. It was a modern start—stark, simple lines that abstracted nature rather than imitated it.

My gazebo, too, was a simplified version of the real thing. Oliver had once done a painting of it as a raffle prize for the town, so I felt extra pressure by using the image, but I knew I had to use it. He loved the structure as much for its beauty as for the symbol of small-town America, and Eleanor loved it because it was a familiar part of home. As I sketched out a large drawing of the gazebo to use as my pattern for the appliqué, I realized suddenly that I was making them a piece of Archers Rest to take with them to their new place in South Carolina.

"It's just their winter home," I said aloud to Patch, the only other creature in the shop with me. She didn't hear me or didn't care. She was busy chasing a piece of scrap yarn around the shop floor, attacking it, then moving back so she could attack it again.

After our guests had left last night, Eleanor and I were so tired we went to bed and never discussed the shop or the house, and what would happen during the months every year she and Oliver were gone. Eleanor could close up the house for the winter, but not the shop. In order to stay profitable, it would have to stay open, and be staffed, through the winter, or close altogether. The thought brought tears to my eyes.

In the morning I'd gone to register for a figurative drawing class, then went to the shop to relieve Natalie, who had to bring her daughter to a doctor's appointment. Eleanor and Oliver were meeting with the pastor to discuss their wedding, but she would be in on time to let me head off to meet the quilt group at Jitters for another one of our secret meetings. The schedule was a carefully choreographed dance as it was. How would the shop manage with just Natalie and me to keep things going? I tried not to think about it.

One thing Eleanor had taught me was that when the big questions of life seem overwhelming, focus on something small that's right in front of you. So I looked at my drawing, which had turned out pretty well. We had several white and off-white fabrics I could use to imitate the color and shadows of the gazebo. The flowers I could either paint or embroider, something that would add color and texture without being too fussy. When would I find the time with the wedding now less than two weeks away? That was another thing I could think about later.

Something loud crashed in the back of the shop; Patch hissed and ran toward me. I grabbed her, tucked her under my arm, and went in search of whatever it was that had been knocked down by our little furry helper.

It was a pattern rack—a heavy round spinning rack that had withstood countless years—through sales and customers and renovations, but somehow a kitten weighing a couple of pounds had gotten the better of it. The yarn was tangled up at the bottom, and in the fall the rack had broken.

"You are trouble," I scolded her. She meowed in response and I smiled. It's hard to stay mad at a ball of purring fur.

I picked up the patterns and brought them over to the checkout table. I'd figure out a display later. In the meantime, I found myself not just organizing the patterns but looking at the photos on the cover, the font size for the pattern names, and the companies that made them. When I had a minute maybe I'd go through them just to see what exactly it would involve to actually make a pattern of one of my quilts. Maybe if the shop closed I would design patterns . . . But as soon as the thought entered my mind, I crushed it. Someday Quilts had been a part of my life since I was a child, when my parents, sister, and I would visit Archers Rest. I would run my hand across the fabrics, make piles with the books, nap under the sample quilts, and get in trouble anytime I went near sharp scissors. I could not imagine it closing, but I didn't see any realistic way for it to stay open.

Eleanor came into the shop with three full bags just as I put the pile of patterns on the table next to the kitten. "Okay, you're free to go across the street to your super-secret quilt meeting."

"Which you don't know about."

"Not a blessed thing. Can't wait to see the quilt you girls are putting together, though."

"Assuming it is a quilt." I gathered my own fabrics off the cutting table before that surprise went out the window as well. "Did you buy out the town?" I nodded toward her bags.

"Nearly," she said. "I bought a few things for the house, to make Oliver more comfortable. It's been so long since a man lived in that house, I wasn't sure what to get."

"Shaving lotion and spittoons?"

"Nearly. But then I bought navy towels—plain, boring navy. The ones I have in my bathroom have flowers on them. I didn't think he'd like those." She held up a bag. "And I got new sheets for the bed and a few plaid pillows for the couch in the living room."

Another change I knew was coming but wasn't quite prepared for. "When's he moving in?"

"Right after the wedding, I suppose. He wants us to take a few days and go to Montreal on a honeymoon. Can you imagine—a honeymoon? At our age."

"But that's what you do when you get married."

She looked flustered. "I imagine the whole town is whispering about how foolish we look."

"The whole town is happy for you."

"I got an e-mail from your uncle Henry. He's not able to make it. Said he'll meet Oliver after the wedding." Eleanor's voice was full of disappointment. "And your parents . . ."

"I haven't heard," I admitted. "They're traveling. I know Mom is excited for you. . . ."

Eleanor rolled her eyes.

"Well, *I'm* excited," I said, then resolved to give the speech I'd been planning since the engagement. "Grandma, I'm going to look for my own place. I know you'll be gone for months at a time, but when you're in town, you'll want . . . I mean, you'll be newlyweds. You might want to run around the house wearing nothing but a—"

"Nell Fitzgerald, don't you finish that sentence. I am still your grandmother."

"I just don't want to be in your way."

She let go of the bags. "You could never be in my way. Or Oliver's. I've treasured every moment since you came to live with me."

"Really. Even last month when I ate the muffins you were planning to give to the church bake sale?"

She smiled. "Good point. Pack your bags and get out." She hastily put her purchases behind the checkout counter when a customer walked into the shop. "It's not like you're at the house much anyway.

What time you don't spend here, or at class, you're at Jesse's." She sighed. "Poor soul. Any word on his friend?"

"Nothing new since yesterday. That I know of."

"That man . . ."

"Roger."

"Yes. He took such a long drive up here, only to go straight to Jesse's and get killed."

"He didn't go straight to Jesse's. He stopped at Jitters for tea."

Eleanor looked puzzled. "I thought he was desperate to tell Jesse something."

I felt myself blush. I had been so busy blaming myself for keeping Roger from talking to Jesse I hadn't put any thought into his visit to Jitters. But now it nagged at me. "Why didn't he go to Jesse's right away?" I wondered. "The police station is just down the street, and Jesse's house only a five-minute walk. Why stop for a snack?"

"And if he stopped there," Eleanor continued the thought, "where else did he go before he found his way to Jesse's house?"

My grandmother was the most reluctant member of our unofficial, and barely tolerated, investigative unit of the Archers Rest Police Department. But she was quickly becoming one of the best. She wasn't interested in credit reports, like Carrie, or good at Internet searches and combing through old documents, like Natalie and Maggie, but she knew people.

"We need to know more about Lizzie," I said. "I need you to ask Jesse's mom—"

"I thought we'd been through this. There's no point in going back."

"But this whole case is about the past. Roger came up here for Jesse. Why? It's probably because of something that happened while they were on the force together, an old case, or another detective. But if it's not about the police force, it's got to do with the time they all lived in New York City. And that means Lizzie."

"Nell, dear, I know how you like to help, and I know that a few times Jesse has even appreciated that help. But maybe this is the case you leave alone. Whatever it is, maybe it would be better for Jesse, better for both of you, if you stayed out of it."

I took a deep breath and considered what I knew was good advice. "It would," I finally answered, "and you're right, maybe I should. But if Jesse's in danger, and too sad or too stubborn to face that, I can't just sit by and do nothing."

"And you're willing to live with what you find out?"

"As long as Jesse's alive and safe, I'll live with whatever happens."

Eleanor nodded. "Okay then. At least we know that whatever we find, it won't change how you feel about each other."

She sounded sure. But for a brief moment I wondered if she was right.

CHAPTER 12

Susanne, Natalie's mother and an award-winning quilter, had sewn all the blocks of Eleanor's wedding quilt together into a queen-size top. In order to see it, the rest of the group—Bernie, Natalie, Maggie, and I—had taken over the back table at Jitters. Carrie handed over the cash register to Rich, her favorite employee and a former juvenile delinquent turned expert barista.

Susanne unfolded the quilt top slowly, as if she were preparing us to gasp and applaud, which we did. I'd been expecting our twelve blocks to be sewn three across by four down, with maybe some borders added. But Susanne had gone above and beyond, as usual.

The blocks were arranged asymmetrically, with Suzanne's hand-embroidered details, including the names of Eleanor's children and grandchildren, Oliver's daughter and granddaughter, the date they met, and the date of the wedding. It was a love story in thread and fabric: Oliver's hugely successful career as a painter, Eleanor's years in Archers Rest, the name of their favorite restaurant, their engagement over the summer—everything was there.

"Well, you've outdone yourself again," Maggie declared, making Susanne blush.

"I think it's the best quilt I've worked on," Susanne said, which was saying something given the dozens of ribbons for her remarkable quilts. "I think it's because it's all of us working together. It's all our creativity."

"I'm going to start quilting it tomorrow," Natalie told us. "I'll do it when Eleanor's not in the shop, and I'll take it off the frame when she comes in."

"Just cover it," I suggested. "She's too busy to pay attention to what's on the longarm machine."

"But make sure Nell puts in the last stitch," Maggie said, to the absolute agreement of the group.

"Which will do what?" I suspected it had something to do with the many quilt superstitions that dated to the beginning of the art form.

"Whoever puts the last stitch in a wedding quilt will be the next to marry," Bernie said.

"Then you do it," I told her. "You're between husbands at the moment."

"Three was enough." She laughed. "At least for now."

"I thought it was that if an unmarried woman put the last stitch into a quilt, she would never marry," Susanne said.

"That's ridiculous." Maggie rolled her eyes. "If that were the case then no woman from the nineteenth century would have found a husband."

"But just in case," Susanne offered. "Maybe the last stitch should be Bernie's. Since she's fine either way."

We all laughed so loud that several patrons looked over at us.

"It's a beautiful quilt." Carrie ran her hand over the patches. "We're a talented group."

Bernie laughed, though more quietly this time. "Now that we've got the wedding gift out of the way, I assume, Nell, you can fill us in on what's going on with Jesse?"

"I wish I had something." I told them about my conversation with Greg, and my concern that Jesse's past had something to do with the case. "There's a license plate that needs looking into. . . ."

"My nephew works at the DMV," Bernie offered. "I'll see what I can get out of him."

I checked that off my mental list. "And there's a matter of a business card." I gave the details and Maggie wrote down the information.

"Nothing else in the car?" Susanne asked.

"According to Greg, clean as a whistle except for a notebook. And no one has been able to see what's in it except Jesse."

"And he's not sharing?" Susanne asked.

"Not on this one. I think he really wants to be the one who solves his friend's murder."

Natalie jumped in. "I did some digging on Roger Leighton. I figured we'd need to know, so I looked into it last night after I put the kids to bed. Roger left the police force about six months ago. Health issues, something with his back, and he had asked for early retirement."

"How did you find that?" I asked.

"I made a few calls. I talked to a friend of my cousin who knew a New York City cop. And he knew another cop who worked with Leighton, and that guy said that Roger ran marathons, worked out a lot. It surprised him that Roger was claiming he wasn't up for the job."

"The cop who knows another cop who knows your cousin's friend. . . ." Saying it made me laugh. We didn't have the normal channels of investigation open to us, so we had a sort of six-degrees-of-separation way to getting what we needed. Between us we all knew someone who knew someone, etc. . . . Of course, in the last few investigations we had Jesse offering information, actually asking for our help, if reluctantly. "Did he know if Roger was having other problems at work? Maybe an old case that got overturned, or an issue with a fellow officer?"

"He didn't mention anything, and I'm sorry, I didn't think to ask. He did say that Roger had been extra careful on arrests and paperwork. He was super insistent that everything be by the book."

"Was that a new behavior?" Bernie asked.

"I don't know, but it seemed like he found it annoying, and he said he liked Roger," Natalie told her.

"Maybe that's it," Suzanne jumped in. "Maybe Roger discovered corruption and was killed because of it. If he did everything by the book, he'd have to turn in those cops who didn't, right? Maybe he quit so he wouldn't have to hurt his friends."

It was a good theory, and one that fit in with what Jesse had said about Roger.

"I'll keep looking," Maggie said. "We'll find everything we can about him."

As she spoke, Jesse walked into Jitters. We had the quilt unfolded across the table, so to anyone looking we were just a group of women talking about our hobby. Under normal circumstances that wouldn't fool Jesse, but this time it seemed to.

"Wedding?" he asked.

"Nothing but," Susanne said. She held up the quilt and Jesse took his time examining it.

"It's amazing. You ladies are gifted." He cleared his throat and nodded toward me. "Can I talk to you for a minute?"

"Sure." I got up and followed him to the back of the shop, feeling like a kid called into the principal's office. When I looked back at the table, I saw the group read the situation the same way I did.

Jesse held my hands and smiled softly. "I know how good you are at these investigations. I know you always get to the bottom of things."

"I can help you, you know."

"I just said that Nell."

"But you're going to tell me to butt out."

"I'm going to tell you, if you give me a chance, to not go behind my back to get information out of my officers."

"You mean yesterday?"

"Yes. Is there a time limit on when I can talk to you about something that bothers me?" His voice was slightly irritated, but he took a deep breath and started again. "I just needed time to think about what I wanted to say."

"I was chatting with Greg," I said, trying to keep my defensiveness to a minimum and Greg out of trouble. "I've known him as long as I've known you. He's my friend. I can't say hi to him on the street?"

"That's not what you were doing."

"What did he say we were doing?"

Jesse smiled. He'd caught me. "I haven't talked to him. Yet. But my guess is you were pumping the guy for information."

"I was talking to him. . . ." I gave up. "What's going on, Jesse? You're not putting everything into evidence, you're not letting me help you. . . ."

"I'm trying to deal with the death of my friend."

"Then that's what you should do. I know you feel that you should conduct the investigation, but maybe it's a mistake. Maybe you should focus on the personal and let the state police handle it. If you do that, I'll stay out of it, too. I'll be whatever you need me to be."

"That sounds like blackmail."

That took me aback. "In what way? I'm saying that you should focus on Roger, and on your loss, and let . . ."

"I heard you." The edge in his voice returned. He was starting a fight with me. I had to decide if I wanted to help it along or stop things where they were.

"I'm sorry," I said, choosing to assume that Jesse was too shaken up to think straight. "I'm here, however you need me."

"Right now, I need my girlfriend, not another detective."

"I've been both for a while."

"Not this time."

I bit my lip, but I couldn't stay quiet. "Why? Is it just because he was your friend or is something else going on?"

"Nell, promise me you'll stay out of it."

I hesitated. If I made the promise, I wasn't sure I could keep it, and if I didn't make it, I wasn't sure what Jesse's reaction would be. "Okay." It was a halfhearted whisper.

"Okay," he said. Then he kissed my cheek, let go of my hand, and headed out of Jitters. As I walked back to the table I was already regretting the agreement. And already certain that I would break my promise. I took a few steps toward the door, to tell Jesse I'd changed my mind. But before I could get very far, I heard a shot.

CHAPTER 13

I t all seemed to happen in slow motion. I ran from Jitters and saw Eleanor coming from Someday Quilts. Carrie was behind me. Natalie, Maggie, and Susanne pushed past us to see what was going on. Bernie yelled out that she would call the police station. I understood the words, but it seemed like they were in an echo. On the sidewalk beside me, a crowd seemed to gather from nowhere. Jesse was on the street, on his back. I wanted to run to him, but Carrie held me back just as another shot rang out, hitting a streetlamp and shattering glass all over Jesse.

"Jesse!" I screamed.

He sat up, then turned to me and barked, "Get back inside. Now. Everyone."

People started running into doorways and shops. A third shot. This one hit Jesse's squad car, causing the windshield to explode.

"Now, Nell. Move."

Eleanor and Natalie went back into the shop. Carrie grabbed my sleeve and pulled me back toward Jitters. Jesse, finally, got up and ran toward us. We made it into the store just as a fourth bullet tore up a second streetlamp.

Then, everything sped up. I saw blood on Jesse's arm. His face was pale. I looked in his eyes. They were clear, angry, and maybe a little scared, but it was obvious that he was in control of the situation.

"I'm okay," he said. He wrapped the good arm around me.

"What the hell is going on?" My heart was pounding so hard I could barely hear myself speak.

"I have to call the station."

"Not necessary." I pointed out the window. Two Archers Rest police cars were speeding down the street, sirens blaring. They stopped in front of Jitters. Greg got out of his car and came toward the store. He moved quickly but didn't run, all the while looking around him. It was one of those brave cop moves that reminded me how far he'd come since I'd met him. He walked into Jitters, looked around for Jesse, and went straight to him, moving past the rest of us without comment.

"Where was it coming from?" Greg asked Jesse. No preliminaries or "how are yous," just right to it. Jesse seemed relieved.

"The park, it seemed like."

Archers Rest had a Main Street going north and south, and a couple of small side streets before it drifted off into houses and, farther out, into farms. Someday Quilts was right in the middle of Main Street, with Jitters directly across from it, and beyond that the cemetery. Around the corner, at the north end of the street, was City Hall and the police station. To the south Main Street dead-ended at a small but well-loved park.

"Did you see anyone?" Greg was writing down Jesse's answers in a small notebook. It was very official, and it made me feel safer knowing that Jesse wasn't going to have to deal with this alone.

Jesse shook his head. "Didn't see anything, just heard shots."

"How could someone have shot from the park without being seen?" Greg asked.

I'd been thinking the same thing. The park was a wide-open space. There was only one place to hide—the gazebo. The street in front of the park was normally a no-parking zone, but I'd noticed that there was a car parked there this morning, a VW Bug. It might have been suspicious except I knew who it belonged to, our town's librarian, Dru Ann Love. I doubted Dru, who rarely stuck her head out of a book, was shooting at anyone in her spare time.

I was standing in the center of the shop, away from the front window under orders from Jesse and Greg to stay back, but I still had a decent view. Dru's car was still at the end of the street. Her VW Bug didn't provide much cover, and since it hadn't been stolen as a getaway car it meant that the shooter would have had to run from the spot to escape.

"No one would have noticed in all the chaos," I thought out loud, "unless the person running still had a gun."

"Not a gun," Jesse said. "A rifle. A bolt-action rifle, if he's a pro."

"Are you sure?"

"The sound, it's very specific," he said.

"But why would someone shoot at you?"

"It wasn't aimed at me," Jesse said. "Unless the guy is the world's unluckiest shooter. There were half a dozen people on the street when the whole thing started, and the only damage is to a car, two streetlamps, and the sign to Someday."

"The what?"

I moved closer to the window, trying to still stay back far enough to be out of the line of fire, just in case. But I had to see for myself. The logo for Someday Quilts was a needle, with the shop's name spelled out in thread. It was painted on a piece of wood that hung above the front window of the store. The sign was big, maybe five feet long, but it was flat against the building. It didn't seem like an easy target unless you were directly across the street from it, and yet there was a hole in the *S* of "Someday" that wasn't there this morning. Why would someone shoot at a quilt shop?

Jesse and Greg huddled at the back of Jitters, talking in low voices. While Bernie did her best to tend to Jesse's wound, I saw Carrie handing out tea and coffee to the shaken patrons. I went for one of the green teas on offer, but as I grabbed for the cup, I noticed my hands were shaking.

"Okay?" Carrie asked.

"So far," I said.

Maggie and Susanne busied themselves making more drinks, and Natalie turned herself into Bernie's assistant. She handed Bernie a bandage from Jitters's first-aid kit and searched in her purse for some aspirin to give to Jesse.

"It isn't a bullet wound," Bernie assured me. "He got hit with some falling debris and he's just cut. It's deep, might need a stitch or two, but he'll be okay. I could go over to my pharmacy and get something to disinfect . . ."

"You're not going anywhere," Jesse told her. "I'll be fine."

He looked fine. Mostly. He could move his arm and he didn't seem to be in much pain. I tried not to think about how it could have been so much worse. Or how much worse it could still get.

All of us—Carrie's customers, my quilt group, Jesse and Greg—stayed crowded in the back. No one, it seemed, was anxious for a place near the window. The minutes ticked by. We waited. Nothing happened, and with each minute I grew more frustrated. Jesse held tight to my hand, probably as much to keep me with him as to comfort me. After a few calls to the station seemed to indicate that the shooter hadn't moved on to another target but stopped completely, Greg and Jesse took the short-cut through the alley to the station to see what could be done. Carrie locked the door behind them and we all went back to waiting. But after five more minutes of silence, I was done with doing nothing.

I walked toward the wide glass window with a clear view of Main Street. The street outside looked quiet. Across from me, I could see Eleanor in the window of Someday. She had the phone to her ear, and my cell was ringing in my pocket. But when she saw me, she put down the phone and pointed toward her arm. She wanted to know about Jesse. I smiled and nodded, hoping that conveyed he was fine. Then she gestured for me to move back and disappeared from the window.

I should have done the same, but I needed to see what was happening. The shock was gone. Sadly, Archers Rest wasn't immune from the violence that hits everywhere. In fact, murders and other crimes seemed to strike the town with an alarming regularity.

As I stood staring at the hole in the Someday sign, and the damage that had been done to the car and streetlamps, I tried to figure out where the shooter could have been. The angle was such that it seemed like he might have been above the shop, but there was no second floor. Next door maybe?

"Nell, get back there." Greg was behind me walking toward me. He had come in the back door and startled me more than I cared to admit. "We have the rest of the force on the street, the sniper seems to be gone. I'm going to take Jesse to see the doctor. If you want to come with us . . ."

"So it's safe now," I said.

"Safe enough to get Jesse to the hospital. I think it would be better if everyone just stayed inside a little while longer. We have some help coming from the state police to do a street-by-street sweep. That should take an hour or so, and then everything can get back to normal. Hopefully."

"Do you think this has something to do with the murder?" I whispered my question, but it didn't matter. Jesse had also snuck up behind me.

"You made a promise," he said.

"You got shot at," I countered.

"All the more reason to stay out of it."

"So you think this has something to do with Roger."

Jesse turned to my quilt group, my friends and co-conspirators on more than a few cases. "If you have to tie her up, keep her here."

"Absolutely," Maggie said.

Jesse kissed my forehead, and he and Greg headed toward a police car. Carrie locked the door behind them, and we watched them get into the car.

"He'll be okay," she said.

Greg sped away, replacing Carrie's reassurance with the piercing sound of sirens.

CHAPTER 14

The siren had barely faded away when I got another jolt. My cell phone vibrated against me, insisting on my attention. I grabbed it from my jeans pocket assuming Eleanor had decided she wanted to talk. But it wasn't Eleanor. And while the number was familiar and comforting, the timing was all wrong.

"Not now," I muttered. I took what I hoped was a calming breath, and answered. "Hi, Mom."

"Everything okay? You sound nervous."

"Not nervous, caffeinated. I'm in a coffee shop with some friends." I just didn't have the energy to explain.

"Oh."

I couldn't tell whether she believed me or not, but it wasn't a lie, and in any case, it was the only answer I intended to give. "Are you and Dad back from Rome?" I asked.

"Istanbul, and yes, we're back. We got back two days ago and we were completely jet-lagged or I would have called sooner. But don't worry, Dad is packing the car right now."

"Where are you going to this time?" My parents had been on an almost nonstop around-the-world trip since my dad retired two years ago.

"Archers Rest. We're coming to see you and Grandma."

I had gotten used to them being a postcard or a Skype conversation away. Seeing them in person was like Christmas arriving eleven months early. Except this wasn't the best time for a quiet visit. "The wedding is more than a week away, why don't you wait . . ." I started.

My mother cut in. "She's going through with it?"

"The wedding? Of course."

"Nell, tell me the truth, is she okay? Is she . . . her mind, I mean . . ."

"What are you asking? Eleanor and Oliver are really happy."

"Eleanor? That's what you call her now. What happened to Grandma?"

"We work together. I call her both names." I could hear my impatience. If she and Dad wanted to traipse around the world that was their business, but here at home things had changed. Eleanor had changed. And so had I. "Oliver's a terrific guy."

"They're in their seventies."

"Which means they're adults who can do what they like."

I heard my mother grunt. "The Philly traffic gets bad in the afternoon, so we'll have to head out now," she said. "I intend to continue this discussion when I arrive."

"Mom, they're very happy. . . ."

She ignored me. "And there's a few things I'd like to talk to you about, too."

I heard my father call to her that it was time to get going, and then the phone clicked off without even a good-bye. I love my parents and I couldn't wait to see them, to introduce them to Jesse, and to show them the changes that Eleanor and I had made at Someday Quilts, but somehow it had already gotten off on the wrong foot. And gun shots on Main Street weren't helping.

Natalie walked up to me, twisting her long blond hair. She smiled, but she looked nervous. "I called the sitter. The kids are okay, but I really need to get home. Are we here much longer?"

"I have no idea. Where's your car?"

She pointed out the window. I could see it across the street toward the end of the block, just north of where the shots had been. I could also see another car, the blue sedan from yesterday, parked behind it. It had been moved from the spot where it had been ticketed, which likely meant that its owner was somewhere in one of the shops waiting, like the rest of us.

"Maybe you should stay here until we get the all-clear," I suggested. I could see her fear and frustration. I felt it, too. Everything in me wanted to walk outside and start examining the evidence. Everything except the part of me that was scared.

"This is about the murder, right?" Natalie asked. "Whoever killed Jesse's friend just shot up our street."

"It would be one heck of a coincidence to have two big crimes in twenty-four hours if they weren't related," I agreed. "But what would be the point?"

"To scare Jesse."

"Then whoever it is doesn't know Jesse very well."

"To scare you?" she suggested.

"Why me?"

"Maybe you saw something the other night when you walked past Roger in his car."

"A man. Cigarette smoke. That's it. Certainly nothing that would identify the killer."

"Maybe the killer *thinks* you saw something."

"But even if that's true, I wasn't on the street. I was in here."

"But the sign," she said. "Why would someone shoot at the sign unless it was a warning to you?"

She had a point. I could buy the idea that someone was shooting wildly, except that Jesse was right, no one was hurt. In fact, the bullets mostly hit things, like the streetlights and the sign, that were well above people's heads. So if the shots were aimed, what would be the point unless it was a message?

I closed my eyes and tried for the hundredth time to remember the scene outside Jesse's house the night of the murder. It was cold and I was annoyed at myself for leaving my purse behind at the shop. I parked my car. The streetlight in front of Jesse's house was out, so I couldn't see too far ahead. The car was an SUV with an open window, a man sat in the front seat. There was cigarette smoke.

If the killer was already in the car, sitting behind Roger, had I seen anything—any glimpse of anyone? Was Roger even still alive? I didn't know. I strained to remember more, but the truth was, all I saw was the outline of a man I assumed to be just an unfriendly smoker, sitting in a car. I turned and walked toward Jesse's door without giving anything about the scene a second thought.

If the killer was trying to warn me off the case, then he, or she, was having the opposite effect. There was nothing I was going to learn standing there. I took one more look out the front window and decided that leaving that way was too risky. Instead, I headed toward the back. I heard Maggie call out for me to stop, but it was too late. I was already out the back door. It was safe, that's what Greg had said. No sign of the sniper. Though even the word gave me chills, I tried not to let it get to me. If the police couldn't find him, I doubted I would. Besides, what were the odds he'd be hiding in the alley?

I guessed I was about to find out.

CHAPTER 15

I made my way south toward the park. From the alley all I could see was garbage. There was no one out except me. Maybe wandering around outside *was* nuts, but I didn't care. If the shooter had meant to harm anyone, it would have already happened. At least that's what I told myself, as my heart beat a mile a minute.

When I got to the end of the block, I watched carefully for . . . I don't know exactly what I was watching for. It was unlikely someone would walk past me with an assault rifle, hand it over, and agree to a citizen's arrest. If I did encounter someone, it was far more likely he'd shoot.

Instinctively, I touched my hand to my right shoulder. It had been ten months since a bullet had grazed me there, and I still remembered the pain. An ill-informed misadventure while trying to investigate a crime, I reminded myself.

"Just like this." It was my voice, but it still startled me.

I stuck a foot out into the street and when it wasn't shot off, I took a full step onto the sidewalk. I could see the park, and the street in front of it where Dru's car was parked. One of the Archers Rest police cars was parked in front of it, and two of Jesse's officers were checking the car for clues. Immediately, I could see that Jesse was wrong. If the shots had come from this direction, there was no way that someone could have hit the Someday sign straight on. The shooter had to have been across the street from the shop, closer to Jitters. It worried me that he was so shaken up he'd gotten such a simple thing wrong. It worried me more that he might have done it on purpose.

There was no point in standing near the car now, trying to test my theory further. I'd just be shooed away by the officers, who had, no doubt, gotten orders from Jesse to keep their distance from me. Instead I headed into the park.

It was small. Mainly our park was just a patch of grass, a children's play area, a white lacey gazebo, and an abstract sculpture that had been lovingly dubbed "Johnny" after our town's founder, John Archer. It would be difficult to imagine someone shooting from anywhere in the park and not being seen by a dozen witnesses.

I walked one side to the other, then examined the gazebo. The park was deserted, which made the job easier, but also slightly eerie. It was a cold day, not much activity in the park. Someone had obviously wanted to enjoy yesterday's snowfall, and brought a sled to the park, abandoned when they ran. Someone else had dropped an entire bag of birdseed. People had been here when the shooting began. But there were no injuries, no ambulances, and, thankfully, no coroner's vans. If the shooter had wanted to do more than send a message, I shuddered at the damage he could have done.

I walked back down Main Street toward Someday. I saw a state police car driving slowly, but otherwise the street was just as deserted as the park. I glanced in the storefronts, but I was more interested in the second floors and rooftops. Most buildings, like the ones that housed Jitters and Someday Quilts, were single story, but there were a few that had apartments above the stores—the movie theater, the bank, and an empty shop that was once Clark's Dry Cleaners. The office space above it was empty, too, as far as I could remember. And its position, two doors down from Jitters, would give it a pretty good angle to shoot all three of the sniper's targets.

"Miss, you okay?" The state police car had stopped, and the officer inside it was looking at me.

"I'm fine, thanks."

"What are you looking at?"

I was about to share the fact that I was trying to figure out where the gunman had been. Jesse had gotten used to my sleuthing, annoyed by it sometimes as he was now, but used to it. The rest of the town seemed to alternately applaud me and worry about my sanity. Out-of-towners, particularly law enforcement personnel, tended to laugh at me.

"The building," I answered. "I'm trying to see if the office above Clark's is occupied. I'm looking for a new office space."

"This might not be the best time. There's been some excitement around here."

"I heard about it. Do you know who did it?"

"We're still investigating. Might be a good idea not to wander around in the open until we're sure everything is okay."

"Do you think the shooter is still in the area?"

"I don't know. That's why you should head directly to wherever you're going and not stand around in the street."

"I suppose that's a good idea." I knew it was a good idea, but Greg had said things were safe now, and that's what I chose to believe. I walked a little farther down the street, but the car kept following me.

"Can I ask your name?" The officer leaned out the window.

"Why?"

"We're just being extra careful."

I almost argued the point, since it felt wrong to have to identify myself when I wasn't doing anything illegal. But arguing the point would take longer, and, in the end, likely put me in Jesse's crosshairs. "Carrie Brown," I said, throwing out the first name that came to me. "I own the coffee shop and I'm thinking of getting into some

Internet sales. T-shirts, pounds of coffee, that sort of thing." I was babbling, but he seemed to buy it. If the officer reported back to Jesse that a Nell Fitzgerald was looking at buildings, I'd be in trouble fast. Of course, Carrie wasn't going to be thrilled that I'd thrown her into the middle of the situation.

When I got toward the end of the block, Natalie's car was gone, but the blue sedan was still there. The state police officer had lost interest in me and turned the corner, so I decided to check out the car. There was another parking ticket on the windshield, this one given about twenty minutes before the shooting began and signed by Jesse. It was for parking too close to a fire hydrant, a ridiculous charge since there wasn't a fire hydrant on this side of the street.

The car itself looked pretty new and well cared for. Maybe another rental. I looked in the driver's side window. The inside of the car was clean. The *New York Post* was on the passenger seat, dated a few days ago. A Starbucks cup in the cup holder meant that the driver had come from somewhere at least fifteen miles away since there were no Starbucks, or any chain restaurants, in Archers Rest or in the towns that surrounded us. The backseat was empty, but I noticed something on the floor, something shiny. I could tell that it was metallic, but beyond that I didn't know what it was. I tried the door, but it was locked. They were all locked. That was probably for the best. I really had no business looking into this car's windows just because Jesse had unfairly ticketed it. And I definitely had no business breaking into it.

I stepped away and moved back toward Someday. The best course of action was still getting Jesse to search the old Clark's Dry Cleaners. That is, if he'd listen, which, for the first time since I'd known him, I was worried about.

"It's you." A man in an army jacket and dark pants, maybe ten years my senior, walked toward me. I didn't know him, but he seemed to know me—at least he had the relaxed stance and friendly smile of someone I was supposed to know. He was average height, average build, in fact all the average stuff except for piercing blue eyes.

"Have we met?"

"No, sorry." When he reached me he held out his hand. "Robert Marshall; Bob. I'm new around here. Might be, anyway. I'm thinking of moving here."

There was a lot of power in his handshake. "Nell Fitzgerald," I said. "I'm a little confused. You know me somehow?"

"That must have sounded odd. It's just that I've seen you a couple of times, in the coffee shop and walking a golden retriever. I used to have a retriever. They're nice dogs."

"They certainly are."

"So where is he?"

"Barney—he's at home or in the shop where I work." I pointed toward Someday Quilts.

"My sister makes quilts. Maybe I can get her something. I was away for a while and she took care of my dog for me."

"That's very thoughtful of you. We do have a lot of nice gifts for quilters. And Barney will be happy to meet a new retriever friend if you do move here."

His smiled faded. "My dog died while I was away. But maybe it's time for a puppy. I kept seeing you and Barney, and now you're standing just a few feet from my car." He pointed toward the blue sedan. "It must be a sign that I'm meant to start a new life here."

"Your car?" I eyed him more carefully, looking for the reason he'd received so much negative attention from Jesse. But I saw nothing out of the ordinary, except for his eyes, which were focused intently on me.

"A bit boring, but it's reliable," he said. "Kind of like me."

"It's nice," I said, unsure of what else to say. "Where are you from? I mean, where would you be moving from?"

"The city. New York City, I guess I should say. I love it there, but it's a bit hectic, if you know what I mean."

"I do. I used to live there, too."

"And you moved up here? A woman after my own heart." His wide smile grew even wider. "Good to see I'm not the only one. I drove up here just on a whim and I really like it. This town has a great vibe, don't you think?"

"It does." I felt like an idiot for being so suspicious of a car, and a stranger. My amateur detective tendencies had been on high alert since Roger's body was found, and it was time to dial it back. "How long have you been in town?"

"A few days. I was on my way to Montreal on a vacation, and I kind of meandered here and stayed."

I tried to size him up. I needed a suspect and here was a stranger up from New York ready to fit the part. But was that just a bit too convenient? People did drive through Archers Rest all the time, and it *was* a nice place. Maybe the only thing wrong about the guy was his timing.

"If you decide to move here," I told him, "you'll like it. The people are very friendly and the town is beautiful. It's a nice community, big enough where you don't know everybody but small enough where even strangers have friends in common."

"Except for the police department," Bob said as he grabbed the ticket off the windshield. He read it and laughed. "This is my fourth once since yesterday," he said. "I don't get it. Do the cops around here not like out-of-towners?"

"Small towns need their revenue," I said, rather feebly. "The police station is just around the corner." I pointed in the direction. "Why don't you go ask the chief about it: Jesse Dewalt. He's a reasonable guy. I'm sure if there's been some kind of error, he'll tear up the tickets."

"You know the guy?"

I suddenly didn't want to answer. Bob Marshall was friendly, seemed harmless, and was, for whatever reason, getting a raw deal from Jesse. But maybe it was his intense eyes or maybe I just couldn't dial back my suspicious nature fast enough. Instead of telling him the truth, I said, "Like I said, it's a small town. Everyone knows the police chief."

He nodded. "Well, Nell, I appreciate the idea. I'll go over there right now and find out what this is all about. But if he arrests me for whoever did that shoot 'em up earlier today, I hope you'll bail me out of jail."

"Did you see what happened?" Instead of stumbling on a suspect, maybe I'd found an eyewitness. In which case I was making up for my bad detective work with dumb luck.

"Nope. Didn't see anything, but I heard about it."

"From who?"

"Small town. Everyone knows what's going on, right?"

"Right."

He smiled, got into his car, and drove away in the opposite direction to the police station.

CHAPTER 16

I loved the Archers Rest Library. It was big and old-fashioned, smelled of books and permanence. It was where the town gathered to plan events, celebrate holidays, and hold local elections. And it was lovingly cared for by Dru Ann Love, who had likely read every one of the thousands of volumes in the place. I'd never seen her without at least one book in her hand and today was no exception. When I walked in she looked up from Nancy Pickard's *The Scent of Rain and Lightning,* as if I were waking her from a dream.

"Are you okay?" she asked. "I heard about the shooting. Anyone hurt?"

"I'm good. Everybody's good. Well, Jesse got cut from some falling glass. But he's fine, it was just a small cut."

Dru looked relieved. "Jesse seems to be having a really bad week. I don't know how his guys are going to be able to investigate two serious crimes at the same time. There are so few of them."

"I'm sure they'll manage."

"Well, you'll help, like always, but still . . ." Dru opened a drawer at her desk and pulled out a little box of cat treats. "I bought this for that kitten you found. I was going to bring it over at lunch. Just as a welcome gift. We had a mother around here a few months ago; I think she had a litter. Your kitten must be one of them."

"What happened to the mom?"

Dru frowned. "There were some rats around the trash area out back, so the library board insisted on putting rat poison out. I found the mom and two little kittens dead about a month ago, right behind the library. I guess your little one was too smart to eat it."

She wasn't a lost kitten, she was an orphan. I had assumed it, but now it was for sure. Smart enough to avoid poison, survive for a month on her own, and find shelter in a quilt shop on a bitterly cold night. It was a lot to go through for such a tiny little thing; I loved her already.

"Has your car been in front of the park all day?" I asked Dru after I'd tucked the cat treats in my purse.

"Since last night. After I closed up, I walked over and the car wouldn't start. So frustrating. Luckily Greg was driving by, and he offered me a ride home."

"That was nice."

"It was. He's very nice."

"Greg didn't look to see what was wrong with the car?"

"He was going to, but I told him I was meeting Charlie Lofton at Moran's Pub and I was running late, so Greg dropped me there and Charlie gave me a ride home instead."

"Charlie?" I smiled a little but tried to squash it. If there was a romance starting between the librarian and the third-grade teacher, it wasn't my place to gossip about it. Dru blushed, which saved me the trouble of asking questions. "Did you try to start your car this morning?"

"No, I walked to the library this morning. I meant to call Larry over at the garage to come look at it, but I forgot."

"You never park it there, do you? That's a no-parking zone."

"I did the monthly reports last night, so I was leaving later than usual. And when I do the reports, I'm the last one to leave the library," she said. "The parking lot in back is so dark, especially in the winter.

It just doesn't feel safe. So yesterday I asked Jesse if it was okay if I left my car in front of the park, where it would be under a streetlight, and he said it was. He's so understanding. You're very lucky."

"I am." My one small hope that Jesse was giving out far more parking tickets than usual as some revenue-raising scheme fell away. Jesse was, apparently, only giving tickets to strangers.

"This has to do with my car being used for cover for that crazy shooter, doesn't it?" Dru asked.

"Did you see anything?"

She shook her head. "You can't see Main Street very well from here, so I didn't see anything. But Greg came over and got my keys about ten minutes ago. He told me that the shooter may have been hiding behind my car."

That made me want to ask Greg what he'd found, but knowing how sweet and eager to please Greg was, he'd tell me, and that would just get him into trouble with Jesse again. I was out of ideas. I turned to leave, but something nagged at me.

"Didn't you just get that car?" I asked.

"About eight months ago. Brand-new."

"And it's already not starting?"

She shrugged. "I guess I got a lemon."

"Had it ever happened before?"

"No, first time. It's actually been a great car, but last night, it just wouldn't start. Wouldn't even turn on."

"Like a dead battery?"

"I guess. It was pretty cold last night. Maybe it just couldn't handle it."

"Maybe. Did Charlie try to jump it?"

"No. It was just easier to give me a ride to my place than stand around in the cold trying to get it to start. We were both heading in the same direction." Another blush punctuated that sentence. "I told him it would keep until today."

Charlie, an exceptionally tall, exceptionally thin man with kind eyes and a good heart walked into the library at that moment, his entire class of giggling nine-year-olds trailing after him. He smiled when he saw me and nodded hello, but his eyes went quickly to Dru.

"I'm doing story time for Charlie . . . for the kids," Dru explained.

Then before I had a chance to tell her what a great idea I thought that was, she hurried to meet the class.

At least today wasn't all bad news.

✂

I walked out of the library into bright sunshine and a cold wind. The Archers Rest police were still by Dru's car, but as I walked down Main, I saw that a few officers from the state police were going up to the rooftops of some of the shops. I guess Jesse's theory about the shots coming from the park was only plausible to the officers under his command. I wondered how he felt about that.

Carrie was outside talking to the same officer who had warned me off the street earlier. I saw her pointing to the sign. She was just giving a statement, which as a good citizen she was required to do, but it felt a little disloyal. This was Jesse's town, and his investigation. Someone other than Jesse taking over the investigation didn't seem right. The hypocrisy of that thought didn't escape me, but at least I was trying to help Jesse.

At the moment, though, I wasn't being much help. All I knew was that Dru's new car didn't start the night Roger was killed; Jesse bombarded a stranger in town with tickets; a sniper shot up Main Street but no one got hurt; and Jesse's old police partner was killed outside Jesse's house . . . all within forty-eight hours. They might all be connected, some of them might be, or it could just be one giant, nightmarish coincidence. Like the fact that, in the midst of all of it, my parents were on their way to Archers Rest to talk my grandmother out of her wedding.

Despite all the frightening events in town, that last part was the only thing that I truly panicked about. I wanted to sit quietly and think things through, I needed to go back to the shop and work on my wedding gift for Eleanor and Oliver, but instead I headed toward home, hoping to figure out a way to keep my mother from dampening Eleanor's excitement and, even more impossible, to keep my parents from hearing everything that had been happening in town.

CHAPTER 17

My mother, Patricia Cassidy Fitzgerald, aka Patty, hates quilts. Well, "hate" is probably too strong a word, but she doesn't like them. Not really. She tolerates them and respects them and grudgingly admires the skills and talents of those who make them, but she doesn't like them. They represent homey, old-fashioned things, and my mother likes only what's new and exciting.

I knew why—at least I'd heard the explanation from my father so many times, I'd memorized it. Growing up, my mother and her brother, my uncle Henry, had been one of the few kids in their classes with a working mother, which wouldn't have been so bad if Eleanor had made any money at it. But in its infancy, Someday Quilts brought in just enough cash to scrape by. And as a young girl my mom had to go to the shop every day after school because Eleanor couldn't afford a babysitter, and when mom was older she had to help stock the shelves. After years of it, and years of listening to women like Maggie and Bernie extol the joys of passing down quilting from generation to generation, my mom had become allergic to the idea of tradition.

Eleanor had tried over and over to get her interested in the craft, but it didn't take. "Even Henry can sew on a button," my grandmother would say, but my mom resisted every effort to see either the practical nature or pure art of a quilt.

My mom left Archers Rest at the first chance, moved to Philadelphia, and met my dad, Michael Fitzgerald. My sister and I got quilts from Eleanor, and treasured them, and my mother dutifully kept one in the family room, but she didn't love it. It wasn't mean spirited; she loved that her mother cared enough to send the quilts. And she appreciated the work that went into them, she just didn't get why anyone would bother when blankets were available for purchase at dozens of stores within driving distance.

When I'd been struggling after my engagement was broken off, it was my mother who suggested I visit Eleanor for a weekend of comfort food and fresh air. Mom and Dad were in London, and she knew, rightly, that I would only wallow if left alone. She hadn't expected me to stay. She tolerated it because of art school, because it seemed temporary, and because it's difficult to yell at your daughter from six thousand miles away. But now she'd be here, face-to-face, and as much as I was excited to see my parents, and proud that I got my sense of adventure directly from my mom, I wasn't up for "the talk" about my future.

✂

I walked down the long, winding driveway to Eleanor's Victorian home, my home, rehearsing my answers to the barrage of questions sure to be coming my way, trying to be excited and optimistic about the visit, trying not to resent that it took away from my work on Roger's murder and the shooting. But as I reached the house, I realized it was too late for rehearsal. My parents' car was in the driveway, between Eleanor's minivan and Oliver's Jeep.

"Mom? Dad?" As I walked into the hallway of the old house, I could hear laughter coming from the kitchen. "You're here already?"

My mom and dad were at the kitchen table with Oliver and Eleanor. Barney was sleeping nearby in his bed of many quilts. Patch sat on the kitchen counter, staring down at the dog, looking ready to pounce and completely unafraid. Of course she was out of the reach of Barney's long snout, so being brave was easy.

My mom jumped up and hugged me. "You look wonderful. Just beautiful. I can't believe it's been more than a year since I've seen my baby daughter."

We hugged tightly. I realized how much I missed her, and how nice it was to have her here. "Are you staying until the wedding?" I asked.

"Well, we're staying for as long as we're needed," my mom said.

I glanced over at Eleanor, who shook her head. "Your mother suggested that instead of getting married, Oliver and I live in sin."

"I did no such thing. Honestly, Mom, you just like to shock people."

"Patty, what other reason would you have for coming so soon after you returned from Europe?"

"To see my child, and to see my mother."

I wanted no piece of this argument, so I went to my dad's waiting arms. "Hey, there," I said. "How was Istanbul?"

"Was that where we were? Your mom has me going to so many countries I'm not sure where I am until I check the stamp on my passport."

"Fitz, Turkey was your idea." My mother shook her head at him, exactly the same way I've seen Eleanor do a thousand times. I probably had the same move and didn't know it.

"Sit down, everyone," I said. "I'm thrilled you're here. We're gearing up for the big day, but there's still a lot to do if you want to help."

"The bachelor party is a week from today," Oliver said to my dad.

"Good God. Are you kidding me?" The words came out of my mother before she had a chance to stop them and I could tell she wished she had.

"Patty." My grandmother . . .

"Eleanor." Me . . .

"Stop calling your grandmother Eleanor." My mother . . .

Three generations of my family, all stubborn and all annoyed.

"Sounds great," my dad said in the silence that followed. "The bachelor party. It's been a while since I've been to one of those. I'm waiting for Nell here to settle down. . . ."

"Fitz," my mother said, in the loudest whisper possible. "Don't pressure her."

"Thanks, Mom."

"You're a young woman, lots of time to decide what you want to do, a lot of places to see, and you have to pursue your career as a painter."

"Did you know that Oliver's a painter?" I said. "A very famous painter. His works hang in dozens of museums in the States, in England, lots of places."

My mom smiled at him. "Fitz and I actually saw one of your pieces in London; a woman almost in shadow, sitting by a window in a run-down apartment. It was amazing. It's an extraordinary gift to be able to capture a scene, the light, the mood. I was awestruck."

"You're very kind," Oliver told her. "Your daughter is a quite talented painter, you know. Though I think her real gift is in fabric. Much like her grandmother, she can create beauty in even very simple quilts. But Nell has her own spin that I find truly inspiring."

I reached out and grabbed Oliver's hand. "Thanks, Gramps."

My mother said nothing about my nickname for Oliver, but she grunted slightly and went back to drinking her coffee.

CHAPTER 18

"He might be busy," I warned them. "It's been kind of a hectic day."

"I want to meet this man. You've told us he's wonderful, he's perfect, he's smart and kind and everything else. Now I want to see for myself." My mother grabbed her coat from the rack and bundled up. It was too late to think of an excuse. We were going to meet Jesse.

"Chief of police," my dad said. "Lot of responsibility in that."

"There is . . ." I started.

"It's a small town," my mother said. "When I grew up here nothing happened. Nothing. I imagine it's the same now."

Once my mother decided something was true, she wouldn't go looking to be proven wrong. To her, Archers Rest was a boring town in the middle of nowhere. And with my parents traipsing all over the world, it was easy to avoid mentioning anything that might conflict with that opinion, especially when it was murder. I didn't want them to worry. And I didn't want to have to explain my role in solving some of those crimes. So I said nothing. I figured the odds were good that when they did come, the town would be the quiet place my mother remembered. But as it turned out, the odds weren't in my favor.

I took the scenic route, driving past the church where Eleanor and Oliver would shortly be married, past the large cemetery, and down the road that led to the Hudson River. Then I turned down Main Street, showed them Someday's storefront and Jitters across the street.

"What are those men doing on the roof of that coffee shop?" my dad asked.

"Probably roofers."

"They look like they're in uniform. And there's a squad car. . . ."

My mother pointed to the broken streetlamp. "Vandals." She shook her head. "I never thought I'd see the day when this town had a crime like that."

"I guess they're everywhere," my dad said.

If only it were that simple.

I parked in front of the station, which my mother said looked the same from the last time she was in town, which I pointed out was only about eighteen months ago, and my dad suggested we not argue about it. Greg was manning the front desk, looking stressed. In front of him he had the chief's logbook.

"Doesn't Jesse usually fill that out?" I asked.

He slammed the book shut. "Just helping," he said. "I can't tell you anything, Nell. I'm under orders."

I shook my head and smiled a wide, fake smile. "That's okay, not to worry. This is my mom and dad. They're visiting town and they want to meet Jesse. It's just a social visit."

He looked over at them and nodded. "Oh, right. He's in his office."

"What do you mean you can't tell Nell anything?" my mother asked him.

Greg seemed even more stressed than he had a minute before. "I'm just . . . Nell just . . . it's an inside joke, ma'am."

"That's right," I agreed. "Greg and I . . . well, it's a long story and probably not funny to anyone else. . . ."

My mother glared at Greg a minute. She knew she was being lied to and she didn't like to be thought a fool—I guess the apple doesn't fall far from the tree—but she had nothing to go on but instinct, so she soon relaxed her stance. "Where's Jesse's office?" she asked.

Greg pointed to his left.

The door was slightly open. I knocked lightly, but I didn't wait for an answer, I just pushed the door open farther. Jesse was inside, his back to me, his arms around a slender blond woman, who was holding tightly to his waist.

"Jesse?" I wasn't sure what to do here. I knew immediately that the woman must be Roger's wife, his widow, but I also knew how the scene looked.

Jesse let go of the woman and came to me. He seemed a mix of embarrassment, confusion, and a deep sadness. "Hey, Nell. What are you doing here?"

I turned to my mother and father, their jaws open and their eyes filled with shock and anger. My mother glared at the woman, who seemed too shaken to notice.

"My mom and dad," I said. "And you must be Anna." I extended my hand to the woman, who took it. "I'm so sorry about the death of your husband."

"Thank you. You're Nell, I'll bet. Jesse's talked a lot about you."

"Really?"

"All good." She smiled. "We've been catching up, and, of course, he's been helping me make arrangements."

"My mom and dad wanted to meet you," I said to Jesse, trying to convey an apology and a warning with one glance.

Jesse looked around the tiny office. "I don't think there's room in here for all of us. We could go to one of the interrogation rooms. It's not comfortable but—"

"It's not meant to be," my dad finished the sentence, and we all laughed a little.

"It's appropriate, though," my mom offered, "since I have a lot of questions to ask you, Jesse."

I tried not to blush.

Greg brought five cups of coffee into the interrogation room, since for some bizarre reason Anna Leighton chose to join us. I thought she'd be more comfortable at a hotel, but she wasn't staying at a hotel, she told me; she was staying with Jesse. This was news to me.

"When Lizzie was sick, I used to come up and stay all the time, remember that, Jesse?" she asked him.

"You were a great help. Everyone was. I don't know what I would have done without the support I got from the folks in this town and from my old friends."

"You have a daughter," my mother said, interrupting Jesse's sad memory with the start of her interrogation.

"Allie. She's seven," I answered for Jesse. "She's absolutely adorable. You're going to love her."

Jesse smiled at me. I wanted to get up and walk over to him and hold him for a long time. Instead I smiled back and hoped he understood what I was thinking.

"And who watches her when you're at work?" My mother continued her questions.

"My mother," Jesse said. "And Allie often goes over to the shop after school to hang out with Nell and Eleanor."

"Allie's a great quilter," I added. "And she's really helpful with rolling up the fat quarters and adding the price tags." I was bragging on her like a parent, I realized, and I could tell that my mother had caught on to it.

Anna sighed. "It's amazing that Allie is such a big girl now. Lizzie would be so proud of her, and so happy that you've found happiness again, Jesse."

"I have," he said. "Nell and Allie and me, we're a great team."

My mother shifted in her chair. She was being polite, she was smiling, and she *looked* happy, but I could tell she wasn't comfortable. "Anna," my mother said, "Nell offered condolences when we first arrived. Your husband passed away?"

"Yes. My husband, Roger, died yesterday."

My mother's look softened, and her voice lowered. "I'm so sorry, dear. Is that what brought you to town? You're not from here because if you were a local friend of Jesse's, you would know his girlfriend."

I bit my lip. Was I that blunt when I asked questions?

"Yes. I just got here from New York," Anna said, seemingly unaware of my mother's rudeness. "It's so hard to accept. Any death is hard, but murder . . ."

"Murder?"

"Didn't Nell tell you?" Anna seemed confused. "I just assumed since she was the one who found Roger's body."

My mother and father turned their heads sharply in my direction. "You did what?" my father yelled. I felt like I was about to be sent to my room.

CHAPTER 19

Tell me if I'm wrong, but the first time you introduce your boyfriend to your parents, murder is not a great topic for discussion.

"Were you scared?"

"Why would Jesse let you near a body?"

"Are you in danger?"

"Is Jesse in danger?"

And the most complicated of all: "What are you doing looking for bullet holes on a dead body?"

I took a deep breath, didn't answer any of the questions, and just waited. Jesse, though more concerned than I was, took his cues from me and also sat quietly. Anna seemed almost frightened.

Finally, when my parents calmed down, I stepped in. "Maybe it's a good idea for Anna to go back to your place, Jesse," I said. "The last few hours have been pretty awful for her, and this isn't something she needs to add to her plate."

"Good idea." Jesse took Anna's arm and helped her get up, as she was suddenly a little unsteady. My parents can do that sometimes.

I let them leave the interrogation room before I spoke again. "In the year since I've been living in town there've been a few incidents. . . ."

"What kind of incidents?" My mother's voice raised an octave.

"Let her speak, Patty," my dad said. "What kind of incidents, Nell?"

"Crimes. A few murders . . ."

"A few murders!" they both said in unison.

I quietly, and with as few details as possible, went through the list of murders, break-ins, arson, and assorted smaller crimes that Archers Rest, like a lot of places these days, had to deal with. I wanted to leave some of the illegal activities out, but I feared a constant trickle of gossip would be a bigger headache for all of us than one long wave of information. I ended by assuring them that Jesse was a capable chief, with an amazing police force and a town that loved and supported him.

"It's a safe place, really," I told them. "It's a lovely place. I'm very happy here."

"What's your role in all this?" my dad asked. "There's more to this story, Eleanor Margaret Fitzgerald."

All three names. I was in trouble. But I was also, I silently reminded myself, a grown woman. I didn't need to explain my actions to anyone. I paused for a minute, trying to think of the best way to explain it, then gave up and just plunged ahead.

"Sometimes I have theories on a case, ideas of what might have happened, and I share them with Jesse. And sometimes other people, friends of mine from the quilt group, have theories and we all discuss them. Jesse listens and," I took a breath to find the right words, "sometimes he acts on our ideas. We help him."

My father looked confused, my mother seemed stricken. "How can he let you put yourself in danger?" she asked. "If he's this great cop, why does he need your help?"

"He doesn't," I said. "He gets it anyway. I'm good at figuring things out, detective things."

"You're a painter, Nell, not a detective."

"I'm actually a quilter, Mom. I've been thinking that maybe I would try to have a career as an art quilter. I'm not sure how exactly, but there are a lot of people who teach their techniques, sell patterns and books. It's just something I'm thinking about."

Saying it aloud for the first time felt scary but right. I wanted to be a professional quilt artist.

My mother got up and took a long breath. I knew I was giving her a lot to take in all at once, but it felt good to unload. "You said the shop has expanded since I was here?"

I got up, too, as did my dad. "Yes, it's twice the size. It's beautiful and it's really successful."

"I think I'm going to have a look," she said. "Fitz, you want to come with?"

He nodded. "There's that coffee shop across the street. Is it any good?"

"The best."

"Then we'll go there after. Your mother and I need a minute to think about everything that's been going on."

"It's not something you need to worry about, Dad. I'm an adult. I can take care of myself."

He kissed my forehead. "I guess you can, but we're still going to worry."

We walked out of the room and toward the front door of the station. It had gone well, considering. I was feeling kind of pleased. I had been calm and clear and they seemed to accept that Archers Rest wasn't any more immune to crime than Philadelphia or New York, or anywhere.

My dad paused at the door. "The officers who were on the rooftops . . . does that have something to do with that Roger fellow's murder?"

"I don't know," I said, honestly. There was no point in evading, they would find out everything soon enough. "Someone took a few shots at a car and the Someday sign this morning. There might be a link, but it might be completely unrelated."

"The Someday sign?" my mother jumped in. "Someone shot the sign above the shop where my mother and daughter work?"

"Yes. But I don't think it was aimed at us directly." At least I hoped not. "No one was hurt."

"Oh dear God," my mother said and grabbed my father's hand.

That last part hadn't gone so well.

CHAPTER 20

Jesse came back to the station just minutes after my parents left. He'd given the state police his office to make some calls, so we went back to the interrogation room. He closed the door and we sat next to each other; we held hands and just enjoyed being alone together. I held on to each second as if we would never have a chance like it again.

"Anna really liked you," he said. "She said you seemed perky."

"I don't think perky is a compliment."

"Really? Well, she said she liked you and she should. And she's glad I'm happy, that Allie is happy."

"This has got to be hard for her, losing her husband and coming back here to all the memories of Lizzie."

"Yeah."

That was all I got out of him, so I continued, "Hard for both of you."

"It is."

"You can talk about it with me if you want."

He squeezed my hand. "I know that. I just don't know what to say. Roger was a great guy, and a great cop. He and Anna had their ups and downs, but who doesn't?"

"Were they separated?"

"Yeah. She said they were talking, trying to work things out.

She said Roger had left the force so she thought it was a good sign. Maybe he would get something nine to five and they could spend more time together."

"Did she say if Roger had any kinds of problems, like gambling or something?"

He looked over at me. "She didn't, and he didn't, at least not the last time I saw him. Why?"

"There has to be a reason he was killed."

"If your theory is that he came up here to borrow money from me to pay off some loan shark, then you obviously have no idea how little the Archers Rest police force pays."

"I don't have a theory. If I recall our earlier conversation, I'm not allowed to have a theory."

"But . . ."

"But what?"

Jesse smiled. "Carrie isn't looking for additional space."

"How did you . . ."

"The state police met two Carrie Browns. One who gave him a statement about the shooting, and the other who was behaving suspiciously. A woman in her twenties, red coat, long brown hair, was standing in the street staring at Clark's Dry Cleaners."

"I didn't think he'd describe me."

"You haven't covered that chapter in your handbook for fake police investigations?"

"That was mean." I sounded hurt, though really I was relieved he wasn't angry I'd broken my promise.

"You're right," he said. "So . . . your theory?"

"I told you, I don't have one."

He relaxed, seemed amused, like his old self. His old self from the day before yesterday.

"What was in the notebook you took from Roger's body?" I asked.

"Nothing. Just the name and phone number of a detective Roger and I used to know in vice. John Toomey. I called him. He hadn't spoken to Roger in a few years. It's a dead end."

"You don't think the shots came from the park, do you?" he asked.

"Neither do the state police, or else they wouldn't be on the rooftops checking for evidence of a sniper," I pointed out. "So why did you say it came from the park?"

"I saw something right before the first shot was fired. A flash. I thought it was a shot."

"Maybe there was someone there. Dru's car didn't start last night."

"Greg checked it. Someone removed the starter. Someone wanted that car in that spot this afternoon."

"So if it wasn't the shooter, it was someone watching the shooter who wanted to ensure there would be cover."

"Seems like it," he said.

"If the shooter were on the roof, then whoever was by Dru's car was a teammate, there to signal the shooter," I guessed.

"Signal the shooter about what?" Jesse asked. But as he spoke I saw a realization cross his face. "The flash was to signal that I was on the street and the shooting could start."

"So the bullets *were* meant for you, as some kind of warning."

"Whatever Roger had to tell me, maybe the killer thinks I already know." Jesse wrapped his arm around me and pulled me tighter.

"But the killer, or I guess killers, would have had to know last night that this shooting was going to happen. They planned for it, maybe watched folks in town and saw that Dru's car was there, in a spot where no one usually parks," I said. "So while one of them was killing Roger, the other was breaking into Dru's car to remove the starter and ensure it would be there the next day? It doesn't make sense. How did they know she wouldn't discover the problem? How would they know she wouldn't have it fixed by the time the shooting started? And how would they know you would be in Jitters?"

"That's a lot of questions, and I don't know the answers, except for the last one," Jesse said. "I'm at Jitters all the time. I'm certainly on Main Street every day. In fact, I'm on Main Street most of the day," he said. "The real question is why not kill me? If they think I know something, why not just shoot me like they shot Roger? Why stage a big show in front of the whole town and leave me with nothing but a cut on my arm from fallen glass?"

It was a good question, and it was a terrible question all at the same time.

"Knowing your routine, that points to someone from town," I said.

"But no one here knew Roger except me. And I think I have a pretty good alibi for the shooting on Main Street."

I hesitated to continue, since things were going so well. Jesse had his arm around me, I had my head on his shoulders. It was the most romantic a police interrogation room could be.

"I met a man in town today," I said. "He's thinking of moving here."

"A quilter?"

"No. His sister is, though. This man drives a blue sedan."

Jesse was quiet for a moment, then spoke slowly and with a forced casualness that made me very concerned. "When you say you met him, what does that mean?"

"I spoke to him. He spoke to me, technically. At least he spoke first. I was by his car, heading toward the shop, and we sort of met. He said he'd seen me at Jitters and walking Barney."

"Some guy has been watching you?"

"Bob Marshall. That's his name." I thought about it for a

moment but decided it had to be said. "You've given him several tickets, Jesse. And for things that he didn't do wrong."

"So you're aware of all the laws in Archers Rest?"

"I don't know if I'm aware of every one, but I do know there's no law against parking across the street from a fire hydrant."

Jesse spoke through gritted teeth. "If you don't know him, then maybe you should be more careful."

"Are you telling me not to talk to strangers?" I asked. "Because I'm not Allie, so don't treat me like I'm a child."

Jesse sat up and took his arm from around me. "We just had a shooting in town. You see someone you don't know who has been watching you. I would hope you would be suspicious."

"You're suspicious of him."

"I might be."

"Then shouldn't you be calling him in for questioning and not just giving him tickets for parking too close to the corner?"

It sounded harsh, and I knew it, but before I had a chance to soften it, Jesse stood up. "This isn't your investigation, Nell, it's mine. So I'm going to handle it my way."

He opened the door to the room, and I knew there was no point in arguing. Grief was definitely skewing Jesse's perspective, but so was something else. And I'd just blown a good chance of finding out what it was.

CHAPTER 21

"Robert Marshall," Bernie said to me over the phone later that night. I was in my bedroom cleaning when she called to tell me her nephew had tracked down the license plate number. Helpful but a little late, unless there was more than a name.

"Is there an address?"

"I knew you would ask that," she said. "So yes, I've got an address. He lives on Waverly Place in Manhattan. He's thirty-nine, has perfect vision, and he's an organ donor."

An unselfish trait for a killer, assuming he was one.

"Strange thing, though," Bernie continued. "His driver's license has been lapsed for over two years."

"Maybe he moved out of state."

"Yeah, but then he moved right back to the same address."

"Okay, maybe we can look into that further. Now that we have all that his driver's license will tell us, we need more. Jesse knows him but won't say how. My guess is that it's connected to Roger, which probably means someone from the New York police force."

"Got it," Bernie answered. "I'll talk to Maggie. I'll bet she has something by tomorrow, because, knowing her, she'll spend the evening on it. Some new computer software that Natalie taught her how to use." She chuckled.

Maggie had become like a teenager in search of the newest technology, sometimes spending hours a day online. But in Maggie's case it wasn't games or Facebook that kept her interest, it was information—tracking down anything she could find on any subject, especially if it helped solve a case. Once a librarian always a librarian.

"On my way out of town tomorrow I'll drop off the rest of the tablecloths for the wedding," Bernie continued. "Can't believe I'm going to miss the last quilt group before Eleanor's wedding."

"There's next Friday, too."

"Isn't that the rehearsal dinner? What are we doing for the bachelorette party?"

"It's a week from tonight. Dinner, here at the house, I think. All of us together."

"I suppose you would object to our giving gifts of sexy underwear."

"If I'm in the room, yes. And I'm sure my mom wouldn't be too thrilled either."

Bernie laughed. "I thought I'd do a tarot card reading for everyone. I'll tell you what will happen to you. Won't that be fun?"

"That depends on what you tell me, so I expect you to see only good things for me, and especially for Eleanor."

Bernie didn't answer right away, and when she did answer, she just said good night and reminded me to call Maggie in the morning.

"Nell?" I heard my mother's voice calling from the kitchen. I hung up the phone, gathered some clothes, and dropped them in my grandmother's sewing room, where Patch was sleeping soundly on a half-finished wool throw from an ill-advised attempt I'd made at crochet months ago. One of the many good things about animals is they don't care about stitches or color placement; they just like soft and warm.

I gave the kitten a quick pet, then went downstairs. My mom and Eleanor were putting the finishing touches on dinner, a Moroccan chicken and rice dish that Mom had learned how to cook in

Marrakech. Barney circled the kitchen counter, happily sniffing at the unfamiliar fragrances.

"I changed the sheets on my bed," I told my mom, "and I left fresh towels in the bathroom, so hopefully you'll be comfortable."

"I feel terrible kicking you out of your own room."

"The pullout couch in the sewing room is fine," I lied. It had worn so thin you could feel the springs through the mattress. "Where are Dad and Oliver?"

"Oliver brought some things over from his house," Eleanor told me. "He and your father are bringing them in."

"I'll go help."

My mother grabbed my arm. "Oliver said it's only two boxes. Stay and help us."

I looked at what was clearly a feast, likely to serve eight or ten hungry people, or in our case provide leftovers for a week. "What can I do?"

"Tell me more about Jesse."

"What do you want to know?" I asked. "He's kind, he's smart, he's handsome . . ."

"And he's very good to her," Eleanor jumped in. "He's a good, decent man who loves Nell and who Nell loves. They make a nice match."

My mom bit the side of her mouth. She used to say my sister and I ganged up on her, now it was clear she felt it was her mother and I doing the same thing.

"What do you want to know, Mom?"

"Why him? He's older than you. . . ."

"Only by a few years. He's just thirty-two."

"He has a child."

"And I love her."

"Yes, but that child needs a mother, someone to look after her, pick her up from school and stay home with her when she's sick. That means sacrifices, Nell."

"I'm aware of that."

"And his job . . . It's a tiny job in a tiny town that will keep you stuck here if you stay with him. Sheriff of Archers Rest!" She threw up her hands. "Nell, you were living in Manhattan, dating sophisticated men . . ."

"Getting my heart broken," I pointed out. "And just because Jesse lives in Archers Rest doesn't mean he's not sophisticated."

"I'm not saying he isn't a good man. I'm sure he is. And clearly he loves you," she said. "But being with him, marrying him, means an instant family and staying in Archers Rest until he earns the tiny pension a town like this can afford. It limits you. Limits what you can do, where you can go."

"But if it's what she wants . . ." My grandmother stepped in again.

"That's not for you to decide," my mother snapped.

"Or you, Patty," Eleanor snapped back.

"Oh, this is ridiculous," my mother yelled at her mother. "I'm trying to have a conversation with my own daughter about the choices she's making. She is talented and smart and beautiful and could have a man who could offer her a future that will allow her to pursue her dreams, travel, have a family when she's ready instead of having one pushed on her. And instead of agreeing with me and doing what's best for Nell, you're encouraging her to marry Andy Taylor and settle down in Mayberry. And a violent, murder-a-minute Mayberry to boot."

The words floated downward as my dad and Oliver came in carrying boxes. Jesse was right behind them. When my mother saw Jesse's face she turned beet red. Before anyone could speak, she walked out of the house into the darkness of my grandmother's backyard.

CHAPTER 22

"I'm sorry," Jesse said. "I didn't mean to interrupt."

"You've nothing to apologize for," Eleanor said. "Come in and sit down. Her comments weren't aimed at you, Jesse, they were aimed at me. My daughter and I don't always see the world the same way."

"I always said the Cassidy girls were stubborn," my dad said. "Beautiful but stubborn. I hope you're prepared for that, Jesse."

"If I get a chance to be," he said. His voice was soft, almost embarrassed. My mother's words had landed on him like a punch to the stomach.

Oliver grunted and dropped the box at his feet. It hit the floor with a thud. Even Barney was shaken by it. Once the box was out of his hands, Oliver dropped into a chair. "Bit heavy for me, I guess."

"What's in it?" I asked.

"Books." My dad put down the box he was carrying. "Oliver's moving his encyclopedias into the house."

"I offered to help," Jesse said.

"I can still carry my own boxes." Oliver's voice was a bit shaky. "I've had the books for years. I didn't go past secondary school and it always nagged at me, not getting to learn all there was to know. So a few years back, I saw these encyclopedias in a thrift shop. No one wants the books anymore since it's all on computers, so I bought them and I've been reading them a little at a time ever since."

My grandmother put a glass of water in front of Oliver, who seemed to be having a bit of trouble catching his breath. He took her hand and they stayed like that, quietly, for almost a minute. I looked over at Jesse and smiled. He nodded. He was okay, at least he wanted me to think he was.

"What are you up to?" my dad asked Oliver. "I always thought one day I'd do the same thing, read the whole lot of them in order."

"You have to read them in order," Oliver agreed. "I'm at 'Y.' Just finished reading the entry about Yemen. Fascinating country. I figure I can't die until I finish, so I have two letters to go."

"Oliver," my grandmother scolded. "Don't say such a thing."

"Why bring the encyclopedias first?" my dad asked. "Why not clothes and furniture?"

"Most of that stuff is going down to South Carolina," Oliver said. "We just bought a house down there."

My dad looked at Eleanor and then at me. "Does your mom know that?"

Instead of answering I looked outside the back window into the cold and dark. "She's not coming back in," I said. I grabbed two jackets and put one on me. "I'm going to get her. It's freezing out there."

"Remind her dinner is almost ready," my dad said. "She's a great cook, and she knows not to let a good meal spoil."

✄

She wasn't on the back porch, so I walked to the path through the trees and toward the river. My grandmother's yard bordered the Hudson, and there was an eerie quietness to it, especially in winter. It didn't help that the river was a sheet of black at night. As a kid I thought the yard was haunted, but now, even on the darkest nights, it seemed peaceful.

"Mom," I called out when I spotted her standing by the river's edge, staring off into the water. "Getting pneumonia isn't going to help anything."

She turned to me. She'd been crying. She took the coat I handed her and put it on. Even though we both were still shivering, it didn't seem as though she was anxious to go inside.

"I didn't mean to sound like that," she said. "I know he's a good man, Nell, and you're smart enough to choose the right future for yourself. It's just that it feels like you were on one path in New York and now . . ."

"And now it's all different."

"After your engagement broke off you came here because it was comforting. And maybe now you're staying because you've gotten used to playing it safe."

"Is it just because you couldn't wait to leave Archers Rest when you were growing up that you think I must feel the same way?"

"No." She hesitated. "It's not just that. I don't have anything against this town. It's filled with good people living good lives."

"But . . ."

She pulled the coat tighter, and I could see that she was considering her words. "When you were a little girl, you would do these giant jigsaw puzzles, the ones with a thousand pieces."

"I remember."

"You would be looking for one piece, a duck's bill or a leaf from a tree, and you would get stuck on it. You would search and search and search. I'd tell you to let it go and move on to another part of the puzzle, but you wouldn't, Nell. You would keep at it."

"And I would find it. Isn't that a good thing?"

"Yes, but sometimes you get so caught up in the details that you don't step back and look at the bigger picture. That attention to detail is probably what draws you to quilting, and makes you good at whatever it is you do to help Jesse with his police work, but it can hamper you, too," she said. "All I'm asking is for you to take your nose out of the puzzle long enough to see what else is out there."

"I promise. I'll look at the big picture. I'll really think about the kind of future I want," I said. "But you can't decide for me."

"If you tell me you want to marry Jesse and live your life in Archers Rest, and you're one hundred percent sure, I'll be happy."

I linked my arm through hers. "What's best for me right now is not freezing to death fifty feet from the house."

As we walked back, I thought about what she said. I did tend to get lost in the details. The big picture can be messy and overwhelming, while focusing on a small spot—a clue, a stitch, the day in front of me—feels manageable. It was always my belief that the small things add up—if you gather enough clues it may lead toward a killer; enough stitches and you finish a quilt—but I could see that it might not work that way with the rest of my life. Focusing just on the day I'm in may not lead me where I want to go unless I had an idea of the destination.

Jesse wasn't much older than I was chronologically, but in terms of his view of life, it seemed sometimes that we were generations apart. I loved Allie, but if I took her on as my child to raise, it would mean big changes for me. And with or without Jesse, did I want to live in Archers Rest for the rest of my life? I hadn't thought about that either, maybe deliberately. I'd always been uncomfortable about wedding talk and I thought one day I would just be sure. Asking myself those questions made it seem like there was a chance I wouldn't be in Jesse and Allie's lives, and even the possibility of that was too hard to think about.

But now I'd spent a year with my nose pressed against a puzzle, looking only at a tiny piece of it. My mother was right. It was time to move back from the thrill of the latest quilt, or the most interesting clue in an investigation, and look at the whole picture of my life.

CHAPTER 23

Jesse couldn't stay for dinner, but he did want to talk. I told the others to start without me, and Jesse and I went to the living room and closed the door. I sat on the couch while he paced back and forth across the area rug.

"Where's Allie?"

"Home, with Anna. She was teaching Allie how to make meat loaf or something."

A twinge of jealousy, quickly suppressed. Anna was an old friend going through a hard time, and just because Allie and I often cooked together didn't mean it was "our thing." I let go of my own pettiness, or at least tried to. "I'm sorry about my mom," I said.

"I'm sorry about this afternoon. About what I said at the station."

"It is your investigation, Jesse, but I am only trying to help."

He sat down next to me, started to say something, then shook his head. It was as if he were rehearsing the conversation and finding a flaw each time. Finally he spoke, but his words were measured and unemotional. "That man you met in town, he's not thinking of moving here. That was a lie."

"So you do know him?"

He stared straight ahead, his hands in his lap. "He was on the force with Roger and me. Years ago. I noticed his car yesterday after

Roger's body was found. Always on Main Street, always parked within a few yards of Someday."

"And so you gave him tickets instead of talking to him?"

"It's an old vice trick. Bob Marshall was the one who taught it to me. We would ticket cars for all sorts of stupid reasons, cars we knew belonged to the bad guys, as a way of letting them know we knew they were there. We were watching them."

"Why not just arrest them?"

"We didn't have enough evidence to arrest them."

"But if you telegraphed that you were watching them, wouldn't it just make them more careful?"

"Not really," Jesse said. "It's a stressor. It made them paranoid. Even when we weren't watching, they thought we were. Instead of being more careful, people under stress make mistakes. Then we'd get them."

"And that's what you wanted to do with Bob Marshall?"

He shook his head. "I just wanted him to know that I remembered the old days. He was always pulling at me to cut corners. He would say he knew some guy was guilty. He just needed help proving it."

"He was a bad cop."

"He was a lazy cop. But Roger made sure we all stayed in line. Even Marshall. Roger wanted it done right."

"So what now?"

"Hopefully he leaves town."

"What if he's the killer?"

"He's not."

"How do you know?"

Jesse laced and unlaced his fingers like a nervous tic. "I don't."

"Then why don't you question him?"

"It's not going to get me anywhere. He's a cop. He knows what I'll ask, and how I'll ask it. He taught me."

"Then maybe I should—"

"No." The first word he'd spoken that had anything close to emotion in it. "Absolutely not, Nell. You just let me handle it."

"What don't I know?" I took a deep breath to prepare myself for whatever he might tell me. But there was only silence. "Jesse, you are a great police officer. Even if Bob Marshall knows how interrogations work, you would find a way to get the answers you needed. You wouldn't let a potential killer just leave town. I know Roger's murder has something to do with your days in the city, with your time on vice, doesn't it?"

"No, it doesn't," he said. "I swear to you, Nell. It has nothing to do with me. I don't know what it's about, and I have no idea why Roger was parked outside my house, but I can promise you it has nothing to do with my time on the force with him. It can't. We pushed the edges here and there, trying to get suspects to give themselves away, but we never crossed the line. Not once."

"Maybe one of those edges, one of those suspects . . ."

Jesse looked into my eyes. While he likely saw concern and confusion there, I only saw sadness in his. "I never broke the law," he said.

"But the tickets you gave to Marshall . . ."

"I told you it was just a reminder. I didn't put them in the system, so they're not on his record. It was just . . ." He seemed flustered.

"Okay, this isn't about you," I said. "I believe that. But there's more to this than you're telling me."

Jesse stood up. "I need to get home to Allie. She barely knows Anna, so she's going to start feeling weird about my being gone too long." He grabbed my hand, pulled me up next to him, and hugged me. "I'm a good man, Nell Fitzgerald, and I love you. Do you believe that?"

"Of course."

"No matter what happens, you keep believing that, okay?"

"Jesse . . ."

"Tell me."

"You're a good man and you love me. And I'll believe that no matter what."

He kissed my forehead and walked away from me. I heard the living room door open, and heard him in the hallway. I stayed where I was until I heard the front door close, then I sat down on the couch. At first I just stared into space, trying to go over the conversation, examining every word. But then I realized I'd fallen into the trap my mother warned me against, and I stepped back, looked at the bigger picture—the murder, Jesse's reluctance to share what he knew with me, the words he'd said as he left. And I burst into tears.

CHAPTER 24

That night and into the next morning it snowed hard. By the time I sat in the kitchen eating Cheerios, there was nearly a foot on the ground and more expected later in the day. My mother and grandmother sparred over me, over my parents' travels and what Eleanor should do with the house during the months she and Oliver would be in South Carolina. While my dad read the paper in what can only be called willful deafness, I ate quietly, still exhausted from thinking about what Jesse had said.

Barney sat staring at his quilt-covered dog bed, which was now occupied by a sleeping kitten. Barney, the ever-protective big brother, didn't seem to mind being kicked out of his favorite napping place. He just stood and watched her. While so many other relationships seemed to be moving toward arguments and tears, Patch and Barney were slowly finding a détente and maybe, hopefully, a friendship.

At nine o'clock, Eleanor drove her SUV into town, with Patch in tow, and I walked Barney the half mile from the house to the shop. I was freezing, but Barney was in the dog version of heaven. He sniffed and sneezed, and rolled around in the wet, cold snow every chance he had. He'd wandered into the street when a car came around the corner, but Barney didn't seem to notice it. With his hearing gone, and the snow a wonderful distraction, the old dog nearly met his end. I grabbed him and pulled him back as the car, a blue sedan, passed by. Bob Marshall waved. I waved back, almost instinctively, but I also felt watched. He knew my path to town in the morning. Not that it meant anything, I told myself. Most of the town knew that I usually walked the dog into work. I debated whether to call Jesse, but decided against it. He would only warn me again to stay away from the investigation, and his reluctance to say why would just make me worry.

Once I got to the shop, I put Barney in the office, but he whined and scratched at the door until I opened it and let him find his favorite spot in the shop, another quilt-covered dog bed near the sale fabrics. It was a popular part of the store, both for the sales and the dog, and Barney liked it because it was near the heating vent. Barney looked for his new friend, hoping to build on the growing trust they'd started to have. But Patch didn't share his enthusiasm. She found herself backed up against the wall with Barney's large teeth blocking her escape. I grabbed the old dog and pulled him away.

"She's playing hard to get," I told him. "Give her time."

Barney, who never had to work this hard to be loved, found the whole thing pretty stressful. Relationships are hard for everyone, I guess. I warned him to stay away from Patch, who'd used the opportunity to jump onto a shelf. After rubbing up against a few fabrics, in the true spirit of a quilter, she found herself a home on a pile of flannel fabrics just out of the dog's reach. At first Barney sniffed and whined about that, too, but he eventually settled down in his bed and napped.

There were no customers in the first hour we were open, and the snow was still coming down. Eleanor went to her office to do the monthly bills, and I headed into the classroom to work on the gazebo quilt. A log cabin with appliqué flowers was unfinished at another table. Before Christmas I'd tried out a new product Eleanor had ordered—preprinted designs for paper piecing. Paper piecing is nothing new for quilters, but designers are always looking for ways to improve the technique. Patterns can be drawn or printed onto paper, and then the quilter sews fabric directly onto the paper, using the lines as a guide, allowing for absolute precision and complicated designs. The trick is using paper that can easily be torn off once the design is complete. The new product promised to be both sturdy enough to hold up to machine piecing and light enough to tear away without leaving little bits of paper stuck in the thread.

The design we had to try was the classic double wedding ring. The pattern uses small pieces sewn in an arc to create the illusion of interlocking circles. An oval with pointed ends, referred to as the "melon," and a diamond-shaped centerpiece made up the background. It's a complicated quilt, not meant for beginners, but that's the point. There are a few quilts that most traditional quilters have on their "bucket list"—beautiful, challenging, and heirloom worthy. The double wedding ring is one of them.

I'd sewn about two dozen arcs, and had lots of cut pieces waiting, without any idea of when I would get to them. I didn't mind the chaos, though. Having multiple, unfinished projects going at once is the sign of a real quilter. At least that's what everyone in the group kept telling me.

My conversation with Jesse had kept me up most of the night, and when I was able to finally let it go, my mother's words would pop into my head. It didn't help that I was on the sofa bed in Eleanor's sewing room, or that I could hear my father's snoring down the hall. I was glad when morning finally came and I saw the snow, because I knew it would mean a quiet day to sit and quilt. And that's what I needed almost as much as I needed sleep.

I moved from the double wedding ring to the gazebo quilt when I tired of sewing arches. The work went quickly. By the time noon came, I had the trees already appliquéd. They were simple, elongated triangles in various greens, with small brown rectangles as the trunks. Nothing flashy or precise, but the colors and shapes stood out well against the sky. I laid the first piece of gazebo on and was pinning it in place when I heard movement in the main part of the store.

"I'm going across the street to get coffee and sandwiches." Eleanor walked into the classroom and saw my appliqué pieces spread out on the worktables. "What's that? Is this a new one?"

"Don't look. It's your wedding gift."

"But you and the girls made the quilt I'm not supposed to know about."

"This one is from just me."

"Can I know about this one?"

"No."

She smiled at me. "Okay, then, I'll bring you back some lunch. And while I'm gone maybe I'll do a thing or two that I won't tell you about."

"That'll teach me to keep secrets, Grandma."

I listened as Eleanor walked toward the front door and went out, then I went back to my work. I'd barely moved my needle when the bell on the front door rang.

"Did you forget something?" I called out.

"Excuse me?"

"Oh, sorry." I dropped my work onto the table and headed into the main part of the shop. Anna was there in blue jeans and a bright blue coat, looking stylish but tired.

"I've interrupted you," she said.

"Not really. It's just such a quiet day I've been in the back sewing. Are you here for some fabric?"

She smiled. "No, I was just wanting to see the shop. Allie was talking about it over dinner and it sounded lovely." She looked around. "And it is."

She walked around the store, stopping at various displays. As she did, she'd run her fingers across the fabric admiringly. "I own an interior design business," she said. "I'm always looking for really unique things to offer clients. Do you sell quilts?"

"No. Just the ingredients. We can teach you how to make one, though."

"I don't think I have the talent. But I do have an eye for beauty. I think that's a kind of gift," she said. "At least I have a lot of clients who think so." She smiled and kept moving. When she reached the flannels, she let out a yelp.

"Are you allergic?" I asked and rushed to grab Patch.

"No, I'm just surprised. It's nice. You have a kitten."

"And a dog." I pointed toward Barney, who had woken up and was now circling in his bed trying to find just the right spot. When he did, he dropped down with a grunt and buried his head in his paws. It seemed he was still nursing his wounds from Patch's rejection.

"No wonder Allie likes this place so much." Anna stared at me, and I waited for her to say something else, but she didn't. She just moved on to the Easter fabrics that were displayed on a rack. I put Patch on the ground and followed Anna as she headed toward the classroom.

"Have you made arrangements yet?" I asked.

"For Roger? I've called his family and as many friends as I could. Roger had a lot of friends, so it's impossible to think of them all. Everyone's asking why it happened. I don't know why."

"Jess will find out."

"Roger used to say Jesse was the best cop he knew. I suppose he doesn't get a chance to do much real police work up here."

"You'd be surprised," I said. "I'm sure Jesse's been filling you in on his progress."

"All we've been talking about are the old days." She sat down in one of the chairs that faced a sewing machine, but she swirled it to face me instead. "They were wonderful times. Jesse and Lizzie would come over to our place in Queens, and we'd have barbecues in the summer and play cards in the winter. Lizzie wanted to buy a house in our neighborhood. They were living in a tiny apartment and Lizzie was pregnant at the time." She sighed. "She wanted a dozen kids."

"It sounds wonderful."

"And sad that it didn't happen." She studied me for a moment. "It's amazing how different life can be from what you plan. Don't you think?"

"I don't know. Last night it was pointed out to me that I don't make plans. I just sort of stumble along."

"That can't be true. Jesse told me you help with his cases. A real partner in crime," she said. "Or, I guess, crime solving."

"I like to help."

"That's where I went wrong with Roger. I didn't take an interest in his work. I harped on him to make more money or to spend more time with me, but I didn't really try to learn about the things that made him happy," she said. "You have. That was smart. Is there a wedding in the future?"

I sat in a chair at the sewing machine next to her. I couldn't tell if the question was genuine interest or a trap of some kind, so I sidestepped it. "Is it hard to be married to a cop?"

"For me it was impossible. Lizzie didn't mind."

"You and Roger . . ." I tried to start delicately, to not let my curiosity turn into rudeness. "How did you meet?"

She laughed. "Oh God, you won't believe me. We met in the police academy. My dad was a cop; my brother was a cop. I thought, why not? So I joined up. I was good, too. Passed all the exams with flying colors, could outshoot the guys, and was voted rookie of the year."

"But you quit?"

"I hated it. When Roger and I got married, I left the force and started working for a small design shop on the Upper West Side. It suited me much better. Maybe that's why we never talked about his work. I loathed it."

"And your marriage . . ." I took a breath. "I'm sorry, it's just that Jesse said you had problems."

"Don't apologize. It's not a secret. Roger and I fought all the time, broke up, and got back together. It was embarrassing, especially when you compared our marriage to Jesse and Lizzie's. They were the happily ever after the rest of us just dream about." She paused. Her voice softened. "Except, of course, they didn't get to enjoy it for very long, did they?"

"No," I said quietly, feeling somehow that it was my fault.

Anna got up and wandered the classroom. She was difficult to read. Shy people are sometimes seen as standoffish, sad people often come across as disinterested. My initial impulse was to see Anna as attempting to manipulate me, but as she walked around the classroom, looking at the sample quilts hung on the walls, she just seemed tired and overwhelmed. Talking about Lizzie might just have been her way of grasping a happier past, and my suspicion just insecurity.

Anna's eyes rested on my gazebo quilt in progress. "This is amazing. Is this yours?"

"I'm making it for my grandmother's wedding. She's getting married a week from Saturday."

"Allie is the flower girl. She told me. She's very excited."

"We all are. It's going to be a great day. Lots of flowers and music, and half the town is bringing dishes to the reception. It's a potluck dinner."

"It sounds like fun. Roger and I eloped, so I didn't have any of that."

"Can I ask, when's the last time you spoke to your husband?"

"A few weeks ago. We met with lawyers."

"So this time you were divorcing?"

"Not divorce lawyers. We were making changes to our wills. It was Roger's idea. Stupidly I didn't realize he was concerned about something happening to him. I thought he was just trying to force a reconciliation. You know, get us in the same room thinking about the future. Roger was very maudlin when he wanted to be. He didn't want the divorce. He'd tried promises, threats, whatever he could think of. I thought it was just another tactic. Honestly, that day he was the worst. He talked about death as if he'd been diagnosed with something terminal."

"Had he been?"

"No." She seemed shocked by the idea. "Not that I'm aware of anyway," she said. Her voice was a near whisper.

"What did he change?"

She smiled, just slightly. "You really do like to ask questions. Jesse told me about that. I think it's what he likes the most about you."

"I'm being rude. I'm sorry."

"It's a strange situation, for all of us. Seeing Jesse with you makes me feel he's cheating on Lizzie. I know he has a right to move on with his life. And I know Lizzie would be happy he's found some-one else, but . . ."

If I heard Anna say Lizzie's name one more time, I thought I might cry. Trying to win a popularity contest with a memory was a stupid, and pointless, idea.

"Ask whatever questions you like," Anna said. "Jesse has his ver-sion of Roger, which, to be honest, is a more idealized man than he really was. I think he's afraid to ask me any questions that might tarnish his memory."

"Okay. Thanks," I said. "You said Roger changed his will."

"He added a codicil. He set up a trust for Allie."

My throat tightened. It might have been a simple, kind gesture from a man who knew his time was running out, but whatever his motive, Roger had involved Allie in something that might have got-ten him killed. "Why?"

"I have no idea."

"How much is the trust?"

"I'm afraid I don't know that either. Roger wanted me to know about it, but then he got very secretive."

"What about you? He must have left you money."

"Roger had a life insurance policy, and I'm the beneficiary. It's enough to pay off the mortgage but not a lot else. Does that make me a suspect? Angry ex-wife?" she asked. "I guess it does. There was no other money as far as I know. Civil servants don't cash big pay-checks. Even the ones who risk their lives. He used to talk about how he had a second insurance policy, but then he'd laugh. He said the only way it paid off was if he didn't die." She rubbed her eyes and stared at me again. She didn't look like she'd had any more sleep the night before than I did.

"Maybe you should get some rest," I suggested.

"I'm fine. If you want to ask me anything else . . ."

I did, though I felt bad asking it. "What did you mean, he wasn't the idealized version Jesse thinks he was?"

"He was a man. Just an ordinary, fallible man. He did his best, and sometimes that was pretty good, but sometimes he went too far." She squinted, thought for a moment, then started again. "I loved Roger. He annoyed me, drove me crazy actually, but in my own way I loved him. I just didn't want to be with him anymore, and he couldn't understand that."

"I know Jesse doesn't consider you a suspect . . ."

She laughed a little. "I spent fifteen years listening to Roger talk about catching bad guys. Even if I wanted to kill him, which I didn't, I know that killers get caught. And I also know that the spouse is the very first person the police look at. I'm not stupid. And I guess, unlike what you were saying about yourself, I do plan. Spending my life in prison is not in my plan."

I heard the door to the shop open. Eleanor was back with the sandwiches. "I should get going." Anna moved quickly into the main part of the store, introduced herself to Eleanor, and then headed back out into the snow.

"She seems nice," Eleanor said, looking back at me. "But you don't like her."

"She is nice," I admitted. "And no, I don't."

I was glad Eleanor didn't question me further. I had no idea what it was about Anna that bothered me. But something did.

CHAPTER 25

The afternoon dragged. My eyes were tired, my mind was restless, and my stitches were huge. I left my project on the worktable in the classroom and wandered into the main part of the shop. We'd been open six hours and so far there had been only two customers. Now the shop was empty. The snow had stopped, but the roads were barely passable. The county had the job of clearing the streets, and they were busy on the highways. Archers Rest was low on its list of priorities. I stared out the window at what should have been a pretty scene, the blank white covering on the streets and trees, giving the town a wintery glow.

But my eyes wandered from the street up to the rooftop across the street where just the day before a sniper had probably stood. If I'd been standing in the same spot yesterday I would have seen who it was. Or been shot.

Some of the murders I'd maneuvered my way into investigating had too little information. This one had too much. Roger came to town, was murdered. There was a shooting, no one got hurt. Different weapons, different targets, but I knew they were connected. And they were planned. Someone had seen Dru's car parked in that spot and saw a chance to use it as cover. That meant there wasn't one killer, there were two. Anna and Bob Marshall—who else could it be? They were the only ones who knew Roger. And if Jesse was right that the murder had nothing to do with his days as a New York City cop, then it might have something to do with Roger's personal life—an affair between Anna and Bob? I was stepping out of theory into fiction, but it was better than standing in the shop feeling lost in a sea of confusion.

"Grandma, I'm heading across for coffee," I shouted. I grabbed my coat and went to the door before she had a chance to answer, but I heard a muffled "okay" as the door closed behind me.

I walked across the street to the coffee shop, but instead of going up to the counter for my usual order I walked straight through, leaving through the alley door.

Carrie called out, "Nell, don't you want . . ."

"No, thanks."

"But we have to talk."

She seemed insistent, but it could wait. Something was pulling me up to the roof.

✄

There were fire escapes bolted to the back walls of each of the stores. I jumped up to the ladder of the one leading to the roof of the old Clark's Dry Cleaners. The old iron slid down with a grunt. I climbed slowly. There was ice on the rungs, making each step slow and scary. My foot slipped as I tried to move higher, my bare hands gripped the frozen metal, which tore at my skin as I tried to let go. By the time I made it to the top I was out of breath and regretting the attempt. In my hurry to get moving, I'd left my boots, gloves, scarf—basically all of the sensible attire for a cold winter's day—back at the shop. All I had to keep the chill out was my coat and my stubbornness.

I moved to the center of the roof gingerly, half afraid the thing would collapse under the weight of the piles of snow that had fallen. I edged closer to the front of the building and could see the street below. I was only one floor up, but I suddenly felt dizzy. The wind was picking up. I pulled my coat tighter. I had an irrational fear that I would be swept off the roof by a strong breeze, but I stayed where I was, hoped for the best, and tried to imagine what the shooter had been looking for.

From my position on the roof, I could see the end of the street where Dru's car had been parked. Someone with a reflective object signaling from behind her car would most certainly be seen from up here.

But why did he do it? If the shooting was a message, as it seemed to be, what was the message? If the killer had followed Roger, or taken him to Jesse's house, then surely he knew that Roger hadn't spoken to Jesse yet. Whatever it was he was going to say, or do, Roger had been killed before he'd had his chance. Trying to threaten Jesse seemed likely to cause more trouble, not less. Besides, why not just leave town? He'd gotten away with murder, all he had to do was slip back onto the highway and head south to New York. But the killer had stayed at least long enough to climb up to this roof.

I stood there a long while, watching people walking down below, unaware that I was up here. Any one of them could have been hurt, or worse, if the shooter had aimed his gun just a little lower.

Today the street was back to its normal level of small-town busy. People were going in and out of stores, and I could hear greetings and complaints about the weather as voices wafted up toward me. The broken bulbs on the streetlights had been replaced, and I knew that there was a new windshield on Jesse's squad car. The only evidence of anything out of the ordinary was the bullet hole in the *S* of "Someday Quilts." Other than that, it was like the shooting had never happened.

I saw my parents' car drive down Main and park in front of the shop. My mom got out and went inside. Through the window of Someday I could see her looking around, but then she disappeared farther into the store.

I watched as Greg walked from the park, cigarette in hand. He crossed the street toward Jitters and briefly looked up at the roof. Instinctively I pulled back. He didn't see me, at least he didn't seem to, but he looked nervous. I heard the bell announcing that the door to the coffee shop had opened. Greg went inside.

There was no point in hunting for clues. Assuming the shooter left anything behind, the state police would have found it or the snow would have covered it up. And yet I was pinned to this spot. There was something here, something that might lead to an answer. I just didn't know what it was.

I tried to put myself in the mind of the shooter, the person who also very likely killed Roger Leighton. If I was sending a message, where would I aim? The Someday sign was across the street, the two streetlamps with broken bulbs were in the direct path of a shooter on either side of the shop, and the squad car with the shattered windshield had been parked just below.

It gave me the shivers. The night Roger was killed, he had sat in the coffee shop watching Someday Quilts. When Carrie told him that Jesse's girlfriend worked there, Roger had muttered something about hoping "she liked heartbreak." If it was meant for me, as Natalie suggested, it seemed odd that the shooting happened while I was still inside Jitters. Why not wait until I crossed the street? Maybe the message was to Jesse, and it wasn't that he was in danger, but that unless he did what the killer wanted, I would be hurt. Maybe that's why he wanted me to stay off the case.

My hands were frozen and my feet, clad only in loafers, were wet in the two feet of snow that packed down on the roof. I turned to head back, and as I did I had a decent view of River Street, which intersected Main. City Hall was the most prominent building on the street, with the police station right next to it. I caught a glimpse of bright blue, Anna's coat. She was walking down the steps of the police station toward a silver car. A man I could see only from the back was waiting for her. They hugged. It was hard from this distance to tell if the hug was friendly, comforting, or something more intimate. But it lasted. I couldn't see the man very well, but he wasn't Jesse, and he wasn't Bob Marshall.

He turned toward his car, and I caught a brief glimpse of him. He was elegantly dressed in a suit and camel hair coat. He had a briefcase. Lawyer, probably. I'd been hoping for another suspect, but he was probably just some old friend of Anna and Roger's making sure papers were in order to take the body home. It was nothing, I decided.

Then he looked up and saw me. Maybe it was the light, or the distance, but as our eyes met, it looked like he smiled.

CHAPTER 26

"Are you nuts? It's freezing out there." Carrie didn't even ask if I needed anything, she just handed me a cup of hot chocolate and wrapped a blanket over me the minute I stepped back into Jitters. "What were you doing in the alley?"

"On the roof," I corrected her. I was shivering, and not all of it was from the cold. The idea that the killer might be after me was sinking in. "I just wanted to see where the shooter had been."

"And?"

"And nothing. He . . ."

"Or she . . ."

I nodded. I almost told her my theory, but I couldn't. I might be wrong, and, either way, it would only worry Carrie and maybe put her in danger, too. "Right," I said. "He or she had a very good view of the center of town. I could see people down below, but if I stayed away from the edge, I don't think anyone would have seen me. With Clark's empty, it's not like there was anyone down below who would have heard footsteps on the roof."

"And his escape?"

"Once the shooting started we all stayed inside, so he could have climbed down the fire escape and been in a waiting car in less than a minute. Or he could have dumped the gun somewhere and just walked toward the library. With all the panic, would anyone have noticed?"

"For all we know, he could have stashed the gun on the roof earlier, and been in here drinking coffee, and just slipped out the back."

"Do you remember who was here?"

Carrie shook her head. "Before the shooting? It was busy and I was focused on Eleanor's quilt and Roger's murder. I didn't pay attention."

Neither had I. It was frustrating. "It's just such a public threat," I said. "If he really wanted to scare Jesse, there are simpler ways to do it. None of this makes sense."

"It never does until it does. We'll figure this out."

I admired Carrie's optimism even though I wasn't sure if I shared it. It did snap me out of my own obsession about the shooter, though. "Before I went out back you said you wanted to tell me something."

She pulled me toward the back of the coffee shop, looked around to make sure no one was within earshot, then whispered, "I don't know if you want to hear this."

I braced myself. "Hear what?"

"I contacted my friends in the banking world. One of them works for the company where Roger and Anna have their accounts. He owed me a favor and now I definitely owe him one," she said. "He wouldn't give me a lot of information. He likes me but not enough to spend time in federal custody. He said Roger and Anna had a joint account, but he didn't tell me the balance."

"You weren't thinking he would?"

"Of course not, but when I told him everything about the case, about Roger and Jesse and everything, he got interested. He told me Roger had an account, in his name only. He said it had more than fourteen thousand dollars in it."

"Okay. That's a healthy account, but nothing out of the ordinary. What am I missing?"

"Roger's account is a money market that's been open for just over three years. And in that time there have been about forty deposits for various amounts. My friend said they were small, nothing over five hundred dollars. Roger has never taken any of the money out. It just sits there."

"I'm not getting this, Carrie. You just said it's a savings account. He deposited money and left it there, which is kind of the definition of saving. It's probably from his paycheck. So what is it you're not telling me?"

She took a deep breath. Whatever it was, she wasn't happy about having to tell me. "All the deposits have been from one source. A direct deposit from the account of Jesse Dewalt."

I replayed the last sentence in my head. "Jesse's been sending Roger money for three years?"

She nodded. "Do you have any idea why?"

"He told me they hadn't spoken since Lizzie's funeral."

"Maybe it was a loan of some kind," she said.

"It must have been," I agreed. "But why open a separate account? Why not pay into the Leightons' joint account?"

"I don't know. Maybe he didn't want his wife to know about it."

I finished my hot chocolate. "Over fourteen thousand dollars?"

"That's what he said."

"That's a lot of money for a police officer to loan a friend," I said. "Where would he have gotten it?"

Carrie didn't have an answer. All she had was another question. "What if it wasn't a loan? What if Jesse was paying Roger for some reason?"

"What, like blackmail?" I meant it as a joke, but Carrie didn't laugh. My stomach tightened at all the possibilities: blackmail, bribery, money laundering. None of it seemed remotely possible, not for the man I loved. "Whatever the reason," I said, "we keep this within the group. Jesse didn't do anything wrong and there's no point in hurting his reputation."

"Don't you think the state police are going to look into Roger's finances and come across all of this?" she asked.

I shook my head. "They're not on the investigation. Jesse is running it. It's his town. The state police were here because of the shooting, and only as support for the Archers Rest PD. Jesse has been absolutely insistent on doing this his way."

Almost as if he had something to hide. The thought crept into my mind and I pushed it out again.

"It's got to be a loan," Carrie said. Sometimes, if you don't know the answer, picking a theory and sounding very sure about it feels like almost the same thing. "When we know the truth we'll both feel silly that we worried for even a second. Jesse's a good man and he loves you."

Which were the exact words he'd said to me not even twenty-four hours before.

CHAPTER 27

Carrie had customers and I knew I should go back to the shop. But instead I finished the hot chocolate she'd given me and ordered another one. I sat at a table near the back. I needed a moment alone, and preferably not standing on a windy, snow-covered roof, to think and strategize.

"Big picture," I said to myself, trying to take my mom's advice. I was getting sucked in to the details of the shooting and there was so much else—the wedding, my parents, school, quilting, and, most of all, Jesse. I wanted to find Roger's killer and, by doing that, identify the person who put a hole through the Someday sign. I told myself it was because I wanted to help Jesse get justice for his friend. But maybe another reason, a more selfish reason, was because I wanted Jesse to need me, to prove that we were a great team. Or worse, maybe I just couldn't leave well enough alone.

Of course, if I was really in danger, then my other motivations were trivial. I had to find the killer before a warning turned into a second murder.

I could see Greg sitting by himself at a table near the window, poring over his police notebook with an intensity that I'd rarely seen in him. I knew that asking him about the investigation would just cause trouble for both of us, but it wasn't clues I needed anyway. It was advice.

"Can I join you?"

Greg looked up. "Sure, yeah."

I put my hot chocolate down at his table and sat opposite him. "Can I ask you a question?"

"If it's about the murder . . ."

"It's not. Not really. It's about Jesse. How is he handling the investigation?"

"What do you mean?"

"Is he doing okay or is he overwhelmed?"

"Are you asking if he needs help?"

I shrugged. I was, kind of. "Is he letting you help?"

"After the business card thing, he's doing everything by the book. Mostly he's doing it without anyone's help, but he's following procedure."

"Do you think he's trying to do it all alone because Roger was his friend and he feels some kind of obligation to solve the murder himself, or do you think there's another reason?"

I could see that he was looking at me differently, trying to figure out what I knew that he didn't. It might have helped us both if I shared what Carrie had found out about the bank account, but that wasn't an option. "He's struggling with something," Greg said finally. "Not sure what it is."

"I know they were very close . . ." I started.

Greg rolled his eyes.

"What?" I asked. "I knew they had some kind of falling out, but I don't know what it was about."

Greg leaned forward. "I don't know the whole story, but Jesse was smart to stay away from that guy. Jesse is a good guy, and a good cop."

"And Roger wasn't?"

"I don't know. If Jesse's not telling you why they stopped speaking, you can be sure he's not telling me. But what kind of guy stakes out the house of an old friend? If Roger was a decent person with no ill intent, he'd have picked up the phone and called Jesse. But he sat in his car drinking coffee and watching the house like he was in the middle of some big undercover operation."

"If Roger wasn't a good guy, wouldn't Jesse expose that if it meant catching the killer? Would he really risk letting a murderer go free?"

"There's a loyalty among cops. I would do anything for Jesse. . . ."

"Not anything illegal."

He shrugged. "No, of course not. But I'd do whatever I could to protect him." Greg sighed. "We shouldn't be talking about the investigation. I know we're both a little frustrated to be shut out, but I can't ask Jesse to do things by the book if I'm going to go behind his back." He put his hand over his police notebook, where I could see the word *Walker* circled. When he saw me looking, he shut the book. "How's the wedding planning going?" he asked.

"Under control. I have to finish my wedding gift, and Natalie is quilting the one from the group, but other than that . . ."

"Cake, band, decorations . . ."

"All figured out," I said. "Are you bringing a date?"

He smiled. "Kennette is coming into town, so we're going to go together." Kennette was Oliver's granddaughter. She'd been studying art in London for the last year, but she was coming back for the wedding.

"You guys have stayed in touch?"

"A little. E-mails mostly. She's a great person and she seems to think I'm okay." He smiled.

Romance was everywhere in Archers Rest these days. "She'd be lucky to have you, Greg."

"I guess I want what you and Jesse have."

"I'm not sure what we have at the moment," I said. "It's not just Roger's murder. Anna is sort of driving a wedge through our relationship."

"She's not after Jesse," he said.

I didn't say anything, but I hadn't been thinking of her as competition. Not just because her husband's body had been discovered only two days earlier and he had once been a close friend of Jesse's, but because I'd learned the hard way that if someone wants to stray there's nothing you can do to stop them, and if they want to be faithful there's nothing anyone else can do to make them cheat. I knew Jesse well enough to know that if he wanted to be with another woman, he'd tell me.

Anna wasn't trying to get Jesse for herself. Either unintentionally or out of some unnecessary loyalty to Lizzie's memory, she kept reminding me that Jesse had already found the love of his life, and I wasn't it.

"She's walking around in a daze, I think," Greg continued. "Full of guilt if you ask me."

"Guilt about what?"

"She's with that guy."

"Bob Marshall?"

"No, the other guy. The business partner. He came up today."

"Brown hair, camel hair coat."

"Yeah. Jesse said he put up the money for her interior design business and I guess it turned into something more."

"Is it a motive for murder?" I asked.

"I think it's the oldest one there is."

CHAPTER 28

Someday Quilts was quiet when I opened the door. No customers, no dog, no tiny black and white kitten. No mom, despite
the fact that her car was still parked outside the shop. And, oddest
of all, no Eleanor.

"Grandma?" I called out. "Are you here somewhere?"

I walked past the register, past the St. Patrick's Day and Easter
fabrics that were displayed near the front, past the cutting table, the
sale section, past the threads and notions wall. I took a left at the
longarm machine, with a quilt in the frame that had been covered
with a large piece of muslin. Natalie sometimes covered quilts to
keep off the dust, but I knew that wasn't the reason this time. Eleanor's wedding quilt was under there. After a peek at the amazing
work Natalie was doing, adding hearts to each block, and feathers
in the border, I entered the classroom.

Eleanor and my mother were quietly studying my gazebo quilt
in progress. Barney was curled up by Eleanor's feet, and Patch was
sitting on a table watching him.

"Didn't you hear me calling for you?" I asked.

Both women looked up at me as if I'd woken them from a spell.

"You guys shouldn't be looking at this," I said when I saw them
with the quilt. "It's your wedding gift, Grandma."

"Sorry. We came in here to chat and when I saw it, I couldn't help myself," she said. "It's beautiful. I can't wait to see what it looks like when it's finished."

There was no point in hiding it anymore and I was dying to share. I moved over to the drawing pad I'd left on the table and flipped through until I came to my sketch. "This is my plan," I told her. "I think I could make simple embroidered flowers for the base of the gazebo. It would be easier than trying to appliqué really small pieces."

"Much," Eleanor agreed. "And you could add some vines up the gazebo. We don't have them in real life, but I always thought it would look pretty with vines."

She was right, it would be the perfect addition. I quickly added vines to the sketch. Vines that didn't break, of course. I didn't believe in quilt superstitions, but there was no point in inviting bad luck.

My mother was sitting quietly, watching us. She had a small, sad smile on her face.

"What do you think, Mom?" I asked.

"It's lovely," she said. "You've always been a very talented artist and I think Oliver was right—you really have a gift for fabric, like your grandmother."

"I'm trying to figure out a way to do this for a living," I said.

"Making quilts?" my mother asked.

"No. Patterns."

Eleanor's eyes widened. "Someday Quilts Designs. We could sell them in the shop, and on the website. . . ."

"You have a website?" my mother jumped in.

I laughed a little. "We have one page that shows a picture of the shop and our hours and directions. I've wanted to expand it, but Grandma doesn't want to sell fabrics online and I didn't know what else to put on it."

"Putting our fabrics online would mean ordering much bigger amounts, changing the inventory frequently, having a shipping department. It's a full-time job," Eleanor said. "But patterns make sense for our size shop. We could sell those. They would be a huge hit."

"Do you think?" It had been sitting in my mind for a while, but doing it, really selling patterns of my work, seemed daunting and even a little cocky. "Do you think my stuff is good enough that someone would want to re-create it?"

"Yes!" my mother and grandmother said in unison. Probably the first time they'd agreed since my parents' arrival.

I flipped through my sketchbook, showing them various ideas I had, getting their thoughts on how to proceed. My grandmother, like me, was a detail thinker. She focused on creating the actual pattern, getting good photos of my quilts, price points, and packaging. My mom thought big. She wondered aloud about other websites to sell my patterns, suggested I look into publishing instruction books. She started looking on the Web for the best shows to enter quilts, even finding international ones in places like Ireland and Australia. It was getting a little overwhelming, but it was nice to feel that my mom saw quilting as a real future for me.

"Will you have time for all of this?" Eleanor asked. "With school and your work here, and Jesse?"

"This is her career," my mother answered for me. "This is something she's building for herself. She shouldn't concern herself with whether it conflicts with a dinner date. Does Jesse leave a crime scene because they have movie plans?"

I laughed a little at that. I was usually at the crime scene with him. As the two women who loved me the most were loudly debating my future, my cell phone rang. "I'll be right back," I said, grateful for any chance to sneak away from the conversation, but especially grateful that it was Jesse.

"Hey, there," I said. "I've been thinking about you."

"Can you do me a favor?"

"Sure."

"Do you have time to pick up Allie from school and take her home? There's some fruit and cheese, I think, if you guys want a snack. I shouldn't be more than an hour."

"The investigation heating up?"

"No. Anna wants to go visit Lizzie's grave. I'm not sure it's the right time for that considering what she's already going through, but she says it will bring her some comfort."

"Oh, sure, I can see that." And it will remind Jesse of how much he misses his late wife, I thought.

"You don't mind, do you?" he asked.

"Why would I mind?"

"I have a lot of responsibilities, and your mother is right—it's sort of an instant family pushed on you when you still have the freedom to go where you want, when you want."

"Like the free spirit I was before we met? Backpacking through the jungles and mixing it up with the jet set?"

"That's great." In order to pick up on my sarcasm he had to actually listen to me, which he clearly wasn't doing. "Listen, Anna is here. Allie gets out at two forty-five and you have to meet her by the north entrance to the school."

"I know where to meet her," I said, but he had hung up. I'd picked up Allie from school dozens of times, but this was the first time I'd felt like the babysitter. Never mind, I decided. Anna will be gone soon and life will go back to normal. After Roger's killer is caught, I reminded myself. And the reason Jesse has for paying Roger is explained. And my parents accept that this is where I live, and Jesse is who I want to be with. Then life will return to normal.

But without Eleanor as my roommate and full-time boss.

CHAPTER 29

I didn't hear the bell to the shop door ring, so I nearly jumped when I heard my name. Bob Marshall was standing in front of me. But as soon as I glanced at him, he walked past me.

"I see a doggy bed but no dog," he said.

"He's in the classroom."

"Teacher or student?"

I laughed. "A little of both, usually. Are you here for your sister's gift?"

"Yeah. But she has a lot of fabric, so I don't think she needs more of that."

I laughed again, which I soon realized seemed rude. "Sorry, it's a quilter's thing. We never have enough fabric."

He smiled. "Sort of like a thief I once knew. He said each time he stole it was because he only needed a little more money. I asked him how much was a 'little more' and he said, 'just the money I don't already have.'"

I laughed. "Same thing, only with fabric."

Bob looked around the shop, seemed overwhelmed at first, then gravitated toward a group of pincushions that Natalie made. He held a small pear-shaped one toward me. "This is pretty, but it doesn't seem like it's enough."

"Can I make some suggestions?"

"You can insist. I'm putty in your hands."

For the next ten minutes we wandered the shop, choosing small items, like charm squares, scissors, hand lotion, and a box of threads. I added a quilt pin from our collection as my gift to his sister. "If you bring these to Cindy's Flowers and Gifts, she'll put them in a gift basket for you," I said. "It's right near the police station. Have you gone by there yet?"

"Not yet," he said. But he seemed distracted. The Bob Marshall Jesse described bore no resemblance to the soft-spoken man in front of me. "This was really nice of you, Nell. I forget sometimes how nice people can be." His voice cracked slightly.

I'd done nothing out of the ordinary, but somehow it had touched him. "Anytime." I watched him walk out of the shop, another puzzle that seemed just beyond my ability to solve.

"What's wrong with you? I'm always finding you in a dream world these days." Maggie was standing less than a foot away from me, holding a large quilted tote bag that she dropped on the counter. "Are you sitting down?" she asked me.

I looked down at my feet in an instinctive check. "Nope, standing right in front of you. Do you need to get your eyes checked?"

She waved me away. "I was making a point. You should be sitting down because this will knock you off your feet. I spent half the night on the Internet checking on the lead I got from Bernie, and I found something. I saw you cozying up to Bob Marshall. . . ."

"He was here buying a gift for his sister."

"Well, your new friend was released from prison six weeks ago after doing twenty-seven months on assault charges."

"But he was a cop. . . ."

"*Was* is right," Maggie said. "He was a corrupt cop."

"And he was Roger Leighton's partner," I added hopefully. If it were true, then we would have a murderer who didn't have anything to do with Jesse's payouts to Roger, and the whole thing would be over by the time the sun went down.

Maggie looked surprised. "Not unless you know something I don't."

"He wasn't Jesse's partner at any time, was he?"

"No. But he was involved in a case where Roger was the arresting officer. A drug dealer—a man named Alex Walker." Walker, the name Greg had circled in his notebook. He was obviously chasing the same leads we were, doing his own shadow investigation behind Jesse's back.

"What about Jesse?" I asked. "Did he have a role in any of it?"

"The arrest happened just two months after Jesse came home to Archers Rest."

"What do we know about the case against Alex Walker?"

"It was thrown out of court. It seems that nearly half a million dollars that was alleged to have been found at Walker's home went missing."

"Bob Marshall stole it?"

"Not that anyone could prove. The money was never found."

"So maybe Roger was his partner, and maybe after Bob got out of prison he came looking for Roger to get his share of the money. . . ." I was getting excited. Maybe we really would solve the case by sundown.

I thought about the money in Roger's bank account, the fact that he was still living in the house he'd shared with Anna, and that for three years after the money was stolen Roger had worked for the police force. If he had access to a large amount of cash, he wasn't living like it.

"You think it might be hidden somewhere in Archers Rest?" I suggested.

"If it is, then it's got something to do with Jesse."

"Nell!" My mother walked in on Maggie and me. "Please tell me I didn't just hear what I think I heard?"

"Depends what you think you heard."

"That Jesse's friend was a corrupt police officer who was murdered and Jesse might be involved?"

"I'm just thinking out loud," I told her.

"I don't know what happened to this town since I was a child, but it's not a healthy place for you to live. Maybe it's for the best that your grandmother is moving away from here, and maybe it would be a good idea for you to do the same."

"That's an overreaction, Mom. And a complete misunderstanding of the situation."

Maggie stepped toward my mom. "Patty, don't worry yourself. What's happening now, well, it's a bit of excitement, but really everything's fine. And Nell is really very good at figuring things out. She's brought quite a bit of intrigue to our quilt group."

"With all due respect, Mrs. Sweeney," my mom said, "Nell should be focusing on her career plans, not murder investigations or boyfriends or quilt groups."

"Speaking of which," I told Maggie, "I can't make quilt group tonight."

"We'll muddle through."

"What exactly are you doing tonight, Nell?" my mother asked. "More traipsing around after killers?"

"No, actually, I'm not. We'll talk later about my patterns and getting them on the Web and in other shops. I'd really like your input, but right now I have to go."

"Where?"

"I have to pick up Allie from school." Before my mother could say another word, I lifted my hand to stop her. "This is my life, Mom. Mine. And right now I have to go."

Maggie handed me the tote bag. It was heavier than I expected. "Take this with you," she said. "There are some interesting patterns in there." From the look she gave me, I sensed she didn't mean for quilt tops.

CHAPTER 30

I fed Allie a snack. We played dolls, and talked a lot about the upcoming wedding. Her duties as a flower girl were a big deal to her, so we went over them carefully until she felt satisfied she could handle the job. When she was bored with me, she went to watch her favorite cartoons and I was left alone in the kitchen with a hot cup of tea and the tote bag that Maggie had given me.

There was a folder in the bag stuffed with various papers, and a thick binder that had to weigh a couple of pounds. I opened the notebook first. Maggie had been busy. There were dozens of printouts on the crime that had ended Bob Marshall's career along with a photo of him from a *Daily News* article as he was entering the courtroom for his trial. In the photo his attorney was a tall, well-dressed man identified as C. G. Kruger. The general consensus in all the articles was that Marshall had been caught skimming drug money off vice arrests, though the word *alleged* was used in every other sentence. The corruption had likely gone back years and involved more than just one bad cop. But Marshall wasn't talking and the silence had cost him. Because he'd been unwilling to cooperate, the district attorney threw every charge he could at Marshall: multiple counts of robbery, tampering with evidence, corruption, and filing false police reports. In the end only one charge stuck: assault with a deadly weapon.

I sat for a minute and looked at the photo until it jumped out at me. C. G. Kruger. That must have been the name on the business card Greg found on Roger's body. The card that Jesse wouldn't put into evidence.

I continued reading the story, going over it for details that might lead to another clue. A rookie named Kevin Findlay had testified that, along with a large amount of drugs and a stash of weapons, five hundred thousand dollars in cash had been found at the scene and bagged for evidence. Marshall had been the one to bring the money to the evidence locker, and somewhere between the drug dealer's home and the police station, the cash had gone missing.

Marshall contended the money never existed. Another officer on the scene backed him up, but Findlay wouldn't change his story. Marshall and Findlay had apparently exchanged words, they fought, and Marshall broke Findlay's jaw with the butt of his gun. It put him in prison for more than two years and ruined his career in law enforcement.

"This is the tip of the iceberg," the prosecutor was quoted as saying in one article. "And the frustrating thing is that guys like Bob Marshall know how to play the system. We're not going to see someone show up with a fancy car, or suddenly take an expensive vacation. These guys are just going to add the money in small amounts, a little bit here and there, and they'll wait out the statute of limitations before early retirements and the good life will begin."

The other officer on the scene hadn't been identified, but if the man was Roger, it would explain Marshall's appearance in Archers Rest. Roger might have been hiding the money all these years and Marshall was looking for it.

As I reread the prosecutor's statement, I felt slightly sick. "These guys are going to add money in small amounts." Like bank deposits in odd sums of less than five hundred dollars over a period of three years.

Could Jesse have been holding the money for Roger and paying it out little by little? No, he couldn't have. Jesse was a good man. He didn't have to ask me to believe it; I did believe it. But what if someone else found out about the deposits Jesse had been making, assumed it was the missing cash, and brought Roger up here to get it? That I could believe.

There was a scratch at the window. It sounded like a branch. I knew it was a branch, and when I got up to check it I could see that the wind had picked up, and, in fact, it was a branch from the overgrown oak scratching against the window. The window that was right next to the back door where someone had entered Jesse's house on the night Roger was killed. Maybe someone looking for the money they thought was hidden here.

I walked into the living room to check on Allie, who was half watching the television and half playing with a loom I'd gotten her—one of those simple weaving looms that allows kids to make squares of about six inches. Since I'd gotten it for Allie, she'd been making potholders for everyone she knew. She was making two blue and white ones as her wedding gift, and she was taking the project quite seriously. I stood watching her, but she was engrossed in her task and barely paid attention.

If the money was hidden in the house I didn't know where to start looking. Or even if I should start. Surely going through his things was a huge invasion of Jesse's privacy. And, of course, I reminded myself that the money wasn't hidden here because Jesse would never be involved in anything that terrible.

But someone had been in this house the night Roger was killed, so it made sense he was looking for something. If I could figure out what, maybe I could help.

The other issue was that searching wasn't really necessary. In the year Jesse and I had been dating, I'd opened nearly every closet and drawer in his house. I'd cooked meals, helped him organize toys and clothes, and even sorted through his receipts at tax time. I never saw large sums of cash sitting around, or anything that might contain large sums of cash, like a locked file cabinet or the key to a safe-deposit box.

Jesse certainly didn't live as if he had more money than his salary. Neither one of us were into fancy restaurants or weekends away. Most of our dates had consisted of dinner in town, or cooking at his place so the three of us could be together.

"Instant family." My mom's words popped into my head.

"Not now," I answered them silently. I debated asking Allie whether Roger had been in the house recently. His picture was on the bookcase, so it would be easy to ask if she remembered the man, but that seemed like a betrayal both to Jesse and to his little girl. I walked back to the kitchen.

"So what if it wasn't money the killer broke in to find? What if it was something else?" I asked myself.

Maybe a key, a piece of paper, the number of Roger's bank account. But the day of the murder, Jesse had been unconcerned about my theory that someone had been in the house. If he knew something was here that tied Roger to the murder, wouldn't he have immediately looked for it?

Questions. That's all I had, questions on top of questions, and no one to answer them since Jesse wouldn't talk to me about it. I sat back down at the table and took a gulp of my tea. It had gone cold.

There was one box I hadn't opened. A large plastic bin, actually, that Jesse had said was full of old stuff he was saving for Allie. When we'd been organizing her room over the summer I found it in the back of her closet. Jesse told me not to bother with that. It was filled with "keepers," he said. But a box of old keepsakes might be a good place to hide something.

I stood in the kitchen for ten minutes debating before I finally went upstairs. The box was where it had been before, on the floor in Allie's closet, underneath a pile of neatly folded clothes she'd recently outgrown. I moved the box to the center of the floor and opened it. I don't know what I was expecting, but it was filled with "keepers" as Jesse had said—baby clothes, photo albums, toys from her baby days. I lifted out the top photo album and looked at the first pages. Jesse in college. He was so very young and very handsome. Lizzie was on his arm; pretty, happy, young. The album told the story of their life together, ending with pages of casual wedding photos, the kind taken by friends and family. The next album was the formal wedding photos. I found that I couldn't look at more than a few of those without feeling jealous and sad, and then petty. My punishment for being so nosy. The last of the albums were Allie's baby pictures. At the end of the last book were a few pictures of Lizzie, looking frail and thin, sitting in the hospital bed holding her daughter for what was likely the last time.

As I put the albums back I saw a stack of letters and cards. There was an envelope with Jesse's name written across it, and without wanting to but not being able to resist, I opened the card it contained. "Happy sixth anniversary," it read. "Whether we have six years or sixty, the happiest moments of my life are the ones I spend with you." It was dated six months before her death.

I could see Jesse's handwriting on the envelopes of other cards, some pink for Valentine's Day and others that just said "I love you" on the front. But I didn't read them. I put everything back where it belonged—the albums in the box, the box in the closet, and the clothes on the box—and went back downstairs to the kitchen.

✂

I looked at the thick binder that Maggie had given to me. I didn't know how much more evidence I could take in, but it gave me something to focus on so I opened it. Instead of items about the case, it was photos stuffed into clear plastic three-ring folders. Unlike the photos upstairs, these didn't leave me feeling like an intruder. There were snaps of Eleanor from when she was a girl all the way through just a few weeks ago at the town's Christmas Eve party. Another plastic folder held pictures of Oliver from his days at school, to his early art shows, to the same Christmas Eve party. A Post-it note on the stack said that Maggie had tracked down Oliver's relatives in England for the early photos, and gotten the later ones from photo albums Oliver had in his house.

"Not stolen," she wrote with a smiley face. "Borrowed."

A slide show of photos for the wedding. I'd insisted on it in September when a January wedding seemed so far away and easy to organize. I liked the idea of showing the very different lives of these amazing two people; how they had met, fallen in love, and found themselves wanting to commit to be together.

My mother had found it odd that two people of an advanced age would want to marry when there were so few years left to share, but all I saw were happy people in love. Besides, what were the guarantees for any of us? Lizzie was proof of that.

I shook off my melancholy. Jesse would be home soon and I promised myself that I'd avoid any talk of the murder, or Lizzie, or the past—his or mine. Instead, we'd just be together and enjoy spending time as a couple. A couple and Allie, which, instant family or not, sounded like a perfect evening to me. I looked up at the clock. It was almost six and completely dark outside. Jesse and Anna couldn't still be at the cemetery, could they?

I went to Jesse's desktop computer and started scanning the photos into a file. The folder was thick; I knocked pens, a zip drive, and a "World's Best Dad" pencil holder off the desk trying to make room. It was a long slow process. Allie helped me by placing the photos in the scanner and keeping track of what had been done. She offered suggestions on the best ones for the slide show and how we could decorate poster boards and display some of the photos in Eleanor's hallway so the guests would see them as they arrived. After each photo was scanned, she took a moment to study it before carefully placing it back in the plastic folder. As excited as Allie was by all things wedding, she was equally fascinated by these images of her beloved almost-great-grandparents as young people.

When we were almost done, I had to take a break and feed us both dinner. A simple task like creating the photo presentation had made me feel useful and clearheaded. And hungry.

"Someday I'll be as old as Eleanor," I told her as we ate. "And you'll be as old as me."

"Unless you die like Mommy did," she said. "Then you don't get old."

I tried to hide it as I gasped. Allie had spoken of her mother before, of course, but never about her being dead. It was mainly about how Jesse had told her that Lizzie's favorite color was lilac, and her favorite day of the week was Sunday. Allie had been barely three when Lizzie died. She had no memories of her, so understandably Jesse tried to give her all that he could. About her death he had told her only that "Mommy got sick and went to heaven." I'd never heard him use the word *die*.

"I wouldn't worry about that," I said, struggling for what words to use. "I'm planning on getting old and cranky, like Eleanor."

Allie laughed. "You're already old and cranky. But Anna said that since you're not family you might not be around when I grow up. Is that true?"

I could feel my face flush. It was one thing for Anna to mess with my head, but quite another to confuse this little girl. "I'll always be here for you, Allie," I said. "No matter what."

Allie studied me then looked down at the salmon on her plate. "Even if I don't finish my dinner?"

Now it was my turn to laugh. Finally an easy question with an easy answer. But even as I was laughing, there was another question forming in my mind, and this one had no answer yet. It had been hours since I'd picked Allie up from school. Where was Jesse?

CHAPTER 31

After dinner, Allie and I read stories to each other. We played cards and watched TV. I tried calling Jesse several times, but it went to voice mail. It was unlike him to be unreachable. I briefly considered that Anna had taken his phone to keep him from being in touch, but that seemed a bit extreme. Besides, Jesse was used to calls from the station and from Allie. If his cell were lost, he'd find the nearest phone and check in just in case.

Not calling, pocketing evidence, and keeping Greg out of the loop of an investigation—the "out of character" moves were starting to add up. There had to be an explanation. And whatever it was, everything would be fine. I'd been telling that to myself for a couple of days now, and as mantras go, it was getting a little stale. He wasn't the latest victim of Roger's killer, I decided, or checking into a hotel room with his best friend's widow. He was lost in the memory of his dead wife, and had forgotten about his girlfriend and daughter.

✂

I was about to suggest that Allie get ready for bed when there was a noise at the front door. Finally. I went to it, ready to fling it open and give Jesse a piece of my mind. But just as my hand reached the knob, I looked through the window and realized it wasn't Jesse. It was Bob Marshall, and he was, for lack of a better word, lurking. It was one thing to stop by Someday, but now Jesse's? We were bumping into each other one too many times for my comfort level.

"Allie, do me a favor and go upstairs."

"But it's not my bedtime yet. I have fifteen more minutes."

"I know that," I said. "I'm not asking you to go to bed. I'm asking you to go upstairs to your room and close the door. Bring the phone with you and call Eleanor on her cell phone. Tell her I'm going to talk to the nice man outside and then tell her all about your day. Don't get off the phone with her until I come get you."

"Why?"

"Because Eleanor misses you when she doesn't see you, and I have to talk to the man outside."

Because, I thought, I might be overreacting, but there was no harm in that. And if I wasn't, someone else needed to know that we were in the house alone in case Bob Marshall gets past me.

I watched Allie go upstairs, then I picked up my cell phone and called Jesse. Still voice mail. I called Greg's cell.

"Hey, Nell, what's up?"

"I'm at Jesse's house alone with Allie. Bob Marshall is outside."

"Who is Bob Marshall?"

"The guy Jesse keeps giving tickets to."

"I'm leaving now. I'll be there in two minutes."

I hung up. I switched the porch light on. Marshall was standing on the other side of the door, looking at me through the window in the center of it.

"Hey, Nell Fitzgerald, we meet again. I guess you're more than a passing acquaintance of the police chief."

"I'm a friend," I said.

He smiled. "Half the town is betting that it will be a surprise double wedding when your grandmother gets married next Saturday. The nice lady who owns the pharmacy told me that she had a vision that you'll announce your engagement there."

Bernie. She meant well, but gossip was her second favorite hobby after quilting. The hairs on my neck were standing, but I decided, one last time, to assume an innocent explanation for his being at the door. "Look, Mr. Marshall, I appreciate that you're new in town . . ."

He seemed both amused and slightly annoyed. "I think we both know I'm not moving to Archers Rest. In fact, I'll bet we both know exactly why I'm here."

"Jesse's busy making dinner right now," I said. "If you want to talk to him you'll have to come back tomorrow."

"Jesse isn't here."

"Yes, he is. . . ."

"Nell." He stretched out my name in a way that was, I guessed, meant to convey he was running out of patience. "His car isn't here. After he told you to pick up Allie from school, he drove off with Roger's widow. I'm guessing you don't even know where he is."

"I know exactly where he is." I hit the number 1 on my speed dial. Jesse's number. I held it to my ear and listened as, once again, it went to voice mail.

"Hey, Jesse," I said to the recording. "Bob Marshall came to the house to see you. . . . He's here now. . . . Okay. . . . I'll tell him to call you at the station tomorrow." I hung up. "Jesse said he'll talk to you tomorrow."

I felt ludicrous doing it, and clearly Marshall didn't think much of my acting skills because he didn't react like a man who believed me.

We stood for a moment, watching each other with only a thin piece of glass surrounded by a wood door that was maybe three inches thick. How hard would it be to kick down a door, I wondered. Marshall looked like he could do it if he wanted to. He'd broken the jaw of a police officer, what could he do to me if he wanted?

His eyes didn't leave me. I tried to match his intensity with my own stare. His face looked older than his years, wrinkled and ashen. Maybe prison does that to a person. But did he look angry? No.

About to pounce? Hard to say. Maybe he just wanted to charm me into some con, and when that didn't work, scare me.

"Mr. Marshall," I said, "I would appreciate it if you left now, and tomorrow you can tell Jesse what you wanted to tell him."

"I'm not here for Jesse."

"Then tomorrow I'll meet you at the police station and you can tell me what you wanted to tell me there."

"Nell, why don't you let me in so we can talk? We had a nice chat this afternoon at the shop, didn't we? I'm not going to harm you. I just want to talk," he said. "And Allie is upstairs, right? She won't overhear what we say."

My throat went dry. "Well, Bob," I said with as much strength as was possible under the circumstances. "Since you're so well versed in the town's activities, you probably already know that Allie is on the phone with my grandmother, and the chief detective of Archers Rest is on his way here right now."

He narrowed his eyes. "Nell, listen to me. You need to be careful," he said. "Your Nancy Drew decoder ring isn't going to help you this time." Then he turned and walked off the porch. I saw him get into his car and drive away just as Greg's car pulled up in front of the house.

"You okay?" Greg asked when I let him inside.

"Don't know yet. Give me a minute." I went upstairs to get Allie ready for bed, and to assure my grandmother that whatever threat I may or may not have been under was over now. Greg was with me.

"Where's Jesse?"

"I don't know."

"If he's not home in an hour, you bring Allie to this house and have her spend the night here," she insisted.

I agreed. There was no way I was letting that little girl stay in the house when Marshall could be back at any minute. I came back downstairs to find Greg making tea. We sat together in the kitchen and I relayed the entire conversation start to finish while he listened, looking more alarmed with each moment.

"I tried the chief when you called me and I left a message," he said.

"Where is he?" It was a dumb question. He didn't know any more than I did.

"I'll stay until Jesse gets home," he said as he sipped his tea. "And tomorrow I'll run a background check on Marshall."

I almost told him that the women in my quilt group had already found out about Marshall's past, but I didn't. I'd been told to stay out of the investigation, so it was probably better if it seemed like I had. In the morning Greg would find out everything we knew about Marshall, and probably some things that we didn't.

"I'm scared of him," I admitted.

"He threatened you."

"Did he?" I was thinking out loud. "It almost felt like he was warning me, as if the danger was from somewhere else."

"From where?"

I closed my mouth tightly, for fear the words would get out. And once they were said, I wouldn't be able to un-say them. But in the end, my lips parted and the sounds leaked out. "I think he was warning me to be careful of Jesse."

CHAPTER 32

It was after nine o'clock when Jesse came home. Allie was asleep, and I was worried and furious. I took comfort in two things: he was safe and he was alone. I wasn't going to have to listen to another round of "Nell's not good enough." I had as much of that as I could stand.

As soon as Jesse walked in the house, Greg stood up from his place on the couch and excused himself with a quick, "See you tomorrow, Chief." He seemed anxious to get out from under what must have seemed like the beginning of an argument.

Jesse didn't ask why Greg was there. He just let him leave and turned his focus on me. "I'm sorry," he said as his first words.

"You're darn right you are." I had to shout in a whisper so I wouldn't wake Allie. "Where have you been all this time? I called your cell about a dozen times."

"It's been a tough day." He dropped onto the couch. "I know you're mad and you have every right to be, but sit with me a minute and then yell."

Reluctantly, I sat. "Are you okay?"

"I'm fine. How's Allie?"

"She's great. Where were you?"

I wanted to give him a rundown on everything that had happened that evening, and I wanted to withhold it as well. Now that I knew he was alive, I resented the fact that he hadn't been here to keep Allie and me safe.

"How was your day?" he asked. There was no interest in the question. He was asking it to avoid answering me. I decided to ignore it.

"Where's your houseguest?"

"Anna's business partner came into town today. He's staying at the bed and breakfast. She went over there with him."

"For the night?"

"No. I don't think so anyway. She went to help him get settled in. She'll be home in a while, I guess."

"Is she, I mean, are they a couple?" I remembered what Greg had said earlier about the man, but I didn't know if he was certain or just guessing.

"I think so. He rushed up to be with her, which is a lot for someone who's just a business partner. Anna hasn't said anything, but I mean, why not? She and Roger have been apart for a while."

It didn't seem to occur to Jesse that the "business partner" was the reason for the separation. If he had one blind spot, it was in his loyalty to his friends. It sometimes didn't allow him to see faults that were so obvious to others.

"Were you at the cemetery this whole time?" I asked.

He put his hand on my cheek and brushed back my hair. His eyes were watery and soft. "No. Just a few minutes. It's freezing out there. We brought some flowers and left them there. I never go. It seems maudlin to bring Allie and I don't know . . ." He trailed off for a moment before speaking again. "After the cemetery, Anna met up with the guy, Ken something, Ken Tremayne, and they went to get some food. I had some work back at the station, and then I took a drive. I didn't realize I was out of cell range. If you drive north on the back roads it gets spotty."

"Why did you go for a drive?"

"I had to think. I'm sorry I left you with Allie all this time. I'm sure you had a million things to do."

"I love spending time with Allie," I said, "but I don't like what's going on with you. It isn't like you to promise to be home in an hour but not come home, or call, for nearly six hours. You scared me half to death."

"I know. I am sorry. You don't know how happy I am to come home to you." Jesse kissed my neck, and slowly moved his hand from his lap to my thigh.

"Not if your life depended on it."

He laughed. "I am a terrible boyfriend and a worse father."

"You are not, on either count. You're in the middle of a difficult time, so you get to have a bad day here and there. I know you don't want me to help, but do you want me to listen?"

As I spoke I wondered if I'd put Maggie's notes back in the tote bag, and felt relieved when I remembered that I had. The binder was still next to the computer, but that was all wedding-related stuff.

"The investigation is at a standstill. I still have no idea what Roger came up here to do, or why he was killed trying to do it."

"It obviously has to do with Bob Marshall. He . . ."

Jesse pulled away from me. "Nell . . ."

"Don't 'Nell' me. I'm an objective ear, a logical, interested person you can talk to. Someone completely on your side, who will love you no matter what. You can say anything about your past, about Roger's past, and I will be a sounding board you can trust," I said. "Tell me you don't need that."

I sat and waited while Jesse considered my offer. I didn't know how much he knew about Marshall's conviction and the missing five hundred thousand, but it was hard to believe he knew nothing. Still, it had happened in the last months of Lizzie's life and just after her death. Jesse would have been too preoccupied to care much about the goings-on of his former colleagues in New York.

"I don't want to talk about it," he said. "It doesn't have anything to do with us."

"But it does." I took a deep breath, then told him about my encounter with Marshall earlier in the evening, and the fact that because I couldn't reach him, I'd called Greg.

Jesse leapt off the couch and checked his cell phone. "Four messages. I'm so sorry. I just . . . I have no explanation. I can't believe I put you in this position."

"Why does Bob Marshall want to talk to me?"

"I don't know."

"Jesse . . ."

"I don't know, Nell. I swear to you. Look, Marshall's not going to hurt you, but you have to promise me that you'll stay away from him."

"I can promise that, Jesse. What I can't promise is that he'll stay away from me. It's time you and I talked, and told each other everything."

Jesse put his hands to his face and rubbed his eyes. "Not tonight," he said. "I just want a peaceful night tonight, but what do you say we pick up here tomorrow?"

He took my hand and led me upstairs, a comforting and familiar exercise. Except this time the other hand was on his gun.

CHAPTER 33

We all have a past. In the sixteen months I'd lived in Archers Rest I'd uncovered things about my grandmother, my friends in the quilt group, even myself. But now Jesse's past and our future were bumping up against each other. It seemed only one of them could win, and I wasn't sure it would be us.

As he checked the doors, windows, and who knows what else, to make sure everything was locked, I called Eleanor.

"You didn't tell Mom and Dad about Allie's call, did you?"

"They were having dinner in town," she said. "But if there's a reason to be concerned I can't keep it from them."

"I don't know if there is, but let's just wait and see."

"Okay." I could hear the hesitation in her voice, and I hated that anything was worrying her when she should be focusing on her own happiness.

"Were you at the quilt group when Allie called?"

"I didn't make quilt group. Oliver's daughter arrived from Canada this afternoon, so they came over for coffee. They were just walking out the door when my cell phone rang."

As glad as I was that Eleanor had been there to talk to Allie, I was sorry another member had missed the group meeting. "Did you give Maggie the key to the shop so they could still meet?"

"I didn't have to. Carrie ended up having to go home to a sick child and Susanne was on deadline for a quilt show she entered. Poor Maggie. She said she didn't think it was much of a group to sit in the classroom alone."

"We'll get less busy after the wedding," I said, then I remembered that Eleanor would likely be leaving soon after. "I'll see you at work tomorrow?"

"You bet. We have lots to do. I can't wait to show you something."

Jesse walked into the bedroom, put his gun in the nightstand drawer, and dropped onto the bed. I said my good night to Eleanor, though a big part of me wanted to stay on the phone and find out what it was she couldn't wait to share.

"All locked up tight?" I asked Jesse after I hung up the phone.

He nodded. "I don't want you to be afraid. Nothing will happen to you. I promise."

"What were you thinking about when you went on that drive?" His smile was sad. "Nothing."

"That's not true." I settled back on the pillow and waited.

"I was thinking about Roger. He was the funniest guy in any room." He laughed a little. "I don't know if you've noticed, but I'm kind of a serious guy. . . ."

"Really?" I smiled. "You hide it well."

He rolled his eyes. "Roger was my opposite. I was careful; he was willing to take chances. He saved lives because he went in without backup. I just wouldn't do that," he said. "I don't know why we became friends, really, but we were friends. And then Lizzie and Anna became friends, and we were like this mighty foursome, together every weekend. When Allie was born, we made Roger and Anna her godparents. And when Lizzie got sick . . ." His voice trailed off. "Roger was there for me in so many ways I couldn't even count them."

"So why did you stop speaking?"

"Because, I guess, after I lost Lizzie I got even more careful. Roger just seemed reckless to me. It wasn't fair of me. He was a guy who wanted to do the right thing. He just did it differently than I did."

"Did he have anything to do with the five hundred thousand that was stolen from a drug dealer in New York?"

Jesse looked at me hard and shook his head. "I should have known better than to expect you to stay out of it." He looked away, stared off into the distance, and I couldn't tell if he was angry or not.

"Jesse, I'm in it. Roger told Carrie that your girlfriend better like heartbreak. Those bullets were aimed directly at Someday Quilts. Bob Marshall came into the shop today for something more than just a gift for his sister. And tonight he was here looking for me. Not for you, for me. He knew exactly where I would be and that I was alone with Allie. You can be mad that you're dating a busybody, but in this case, I'm not sticking my nose where it doesn't belong. This is my life we're talking about, so it is my business."

He didn't look at me, but he nodded. It wasn't me he was angry at, I could tell that much, it was himself.

"I think there's something about Roger that you're not telling me," I said.

"I just told you everything you need to know." He was shutting down, physically and emotionally. He seemed on the verge of collapse. There was no point in trying for more information tonight.

"Sleep," I said.

"Yes, please."

We got under the covers and curled into each other's arms. Despite the warmth of his body wrapped around me, I felt a chill.

"You need a quilt," I said, trying to mend fences.

"My girlfriend must not like me enough to make me one."

"She likes you plenty."

He rested his head against mine, and within minutes he was asleep. But I lay there, wide awake, listening for every noise. Just as I started to drift off, I heard one. The door was opening downstairs.

I listened. The person was moving around downstairs, opening cabinets and drawers. Not making a lot of noise, but hardly doing anything to avoid being detected. Anna.

I got out of bed carefully so as not to wake Jesse, grabbed his sweatshirt to keep out the cold, and went downstairs. The light was on in the kitchen, and I could hear more opening and closing of drawers. At this rate she would have inspected every one of them.

"Can I help you find something?" I asked as I walked into the room.

She looked up. "I didn't mean to wake anyone."

I glanced into the drawer she had open. It was the catchall, with everything from batteries to pizza coupons. "What are you looking for?"

"Matches."

"Do you smoke?"

She plopped down on one of the kitchen chairs and let out a heavy sigh. "I wanted to light a candle. I thought I might take a bath, and it's more soothing by candlelight."

I searched through the drawer until I found a book of matches. "Do you have a candle?"

She grabbed a large white-and-pink-striped pillar candle from behind her purse. "I bought one at this cute little store. I can't remember the name, let me find the receipt."

She grabbed her purse and started fishing through it, placing things on the kitchen table as she searched. Women's purses, including my own, are like clown cars. We fit far more into them than it would seem possible. Anna's purse had a wallet, tissues, a set of house keys, her cell phone, two more sets of identical house keys, a business card holder, and a handful of change from the bottom. I wondered why she didn't just turn over her purse and dump it. It would have been faster. Finally she fished out the receipt.

"Burke's," she said. "Do you know it?"

"I do." Burke's was exactly what she had described, a cute little store that sold the kind of knickknacks that no one needs but for some reason, once you see them, you can't live without. "We had a visitor. Bob Marshall stopped by."

She blinked a few times, slightly bit the side of her lip. "What did he want?"

"You know him?"

"He was on the job with Roger. I barely knew him but, you know, weddings and funerals, that sort of thing. He must have wanted to offer his condolences."

There was no surprise that he was in town, no questions about how he had known to come to Jesse's house. And she'd assumed he had been there to speak to her. Maybe he had been, and when he found me alone, he decided to scare me instead, perhaps to throw me off guard. And then there was the fact that Bob knew a lot about me. Maybe Anna was his source, and his partner in killing Roger and shooting at Jesse. Whatever the case, I wouldn't get the answer from Anna.

I yawned. "I need to go back to bed."

"You're spending the night?"

I almost answered, then paused. I knew what I wanted to say, but Eleanor's voice in my head suggested I keep my smart remarks to myself. "Enjoy your bath, Anna."

CHAPTER 34

There's something about the sunshine as it reflects off snow. It's almost blinding. As Barney and I made our usual trek into town, I felt like I was in danger of getting lost. I was in an odd mood. I'd woken up early from Jesse's and headed back to Eleanor's for a change of clothes, just as the sun was creeping upward. I showered, got ready for work, and felt energetic about the day. But as I was heading downstairs to make myself breakfast, I saw that Oliver was in the kitchen, sitting quietly and staring off somewhere, deep in thought.

"I thought I was the early bird," I said.

He smiled a little, but I worried I'd been wrong to interrupt him. "Felt a bit of pressure lying down. Couldn't catch my breath," he said.

I rushed over to him. "I'll call the doctor."

"You'll wake him up."

"Then I'll drive you to the hospital."

He patted my hand. "I'm okay now. Your mother's been cooking all sorts of exotic dishes and I'm afraid they're too much for this old stomach."

"It could be your heart."

"Nothing to worry about. My heart is fine. But I'll make an appointment as soon as the doctor's office opens. Not just an appointment. I'll see him today."

"Oliver, if something's wrong . . ."

"This, too, shall pass." He took a deep breath, as if to prove he could. "It goes so fast," he said. "Enjoy it while you can."

"It's not over yet. Don't forget, you've got a big day ahead," I pointed out. "You're going to dance with my grandmother a week from today. Okay?"

He mocked me with a stern expression and a firm nod. "Yes, mum."

"Oliver, I really think the doctor . . ."

"I'm fine. It's just indigestion." He sounded frustrated with me. I wanted to push but I didn't. As I had pointed out to my mother, Oliver and Eleanor were adults capable of making their own decisions. Even if this one made me nervous.

He decided to go back upstairs and try for another hour's sleep. The changes were hard on him, too. I hoped that was all it was. I decided against my original plan of getting to the shop early to work on my quilt. Instead I waited in the house, making a batch of blueberry muffins and generally keeping myself busy and close until eight o'clock, when my grandmother came downstairs, followed by my parents, and finally by Oliver and Barney. Oliver winked at me, making me a co-conspirator. He wasn't going to say anything to my grandmother, and I was going to give him until the doctor's visit to change his mind.

An hour after that, as Barney and I walked into town, we were passed by Eleanor, my mother, and little Patch on their way into the shop in Eleanor's car. Patch was standing on my mother's shoulder, watching the world out the passenger-side window. She was getting more sure of herself and her place in the world, and maybe she also wanted to show Barney that while he rolled around in snow, she rode in luxury. I took a longer route than usual and walked past the bed and breakfast in town. Anna's friend had spent the night there. I checked my watch. The owner, an old friend of Eleanor's named

Jackie Greene, usually served breakfast until about nine-thirty, and it was that time now. Her guests would either be checking out or heading into town for some sightseeing. It was too cold to just stand there, and Barney was getting anxious, so I decided to go in and just ask Jackie if Anna's friend was still there.

But I didn't even have to go that far. The man in the camel hair coat came out of the bed and breakfast just as I was heading to the door. He smiled as he passed me, but it wasn't a smile of recognition. Just a friendly morning nod as he turned left onto the road that led to Main Street. If he remembered me as the lady on the roof of Clark's Dry Cleaners yesterday, he didn't show it.

Barney and I hung back for a moment then followed. The man, Jesse had said his name was Ken Tremayne, walked quickly, but given that the temperature had dipped below freezing, it didn't surprise me.

I stayed behind Ken, and Barney helped to give me cover by sniffing at everything he could find. When Ken stopped at the edge of the cemetery, I watched him while Barney stuck his nose in the snow to his absolute delight. It was sort of the same reaction I have when a new shipment of fabric comes into the shop, though I don't actually plunge my nose into it.

Ken just stood there. Was he going into our cemetery, which housed residents from as far back as the seventeenth century? What would be there to find? I suddenly had images of a suitcase filled with the missing money hidden in an empty grave.

But no such luck. Instead of walking through the gate, he reached into his pocket and grabbed a pack of cigarettes.

While he smoked, I tugged at Barney to keep walking. I didn't want to be spotted staring at the man.

I walked quickly trying to pass Ken by without being noticed, but Barney was having none of it. A goose, one of many that made a home in the cemetery, waddled toward us and Barney loudly announced its presence. Ken turned and saw me again, and as he did he dropped his lighter. I walked over and retrieved it from the snow.

"Thank you. You must be a resident of this lovely town. Everyone's so friendly."

I looked over at the man, who I guessed was in his fifties. There was a slight gray in his brown hair, and a general no-nonsense quality to his appearance, but he was dressed like a man who had money and wanted the world to know it. "I am," I said. "And thank you. We like it."

"Ken Tremayne." He shook my hand.

"Nell Fitzgerald."

"Nice dog you've got."

"He is." I patted his head. Barney had lost all interest in the goose and now sat between Ken and myself at full attention. "He loves the snow."

Ken took a drag of his cigarette. "I'm a little lost. I'm supposed to be going to one of the coffee shops in town to meet a friend."

"There's only one: Jitters. And you're headed in the right direction. In fact I'm heading there myself." All the better to question you, I thought.

We started to walk, and I knew I didn't have much time since there was only a block to go. No point in wasting it with small talk.

"You're Anna's friend," I said. "I'm Jesse's girlfriend."

"Wow, this is a small town. I met Jesse yesterday. He seems nice."

"You didn't know him before?"

"You mean in New York? No. That's a pretty big town," he said with a laugh.

"I guess I assumed you were a cop."

"Based on?"

I shrugged. "Gut instinct." In truth I was just fishing for his profession.

"No, actually I'm a former prosecutor. But good guess. I believe in law and order. I just decided to go another way."

"Another way?"

"I still get to catch bad guys, but for more money."

"Not anymore."

"Excuse me?"

"You said 'former prosecutor.' What do you do now?"

"Defense. It pays even better."

"Someone yesterday said Anna's business partner had come into town. Is that someone else?"

"That's me. Well, actually I'm more of a silent partner. I put up the money, provide legal counsel, and Anna does everything else."

"Why interior design?"

"I have money in a lot of businesses. I'm an amateur magician, so I own half of a shop in the East Village. I have a stake in a tapas restaurant in Brooklyn. I'm looking into investing in a bakery in Brooklyn."

"Busy guy. It's amazing you can find the time to come up here."

"Anna and Roger are old friends as well as clients. It's so sad to think he's gone. And she's heartbroken, of course. I wanted to do whatever I could."

"Anna said they were divorcing, only Roger didn't want the divorce."

"He had no choice but to go along with it whether he wanted it or not."

"Because you and Anna are a couple and maybe Roger was holding up the divorce."

Ken stopped. He turned his body toward me. Barney pushed his way between us, growling slightly. "What's your role in all this?"

"Curious bystander," I said. "This is a small place and when someone is murdered, even a stranger like Roger Leighton, the whole town is interested."

"Maybe the town should get cable."

Behind Ken, I saw a familiar but unwelcome figure coming toward us. Bob Marshall. "Miss Fitzgerald, we never stop running into each other, do we?"

Ken looked over at Bob, and was just as displeased to see him as I was. But given Barney's reaction to the lawyer, I wasn't sure if one bad guy was accidently saving me from another.

"I wouldn't say we run into each other, Mr. Marshall," I said. "I'd say you keep looking for me."

"You're right there. I saw your mom and grandmother opening the shop, just as I was coming out of Jitters. Carrie makes really good coffee, doesn't she? By the way, Ken, Anna's waiting for you. And she's not a lady who likes to be kept waiting." He smiled at me, and then at Ken, before continuing his walk past us.

"Do you know Bob Marshall?" I asked.

Ken swallowed hard. "I know of him," he said. "The fact that you clearly dislike him is the strongest piece of evidence I have that, despite your earlier comments, you are a sane and sensible young lady."

Ken hadn't acknowledged Bob Marshall, who clearly liked to stir up trouble and must have been looking for a reaction. Or maybe they were trying hard to seem as if they were not friends. I'd been linking Anna to one man and then the other, but what if they were the partners who killed Roger? Of course, at least right now, I had no idea what could join them together.

Ken started walking again. Jitters was up ahead. This conversation would be over soon and I felt like I had only scratched the surface.

"You said you're a defense attorney now," I said. "There's another lawyer's name I ran across, C. G. Kruger. Do you know him?"

He let out a half cough, half snicker. "A crooked lawyer for crooked cops. He represents all kinds of lowlifes, but cops are his specialty."

"And that information is well-known among police officers in New York City?"

"Among the dirty ones, yes. Why do you ask?"

"As I said, I'm a curious bystander."

Jesse took that card, and kept it out of evidence. He knew what it meant. There was a knot growing in my stomach that was getting very difficult to ignore.

CHAPTER 35

"It needs to have more stitching over here. It should have a balance between the blocks and the borders."

Susanne was standing behind Natalie, instructing her daughter on how to finish Eleanor's quilt when I came into the shop, still focused on my conversation with Ken Tremayne. I debated whether to talk to Jesse, and my reluctance made me feel as though I were doubting him, which I wasn't.

I looked around. There were a few customers, but they all seemed in the hunting phase. I grabbed the newest book by husband-and-wife design team Weeks Ringle and Bill Kerr and started paging through, calming myself with the images of their beautiful modern quilts.

"And you should add some hearts there," Susanne continued.

Natalie looked up at me for help. She had only been doing long-arm quilting since March, but in that time she'd completed dozens of quilts and, to my eye anyway, was an accomplished quilter. Her mother was an award winner and perhaps had a tougher standard, though Natalie's work was amazing. I was about to make a statement to that effect when my own parent troubles came toward me.

"Nell." My mother came out of Eleanor's office with a sense of purpose I hadn't seen in her in years. "Grandma and I have it all figured out. Let me show you."

As my mother pulled me back toward the office, I caught Natalie's eye. It was too late to save either of us from the well-intended advice of our moms.

Eleanor was sitting at her desk, glasses perched on her nose, eyes firmly fixed on the computer screen. "I found a company that will do all the printing for the actual pattern and the cover photo," she said. "You just upload the design and they take care of everything. They have thin paper or a heavier cardstock; which would you prefer?"

I looked at the screen. "Wow. We've gotten that far?"

"Not if you don't want to."

My mother sighed. "Of course she wants to. We talked about this yesterday. This is the next step if Nell is going to start her own business."

"It wouldn't just be my business," I said. "It would be part of Someday Quilts."

"I was thinking about that." Eleanor swiveled her chair toward me. She had a blank expression on her face, the one she used when she was doing her best not to influence me. "I sort of jumped the gun with that name. It's your pattern company. You should decide what to call it. I was thinking maybe Nell Fitzgerald Designs."

"Or Manhattan Modern Quilts," my mother suggested.

"But I don't live in Manhattan."

"But you could. I mean, this is exactly the sort of career that would allow you the freedom to go anywhere."

She reached into her oversize purse and pulled out a stack of eight-and-a-half-by-eleven sheets of paper. There was something about quilting printed on them, but it wasn't until she handed them over that I could see where she was going with this.

"Tokyo?" I asked.

"Did you know that quilting is huge in Japan?"

"Yes. But I didn't know that you knew. And what does that have to do with my little quilt patterns?"

"That's my point. They're not little quilt patterns. They could be the start of a major company. I printed this off the Internet yesterday. There's this big festival there, lots of really amazing things. You should go and see what they're doing."

"Mom, I've never even been to Houston."

"Texas? What does that have to do with anything?"

My grandmother took the papers from me and set them on the desk. "It's a quilt show, Patty. And your mother has a point, Nell. You should see the trends, see what's hot, what's changing. If you're going to make a go of this . . ."

Some people have families who laugh when they announce their dreams. Mine went into uber-support mode. My head was swimming. All I wanted was to make a pattern of one of my quilts and maybe sell it at the shop; make my way slowly toward a career in quilting. But my family wouldn't be happy until I was the Bill Gates of the quilt world.

I sat opposite Eleanor and pushed back my chair to give me a little room to think. Unfortunately, I accidently hit Barney in the leg. He sat up with a start, accepted my apology, but left the room. No doubt in search of a place less crowded and dangerous.

"I think I'm going to start with a couple of patterns," I said. "The gazebo quilt and maybe the Amish bars quilt I made. They're easy to re-create and both have some nice appliqué elements that would be simple for anyone. I'll sell the patterns at the shop and on our website, and see how it goes. If more than ten people like them enough to buy, then I'll make more."

"Nell . . ." my mother started.

"And we'll call the company Someday Quilts Designs because it is part of the quilt shop and it should remain that way. We should sit down later and figure out a logical amount to print, and also the profit split. Natalie kicks back a percentage of her fees for longarm services to pay for the machine and the space. If it's okay with you, Grandma, I'd like to do the same. Any questions?"

My grandmother smiled. "I think you've covered it."

"Thanks, both of you, for the help. Mom, I do like the idea of checking out quilt shows and the wholesale market shows to see what the trends are. And if there's ever a time I can afford to go to Tokyo, I'll do it in a heartbeat. Right now, though, we have customers in the shop, so I think I'll go to work."

I got up and left the office, just in time to see Susanne and Natalie sort out their differences on the quilting.

"We're going with stippling in the background of the feathered border," Natalie said, referring to the squiggly quilt design that was often used to fill in spaces and flatten areas. I imagined Susanne liked the idea of the quilted feathers popping from the background, and stippling would certainly help with that. "And my mom has some ideas about how you should quilt your gazebo quilt."

"Wonderful." I tried to suppress a smile but couldn't.

Jesse and Allie weren't the only instant family I had. The quilt group had given me a large group of sisters, all of whom were pretty open about telling me how to live my life.

"Dru!" Natalie called out as the door opened. I turned around to see our librarian come into the shop. She'd visited before many times. Dru had become a quilter after the town had joined together to make a cathedral windows quilt as a Christmas project for Charlie when he was down on his luck.

"Strange to see you outside the library," I said.

She laughed. "I know. People think I live there, which I practically do." She handed me a large hardcover book. "This is for you."

"*Designing Patterns*," I read. "*Taking Your Artwork and Turning It into a Business*."

"I heard you were doing that with your quilts," she said. "So I brought this over. I checked it out for you for two weeks, but if you need it longer let me know."

"How did you find out about the patterns?"

"Jake over at the butcher shop told me when he came to return some DVDs to the library. His wife overheard it when she was getting coffee at Jitters. He knew I'd be interested because I'm always talking about how beautiful your quilts are."

My instant family had expanded once again, to the entire town of Archers Rest. "This will be very helpful," I told her. "I'll read it cover to cover. How's your car these days?"

"Perfect. Except for the scratch."

"What scratch?"

"It's weird. Right on the door handle of the passenger side. I would never have even seen it, except I gave Charlie a ride and he noticed it. You want to see?"

Not only did I want to see, but Natalie quickly covered Eleanor's quilt with the muslin and she and Susanne followed me out of the shop without our coats. Susanne, at least, had the sense to grab her sweater, and as she joined us, she wrapped her Irish wool fisherman's cardigan tightly around herself.

I leaned over to examine the handle. Dru was right. Two lines had been scratched into the handle. "They're perfectly straight," I said. "Hard to do if you are keying a car."

"It looks like something left by a clip," Susanne suggested.

"As if something were attached?" I asked. Susanne nodded. I looked at the door handle again. "Dru, your car was parked facing west on the day of the shooting?"

"Yeah. The passenger side was to the street, and the driver's side was to the curb. Why?"

I stood up. "I've been wrong about something," I said. "Completely wrong."

CHAPTER 36

I had assumed that whoever shot up Main Street was working with a partner. It made sense given the evidence. Jesse had seen a flash coming from that direction just as the shooting began. The logical conclusion was that a partner might have been standing there signaling the shooter that Jesse was on the street. But if the shooter acted alone, everything about the investigation had changed.

✂

Dru had to hurry back to the library, but Susanne, Natalie, and I rushed into Jitters for hot drinks and a huddle. Carrie saw us shivering and knew even we weren't dumb enough to go out into the street on a freezing January morning without coats—unless a clue had lured us. She immediately left Rich to deal with the customers and joined us to talk over this development.

We sat on the purple couch in the front, as if we needed to look out at the crime scene, but we stayed close, whispering our suspicions and questions.

"How could the shooter have made the flash from the roof?" Susanne asked. "Didn't someone else have to do it?"

"No," I said. "You were exactly right about the marks on Dru's car being made from some kind of clip. What if the shooter had fastened a device to the door handle? Something small that wouldn't have been noticed in the ten or fifteen minutes it would have been on the car. In the winter people tend to hurry from place to place. And usually they're so covered with hats and scarves and upturned collars it could have drawn little interest. The shooter, acting alone, could have attached the device, climbed up on the roof, aimed at my grandmother's shop, and pulled the trigger. Then, with people running for safety, anyone looking around would have had their attention drawn toward the flash."

Carrie jumped in. "Just those moments of distraction would have given the shooter time to get off the roof and into the alley. Right behind my coffee shop."

We all instinctively looked toward the back door—the only thing between the killer and the rest of us on the day of the shooting.

"That's all well and good as a theory, but what kind of device?" Natalie asked.

"I'm not sure about that," I admitted. "It could have been a mirror, and he positioned a light at it to create the reflection of a flash, or maybe it was a small firecracker. Something that would have drawn Jesse's attention as the shooting started." I didn't know much about creating a diversion, but I knew I was on to something. "The shooter did something to make that flash happen once he was on the roof."

"If you're right about the flash," Natalie said, "the only person likely to look for a source would be a police officer. It seems like a lot of trouble to go to unless you wanted Jesse on the street."

"I agree," I said. "When I went up on the roof yesterday I could see people walking in the street. I could see Greg walking into Jitters, almost to the point where he was at the door, so the shooter would have been able to see Jesse walking out. And that's when he set off the flash."

Susanne wasn't buying it. "And you're sure you wouldn't be seen from up there? Most of the buildings on this street are only one story high."

I thought about that. The state police had been on the roof the day of the shooting. They were easy to spot, but they hadn't been trying to hide. "When I made a small attempt to conceal my presence, I was only seen when I walked closer to the River Street side of the rooftop," I said. "Other than that, unless I went close to the roof's edge like the state police, I doubt I would have been noticed."

"And if you were crouching down," Carrie added, "maybe wearing dark clothes, would you have been noticed even from the River Street side?"

"Probably not."

Though the memory of it did bring back Ken's smile when he saw me on the roof. Was he amused to see someone standing there, trying to maneuver her way around on a pile of newly fallen snow? Or did he realize I was investigating the shooting?

"So bring this to Jesse and see what he can do with it," Susanne said. She got disapproving looks from the rest of us, especially Natalie, but she held her ground. "We're talking about a pretty sophisticated killer. This is someone who planned a big, middle of the day, middle of the street, shooting without getting caught. This is out of our league."

Susanne joined in our investigations, but like Eleanor, only with reluctance, and only, I suspected, because talking about murder had become such a big part of our quilt meetings. I'm sure, given the option of a vote, she would have lobbied for a return to discussions of normal quilt-related things: fabric storage, the newest trends in design, chocolate, and who in town was starting a new romance.

Which reminded me, I needed to bring up Dru and Charlie when the group met next—if the group met again. Eleanor and I still hadn't discussed what she planned to do with the shop while she and Oliver were away.

"Susanne's right about it being sophisticated," I reluctantly agreed. "This is someone who pulled off a murder in front of the police chief's house, and a home invasion to boot. Then planned ahead to create a diversion for a shooting that served as a warning for that same police chief."

"Or you," Natalie corrected me, "because you saw something when you went to Jesse's house the night of the murder."

"That makes no sense." Susanne jumped in.

"What makes no sense?" I asked.

She narrowed her eyes, and smiled. "I'll tell you if you promise to take this to Jesse."

"Mom!" Natalie protested.

"I'm serious. It's okay to look things up on the Internet or discuss possibilities of who might have killed whom. That's not dangerous."

"We've done more than that," Natalie stepped in again.

"Fine, maybe we have. But we've always had Jesse to do the actual police work. Nell has shared our findings with him almost every time."

The operative word there being *almost*, but she was right. "I promise," I said. "Tell me what doesn't make sense."

Susanne took a deep breath and looked at all of us separately as she spoke. "If the killer took the starter out of Dru's car the night before, before he'd even committed the murder, then how would he know that Nell would happen to walk past and see Roger sitting in the car? How do we know the killer was even in the car when Nell walked past?"

We each sat back and went over her words in our heads. She had a point.

"So maybe the killer didn't know," Natalie said. "But then why seem to target Someday?"

There was no arguing that all four targets—the sign, the streetlamps on either side of the shop, and Jesse's patrol car parked right out front—seemed to be a warning specifically directed at the quilt store. But if it wasn't a message for me, then it had to be a message to Jesse about me.

"So either the killer knew who I was before the murder took place," I said, "or he found out once he arrived in town. If he was following Roger . . ."

Carrie gasped. "I told Roger that Jesse's girlfriend worked at the quilt shop. Do you think it's possible the killer overheard? I don't remember if there were people in here I didn't know. Aside from Roger, I mean. And Rich waits on about half the customers. . . ."

"Maybe Rich will remember. . . ." Natalie started to say, then she laughed. "Forget it. Unless the killer is a cute eighteen-year-old girl he won't remember."

"Don't be too hard on him," Carrie said. "I don't always pay a lot of attention if the person doesn't stand out, like Roger did by staring across to Someday for so long."

"But if Carrie's right and the killer did overhear, half the town would have identified you as that person, Nell," Natalie said. "Look at all the information Bob Marshall has put together on you. The killer could have done the same."

"Assuming the killer isn't Bob Marshall," I said.

Susanne wrapped her cardigan tighter. It wasn't cold inside of Jitters, but she felt a chill. "So even if you weren't the target before Roger's murder, you might be now."

Susanne was right again.

CHAPTER 37

"I'll call Jesse," I said. "Maybe we can have a quiet moment together and talk. I'll tell him everything I've found out and we'll go from there."

I wasn't sure Jesse would be open to my theories. This wasn't like other times I'd pitched in on a case. Jesse was hiding something from me. I knew it in my gut, but I just didn't want to share it with the rest of the group. They loved him nearly as much as I did. My small nagging doubts were difficult enough; I couldn't bear the idea that my friends would feel them, too.

Carrie was the first to pull away from our tight circle. She looked around at the new customers that were coming into the shop, lining up for a midmorning pick-me-up of caffeine and sugar. "I only have a few more minutes before I have to relieve Rich, and you do realize the bachelorette party is in five days. Have we done anything for it?"

Natalie grabbed her cell phone. "If we're going to huddle on that subject, we need Bernie and Maggie. From what I understand, Bernie has very specific ideas on what we should do."

I went to the counter to refill my coffee. Natalie made some suggestion for the party, which left Susanne looking shocked and Carrie laughing hysterically. I didn't want to know.

Greg had the same need for a caffeine fix that I did. Rich was waiting on him, pouring a strong black coffee while Greg looked through the display case at the dozens of scones, donuts, coffee cake squares, and giant cookies. While he picked out just the right sugary snack, I went behind the counter and refilled my own cup. In Jitters, much like in Someday Quilts, when it was busy, friends sometimes helped themselves and settled up on the honor system.

"Cold day out there," Greg said, a little louder than his normal voice.

"It's just about this time of year when I wonder how long 'til spring."

"That's true for me, too." He jerked his head slightly. It took me a moment to realize it was a signal. He walked toward the back door and I followed.

"Everything okay with Jesse?" he asked.

"Yeah. He said he went for a drive and lost cell service."

He clenched his jaw a little, nodded a bit too much. "I'm glad it worked out. And Nell, you can call me anytime. Not that Jesse will be MIA again."

"No, hopefully not. And thank you for last night. I don't think I can say enough how glad I was that you picked up your phone."

"Has Bob Marshall given you any more trouble?"

I told him about my walk into town, about Ken Tremayne, and about our encounter with Bob. I didn't tell him about my switch in theory from two killers to one. I figured I'd save that for Jesse.

"Ken Tremayne lost his law license six months ago," Greg said. "I did a background check. Apparently there's some malpractice suit against him."

"What about?"

"Nothing to do with Roger or the case. Just some guy who didn't like his representation. He filed some kind of complaint, and it cost Tremayne his license, and now there's a lawsuit."

"Why did you look in the first place?"

"Because he was here, fussing over Anna. It seemed a little weird that he rushed up to be with his girlfriend when her husband's body wasn't even out of the morgue."

"Maybe she needed comforting," I suggested, then realized how unlikely it was given her actions. "Except she is doing everything she can to make sure Jesse is the one doing the comforting."

"Maybe that's why Ken's here. He doesn't trust her."

Well, that was something I hadn't considered. Had Roger been killed because he was competition, and had the bullets that whizzed over Jesse's head been a warning?

"What's he doing now?" I asked.

"Consulting. I'm not sure what that is, exactly. Plus he has money invested in several businesses."

"Can I ask you something else?" I didn't wait for a response because I wasn't sure what it would be. "Do all police officers train on those automatic weapons?"

"Are you asking if the shooter was a cop?"

"Or at least trained to be one, yes."

"Those weapons aren't as hard to shoot as you think, I mean for someone with a little training. We're not talking about a huge distance here, just across the street. And it's not like we know for sure that the shooter aimed at the *S* in the 'Someday' sign, or at Jesse's windshield. He could have just aimed at the sign and the car, and happened to hit those targets. And in terms of the streetlamps, they would have been closer, height-wise. Good shots, no doubt, but we're not talking military marksman."

"So not necessarily a cop?"

"You know how easy it is to get your hands on one of those things? Too easy," he said. "I'm not sure who you're trying to eliminate from the suspect list, but anyone with money enough to buy a weapon, and willing to put in the practice, could have been up on that roof."

But still, I thought, at least a working knowledge of crime scenes, cop behavior, and guns. Like a disgraced ex-vice detective, former cop, or a criminal lawyer. He was right—that didn't eliminate any of them.

Greg sipped at his to-go cup. I was keeping him from somewhere. "Thanks for your help," I said.

"You know I would do anything to protect you and Jesse. You guys mean the world to me." He drew a long breath. "And, you know, if Jesse needs to take a break, maybe a leave of absence to deal with all this, I'm here to step in."

I decided to ignore it. Greg was a lovely person and a loyal friend, but as Jesse once said, his ambitions sometimes got the better of him. I gave him a quick hug and looked for happier news to share. "Kennette arrives Tuesday," I told him. Greg's face lit up. "I guess you already knew that."

"I can't wait. She told me she likes to dance, so I guess I'll be making an idiot out of myself at the reception."

"That's why they exist."

He waved a quick hello to Maggie and Bernie as they entered the coffee shop. Instead of immediately joining the group, I stood watching him walk outside into the cold. He opened the door to his police car but didn't get in. A moment later he emerged again with a Jitters to-go cup that he dumped in the trash. When he saw me watching, he shouted. "I'm an addict. This is the old cup from this morning."

I smiled and raised my own coffee mug in a toast. Then Greg took out a cigarette pack from his coat pocket and lit one before getting back into his car.

Maggie, sitting on the couch with the rest of the group, unexpectedly howled with laughter. The plans for the bachelorette party were well under way, and it sounded like something to make both grandmother and granddaughter feel slightly awkward. I could hardly wait.

CHAPTER 38

By the time I returned to the table the group had most of Eleanor's bachelorette party planned, and it centered around food—a long, calorie-laden meal, a few bottles of wine, a half dozen desserts . . .

"The tiny ones," Bernie declared, "so we can taste as many as we like."

"And gifts. Something personal for Eleanor."

"Keep it clean," I demanded.

Maggie stared at me. "Honestly, Nell. What can you be thinking? We've already decided on what to get her."

"A baker's dozen. It's a quilting tradition that every bride have twelve quilts for ordinary use and one for special use," Susanne explained. "We're making her the special use one as a group, so we're each digging into our stash of finished quilts as a gift."

Natalie jumped in. "We figure when she moves to South Carolina she'll need quilts for the new house. She can take five of her own, our six stash quilts, and one that Grace made her. That way she has a piece of all of us with her."

I liked that. Grace Roemer was the woman who had taught Eleanor how to quilt years before, and she was the unofficial patron saint of the group.

"They can be anything?" The gazebo quilt would qualify as my contribution, but I also had a blue and cream bow tie quilt I'd made over the summer that Eleanor had liked. I decided to give her both.

"A baker's thirteen," Susanne said. "Why not?"

"That sounds like a great bachelorette party."

Bernie looked over at me. "Then, after we open presents, the stripper will arrive."

At that the group burst into laughter, in large part because of the stricken look on my face.

✂

Natalie and I had been away from the shop for the better part of an hour, but I had an errand to run before I went back to work. I snuck back into Someday, grabbed my coat, and left. I wasn't trying to avoid helping customers, just an overly involved pair of women I loved deeply. When they weren't driving me nuts.

I headed toward the police station. I was intent on keeping my promise to Susanne. The more I thought about it, the more convinced I was she was right. We were in over our heads. Jesse knew Bob Marshall and Anna, and he had met Ken Tremayne. He might have come to the same conclusions about them that I had—which was that any one of them could have done it—but without knowing about the scratch on Dru's car, he could be looking to match up the right pair of killers, instead of singling out one.

At the station, I walked past the front desk without bothering to stop and ask for Jesse. I just went to his office door and knocked.

"I said I didn't want to be disturbed." The voice from inside was Jesse's, and he was annoyed.

"It's me."

I waited. For a half second I contemplated opening the door, to catch Anna and him in the act of . . . I didn't know. Jesse wasn't that kind of man. I didn't have to imagine scenarios for too long, though. Jesse opened the door wide.

"Hey, there." Now his voice was gentle. "How did I get so lucky?"

"I wanted to talk with you."

He grabbed my hand and pulled me into his office, closing the door behind us. "What's on your mind?"

He was alone in his office. Aside from his laptop, his desk was empty, as usual. He hadn't been working on a case file, so I couldn't figure out why he'd been so gruff at the knock.

"Am I catching you in the middle of something?"

"No." He paused. "Yes." He turned his laptop around so I could see the screen. Caskets. "Anna asked me to work with the funeral director in New York to pick out the casket and music. You know, just make the arrangements."

"If she doesn't want to do it, surely he had other family . . ."

"Not in the area, and nobody close."

"Can I help?"

Jesse sat at his desk. "I did this twice before. For my dad twelve years ago, and for Lizzie. It just doesn't get any easier."

"When's the funeral?"

"The wake is Tuesday in Queens, the funeral is Wednesday, and then back home for Oliver's bachelor party."

"I'm sure Oliver would understand if you skipped it."

"I wouldn't. We're taking over Moran's Pub, drinking good scotch, eating bad pizza, and playing pool. That type of event is easy to plan." He sighed and looked back at the screen filled with rows of caskets.

It seemed like a lousy time to discuss the case, so I sat with him and together we chose everything necessary for Roger's friends to say good-bye. When we were done, Jesse was blinking back tears.

"I don't know what I'd do without you," he said.

"You won't ever find out."

"Promise. Because when this is all over with we should have a long talk about, well, everything."

"*You* want to talk about our relationship?" I lightly mocked.

"Let's get through Roger's funeral and Eleanor's wedding first, then I'm all ears. In fact, there's a lot to discuss."

"All good?" he asked.

"Are you nervous?"

"Your mom . . ."

"Isn't in charge of what I do with my life. And she likes you, Jesse, she just doesn't know you yet. And she hasn't met Allie."

"We should change that," he said. "How about tomorrow?"

"How about tonight? Eleanor and Oliver are going to stay at the house and have dinner with my parents, so why not let Allie hang out there as well? And we can go to dinner and talk."

"I thought we were going to wait until next week to talk."

"Different subject." Dinner, just the two of us, sounded romantic except for my plan to tell him everything I knew about the murder case.

"Okay. Dinner." He got up and I did, too. He kissed me lightly. "Don't get into trouble."

"I'm going back to the shop. How much trouble can I get into?"

$\mathcal{C}$HAPTER 39

As it happened, I didn't get into any trouble between the police station and the quilt shop. I walked quickly, kept my head down, and although I thought I saw Anna walking into one of the shops at the end of the street, I said nothing and kept moving.

I pushed open the door to Someday ready to get back to work after the longest coffee break on record, when Natalie whispered to me, "Stop. Don't move."

I stopped. "What's going on?" I whispered back, ready to dash out and get help.

"Walk quietly. I'll show you."

Together we crept toward the back of the shop where the sale fabrics and Barney's workplace bed were kept. Sure enough, Barney was curled up on it, nose to tail. Natalie put her finger to her lip and then pointed. I looked toward the spot and saw a little black and white tail coming out from under Barney's chin.

Patch was curled up just like Barney, only her tiny body fit perfectly in the circle between his graying snout and his back paws. They were both sleeping soundly. We backed away slowly until we reached the checkout counter at the front of the shop.

"When did that happen?" I asked.

"No idea. I noticed it about twenty minutes ago."

"Has Eleanor seen it?"

"Not yet. She and your mom went out to buy a dress your mom could wear to the wedding. Where were you?"

I told her about my time with Jesse, and got her advice on the best way to tell him all we'd learned despite being told to stay out of it. Then we heard stirring from Barney's dog bed. Rather than wake our furry friends, we stopped our conversation and Natalie went back to working on Eleanor's quilt and I went to the classroom to work on the gazebo piece.

><

I've heard that meditation is a great way to calm down and refocus. For me, quietly sitting with a piece of hand appliqué has the same effect. As I slowly added to the gazebo, making layers of white and cream fabrics into a representation of our town symbol, my breathing calmed. Time was slipping by, and I felt centered.

In two hours I had sewn on most of the gazebo. There was the quilting to do, and when that was done I would add on the embroidered flowers, but in a few short days I'd accomplished a lot on the quilt. There was even a chance I'd have it ready for Saturday. I went back into the main part of the shop to see if Natalie would be able to quilt it for me with such a short turnaround.

But Natalie was too busy to approach. She had left Eleanor's quilt in the frame and was cutting fabrics for a regular of ours, a man who came up from Dobbs Ferry every other month for fabric to make pillows he sold to high-end design shops in New York.

There were a few other customers looking for fabrics, and I made the rounds to see if anyone needed my help. One woman was gently petting my Amish bars quilt with the appliqué flowers.

"We're making a pattern of that," I said.

"Good. I like the soft, rounded shapes of the appliqué against the stark design. You wouldn't think the two things go together, but they do." She pointed toward Barney and Patch, now awake, but sitting together. "Like those two."

A big yellow dog and a tiny black and white kitten did seem an odd match, but they did go together. Barney laid down, stretching his paws in front of him, and he leaned over and touched his nose against Patch's. I grabbed the camera from Eleanor's office and every time they did something cute together, I took a photo. I had my logo for Someday Quilts Designs.

The woman who liked my quilt went back to shopping and eventually got about twenty fat quarters that she brought to the counter along with a book of traditional quilt patterns. "What do you think of these? I'm making a Chinese coins for my nephew. Lots of blues with a brown border. Very male, I think."

Chinese coins was a simple pattern, vertical rows of fabric strips, set apart by sashing. Since the strips and sashing could be any length or width, the pattern was easy to translate from wall hanging to bed size, and fast to make.

"It's great," I said. "And you've got the right colors there for any guy."

Maybe this would be the quilt I made for Jesse. I'd put it off, wanting to find just the right pattern, but I was overthinking it. I made quilts and he needed one. There was a quilting superstition that the first night under a new quilt, an unmarried person would dream about their true love. I liked the idea of being in his dreams.

The customer flipped through the book to show me another choice. "I have another nephew, and I'm thinking maybe this for him, but I don't like the name."

I looked at the photo. "A double wedding ring."

"I'd love the challenge, but I'm afraid if I made it for him, he'd think I was dropping a hint to finally meet a nice girl and settle down."

"He would."

"But it's pretty, don't you think?"

"I've got one started in the back," I told her. "I just didn't know what to do with it."

She nodded emphatically, as if we had stumbled across one of life's great mysteries. "It's more than just a nice bedcover, it's the sort of quilt that says 'forever,' doesn't it?"

"It does," I admitted. I lightly traced the blocks in the photo with my finger. Sometimes you can stare at a puzzle piece for hours and not know where it fits, and then suddenly you know. Like my relationship with Jesse, the double wedding ring was complicated but worth the effort. No matter how much work it was, this was the quilt I wanted to make for him.

I still had several unfinished quilts, including the gazebo quilt, but there's an urgency when an idea hits you. After the woman left, I headed back to the classroom and grabbed the paper-pieced arcs I'd made. They were in blues and greens, perfect for the quilt I had in mind. I rushed back into the main part of the shop, looking for a neutral background, going through a half dozen fabrics before I came up with the perfect choice: a creamy white that looked hand dyed. I wanted to piece at least one complete block of the quilt before I lost that feeling. Once a quilt like this was on its way, I knew I would finish it.

One block turned into two, which turned into ten. I wanted a nap quilt, large enough to fit Jesse's tall frame, but not big enough to be turned into a bed quilt. I pictured him curled up on the couch and watching TV, wrapped in something made just for him.

The blocks were large, but each one had dozens of pieces. Natalie helped out by cutting the background pieces while I sewed. By closing time we had half the blocks already pieced and a few more ready to go.

"Why has it taken you so long to do this for him?" Natalie asked. "I made my husband a quilt on our third date."

"I don't know," I said. "It's bugged me that I haven't done it. I've made quilts for Allie, for charity, for Eleanor; I just wanted something perfect for him."

"You know it's not going to be perfect. No matter how hard you try, you'll just have to accept that nothing is exactly the way you want it to be, but that's okay."

"We are still talking about quilting, aren't we?"

She laughed. "If we're talking about marriage, then it's definitely not going to be perfect. But it is good, if you let it be. The question we all want to know is, are you going to let it?"

As Natalie talked, I examined my sewing. I'd been leaning close to the fabric, checking my seams, which were a little crooked. I could have focused on that and been satisfied. But when I pulled back, the inaccuracy wasn't even noticeable. Maybe all I needed was a little change in perspective to answer Natalie's question, and to figure out my future.

CHAPTER 40

"I picked up a board game on the way home from work, and there are some toys that Allie left here the last time." I put my earrings on and tried to remember where I'd left my black boots.

"I have met Allie," Eleanor said, just amused enough to annoy me.

"I know, but Mom and Dad haven't, and I want it to go well."

"She's not auditioning for them. She's a little girl, and a lovely little girl at that. She'll have a nice evening, and so will we."

I took a deep breath. "You're right, Grandma. Now, boots."

Somehow, miraculously, they were found, as were the red leather gloves I wanted to wear with the gray wool coat and handmade red scarf. I had my favorite black dress on, nothing too dressy but not too casual either. And it had long sleeves. It was freezing out there.

It had been less than a week since Roger's body was found in front of Jesse's house, and only a few hours since Jesse and I had been in his office together, but somehow I was nervous, first-date nervous. I worried about how to tell him that, despite his request, not just me but the whole the quilt group and I had looked into the murder. I hoped, if I laid it all out, we might each have seen something in the investigation that the other had missed.

Jesse and Allie arrived promptly at seven. Everyone went into the living room to chat and have a glass of wine before we left. My mom and dad asked a lot of questions about Jesse's job and how things in town had changed or stayed the same. He asked them about their next trip, which was planned for March. This time they were headed to Malaysia.

"Have you ever tried Malaysian food, Jesse?" my mom asked.

"Sort of an Indian and Thai mix, I would think," he answered with an easy charm. "But no, I don't think I have. We don't have many exotic flavors in town, and, as Nell can tell you, I'm not exactly a gourmet cook."

"You make a great macaroni and cheese," Allie said.

"If there's a box and a microwave involved, I'm your man."

My mom laughed.

"The plan," I told everyone, "is for Jesse and me to have dinner and then Eleanor can bring Allie home, put her to bed, and wait for us."

"Unless Anna is back at the house, then you can just drop Allie off," Jesse said. "She told me she would be home early."

"Either way," I promised, "we won't be late."

"Be as late as you like."

I looked over at my mom and dad as they chatted with Jesse's little girl. My dad took to her immediately, but my mom held back. Loving Allie would be tantamount to accepting my role as a potential stepmother and a forever resident of a small Hudson Valley town. And I could tell she wasn't quite ready for that.

Oliver had been avoiding eye contact ever since he arrived at the house, and when he saw me watching him he immediately got into a conversation with my dad about the English sport of cricket. Before we left the house, I was determined to get him alone. So I delayed for just a few minutes and watched. When he went to the kitchen to open another bottle of wine, I followed.

"What did the doctor say?"

He shrugged. "I felt much better as the day went on."

"So you didn't go?" I asked. "I'm going to tell Eleanor that you weren't feeling well this morning."

"No, you aren't. When you get older, you'll see that the bones creak and the muscles ache. It's just a part of life."

"That's not what was happening with you. It's not just this morning. The other night you were short of breath. . . ."

"I think it was too heavy a box." He put his hand on my shoulder. "Please don't worry your grandmother with this. It's nothing. I'm not a reckless man. Well," he smiled, "not anymore. I would go to the doctor if I thought it was warranted."

"But . . ."

"But nothing. Go enjoy dinner with Jesse. Love each other. Enjoy each other. Life is short, Nell, and arguing with an old man is a waste of valuable time."

I wanted to protest, but as I reminded myself again, Oliver was an adult. I couldn't force him to go to the doctor, and I wasn't sure it was my place to go to Eleanor against his wishes. I gave in and let him have his way. "Okay. Bland food from now on. Don't let my mother's cooking do a number on your digestive system. And the next pain, I don't care where it is—your stomach, your chest, your big toe—you are going to the doctor."

"You're going to be a very bossy granddaughter, aren't you?"

"Runs in the family."

CHAPTER 41

At the restaurant, Jesse ordered steak and I ordered pasta. We chatted about the wedding and the weather, and any subject we could think of that was noncontroversial. I was trying to find a way into the murder case, but instead I told him about my idea to create a design company as an offshoot of the shop. His eyes lit up. As we got into the details, he asked a ton of questions and had ideas of his own. The whole thing was becoming more real with each person who heard about my plans.

"Your mom is right about seeing the big quilt shows, really getting out there," he said.

"We get most of the info on trends right at the shop. But yes, I'd love to do that. Maybe when I'm finished with school this spring, I'll have more time."

"Of course, if Eleanor's gone and you're traveling, that means taking on extra help. Or is she thinking maybe it's time to close its doors and just go online? I think lots of businesses are doing away with the brick and mortar these days."

"No Someday Quilts at all?"

"No building, except maybe as a shipping department. But Someday will always exist. You'll sell your patterns, write books, and maybe get into designing fabrics. You're always telling me about fabric designers you love, why not you?"

Dessert arrived as I was trying to wrap my mind around yet another suggestion for my career. It was time to switch topics. But just as I was about to mention the investigation, Jesse's phone rang. He saw the number on his caller ID, answered with a quick hello, and excused himself.

While I waited, I saw Dru and Charlie enter the restaurant and sit at a table in the corner. He took her hand. She looked into his eyes. I got lost for a second in the nostalgia of the early moments of Jesse's and my courtship.

"Sorry." Jesse returned to the table. "Where were we?"

"Look over there." I nodded toward Dru and Charlie.

"Are they on a date?"

"I think it's more than that. I think they're falling in love," I said, and turned back to look in his beautiful green eyes. "You remember that moment when you knew that the person sitting across from you was the person you wanted to spend your life with?"

"We were in college so it was probably over pizza."

I'm sure my face went white. I certainly felt the blood leave my body. Jesse looked up at me. At first he seemed puzzled, then finally an awareness crept across his face.

"Nell, I'm so sorry. It's just . . ." he stammered. "I mean, she's been on my mind a lot."

"Tonight?"

"Well, no, no, earlier. But that was Anna on the phone. She's at my house, so when Eleanor's ready to drop Allie off . . ." More stammering. "She saw a picture of the four of us, her and Roger, Lizzie and me. She started talking about old times. I guess it got me thinking."

I tried hard not to react. In my head I threw down my napkin and stormed out of the restaurant, or ran into the ladies' room and burst into tears. But in real life I sat there silently, stabbing at my flourless chocolate cake and trying to seem calm.

"I'm sorry," he said. "I'm completely thoughtless. Let's forget it, okay? I'm glad you told me about your new business venture. When you came to my office today I couldn't figure out what it was you had on your mind."

"Relieved?"

"A little. I figured you were going to spill some theory about Roger's murder."

"Would that have been so terrible?" Despite my best efforts, I felt my eyes start to tear up. "I know that I can't compete with Lizzie's sweetness, or be your first love, but I *have* helped you. You've actually come to me for help with cases."

"I know. Nell, I love you—you must know that. I wish I could explain how much. And I do remember the moment I fell in love with you. You were interfering with one of my cases." He smiled. "I wanted to be mad at you, but you were solving it for me, and you were so cute doing it. I couldn't get over the fact that the same person who could look at a bolt of fabric and see a quilt, could look at a blood spatter report and see a killer."

Against my better judgment, I smiled a little. But then the thought of Anna, waiting at Jesse's house to spoil whatever we managed to salvage, crept into my mind. "Don't take this the wrong way, Jesse, but I'd rather go home now."

His jaw clenched, but he nodded. "I didn't mean to hurt you." He said the words almost to himself.

CHAPTER 42

Sunday I worked at the shop, busying myself with customers and the gazebo quilt. By the end of the day I had finished all the appliqué and had turned it over to Natalie to longarm. She'd finished the work on Eleanor's quilt and taken it off the frame. It was a masterpiece. The individual blocks made by the group had been turned into a cohesive story by Susanne's piecing of the top, and that story was now enhanced by hearts and feathers and even a few quilted birds.

"Stunning," I said, and it was.

Natalie beamed. "I'm bringing it to Maggie. She's doing the binding and label, and then it's done. So tomorrow I'll quilt the gazebo and help you sew the rest of the blocks for Jesse's quilt."

"Great." I hadn't said much about my dinner with Jesse except that I couldn't find the right moment to tell him what the group had learned. There are times when you don't want even your closest friends to weigh in on your life, and this was one of them. I certainly didn't want to work on the quilt. Making him a double wedding ring pattern now seemed more delusional than romantic.

"And I can work for you Tuesday," she said.

"What's Tuesday?"

"Roger's wake. Aren't you going with Jesse?"

"If I can," I said. "I have to see if everything's ready for the wedding."

Natalie looked a little skeptical. "Everything's ready. So unless there's another reason . . ."

"And all our suspects are leaving town."

"We can solve the murder without them." She turned off the lights in the classroom, said good-bye to Eleanor, who was still in her office, and headed out. "Have a great night." The bell on the door tinkled as it closed.

Jesse had called during the day, and while it wasn't unusual for me not to pick up in the middle of a busy weekend at the shop, it was unusual for me not to call back. But I didn't. Instead, I went home and sat with my parents, looking through the photos of their adventures abroad, and then went to sleep on the lumpy mattress in the sewing room.

Monday morning I got up early and walked Barney along the river's edge. He sniffed and rolled, and did his business, but he seemed anxious to get home to his new friend. At least his love story was working out well.

When we got back, I was confronted with a stack of boxes littering the hallway. Eleanor was in the kitchen, packing.

"Oh, good," she said when she saw me. "I made French toast, but I think I overdid it on the cinnamon. Fry up a slice and see what you think."

"You're packing."

"Yes. Obviously."

"Are you packing everything?"

She looked at me standing there doing nothing. "The French toast."

I moved to the stove, dipped a slice of bread into the egg and cream mixture, and put it on the already sizzling griddle. "You haven't answered my question."

"I have so much of everything. I have dozens of bowls and pots and whisks." She held up three potato peelers. "Now how do you imagine I needed three? I figured I would pack up the extras for the Carolina house."

"But you must have twenty boxes in the hallway. How much extra stuff do you need?"

"Blankets, pillows, clothes. I'm leaving most things here, of course. This is still my home, but it's amazing what you need just to get through the day." She fished around in a drawer until she came up with an odd little tool, a long metal rod with a tiny ice cream scoop on either end. "When did I ever need a melon baller?" She tsked at herself and dropped it into the box. "Just in case it's the sort of thing one does to melons in South Carolina."

I flipped over the toast and let it finish cooking, then plated it. I grabbed the bottle of maple syrup, sat at the table, and ate a bite. I wasn't hungry, but I didn't quite know how to start the conversation that needed to be started. "Not too much cinnamon," I said. "It's perfect."

"Wonderful. I'll start another slice for you when I'm finished with this box."

"How's Oliver been feeling?" I asked. Maybe if Eleanor mentioned something she'd seen I could, too. I was almost his granddaughter, so the way I saw it, I could almost interfere.

"You think he's getting cold feet?" She laughed.

"I mean the other night with the box of encyclopedias."

"He was trying to show off for your dad, but he's fine. I can barely keep up."

Maybe that was good. They were spending most of their time together, so if Oliver was having problems, she'd have seen it. And there were other things to talk about. The boxes made the topic seem urgent. "We have to talk about the shop."

Eleanor stopped her packing and looked at me. "We do." She left the packing, poured herself a cup of coffee, and sat opposite me. "What shall we do about it?"

"It's not my decision."

"It is, at least in part," she said. "Oliver and I have three plans, and you can help me decide which one. In plan A, Oliver and I leave for South Carolina after the honeymoon. We go down until Memorial Day and then come back up for the summer and fall. I love the fall in Archers Rest. I don't want to miss even one. In that plan, I would need someone to run the shop. I can pay the bills by computer. I do that for most of them anyway. But someone on hand needs to keep track of inventory, make sure the shop is opened and closed at the regular hours. Someone who could pick out the fabrics to order for next season . . ."

"I do some of that now."

"Exactly. Which is why I would turn the shop over to you. It would be yours, and I'd pretty much retire. It's about time. I know you have school starting at the end of the month and that goes until spring, so obviously you couldn't be there full-time. Plus, there's your pattern business. So if you decide to take over now that means hiring extra help."

"It's a big responsibility to run a business."

"Yes, it is, so in plan B, Oliver and I wouldn't go down to the new house for a few months. We'd stay here and I'd help transition you into taking over the business until you feel you're ready. Of course, plan A and B assume you want to take over the business. The way you've been talking about earning a living as a quilter, you could see having your own shop as an asset, or as a liability."

"How would it be a liability?"

"It would take a lot of your time and attention. And you just never know how things go. We've had a few good years, this last year especially, and that's a lot to do with you. You've had great ideas. But next year or the year after . . . there are no guarantees."

"And what's plan C?"

"We close Someday Quilts."

It took a moment for the words to sink in. "It's just that easy for you, after all these years?"

"It's not easy. I just don't let myself think too much about it. That shop has been my home for a long time." She blinked back a tear. "I am tired of working so hard, and I do hate these winters. I know I should have come to this decision months ago, but the house in South Carolina came up suddenly, and truth be told, I guess I didn't want to face it. I'm sad to let go, but I'm ready."

"If I weren't here. If I hadn't come to Archers Rest . . ."

"I wouldn't have met Oliver, and I wouldn't be packing half my kitchen to move it to South Carolina."

"But eventually you'd want to retire."

"I had thought I'd sell it, but I don't want a stranger in my shop. And who else is there? Natalie has those babies, it's all she can do to work part-time. Susanne has told me a thousand times she'd be lost trying to run Someday. Maggie's my age, and Carrie and Bernie have their own businesses to run."

I could hear the rustle of other people in the house waking up. My parents would soon be downstairs, and as much as I valued their opinions, this wasn't a group decision. Eleanor got up from the table and dipped a few more slices of bread in the batter. I heard them sizzle as they hit the hot pan.

"Don't decide right now," she said. "And Nell, you don't owe me anything. Someday Quilts was my dream and I've achieved it. Pretty well, if I do say so myself, but if it's time to say good-bye, so be it. You can keep the name for your patterns. I'm honored you would want to. But if running a quilt shop is too much, and I'm here to tell you that sometimes it's all consuming, then say no, and I will be proud of you for knowing your own mind."

Unsure of what to say, I said nothing. I didn't want Someday Quilts to close, but did I want to make owning a quilt shop my career? Could I do it and also launch a career designing patterns?

Then there was another thing to consider. After my date on Saturday I'd begun to realize I could never live up to Jesse's memory of his wife. Did I want to stay in Archers Rest, bumping into Jesse at every turn, if we were no longer together? As my mother had pointed out, I could run a pattern company from anywhere. Heartbreak had brought me to Archers Rest, maybe heartbreak would be the reason I left.

I didn't say any of this to Eleanor, though. I just got up from the table, gave my grandmother a quick hug, then grabbed my coat and gloves and went out into the cold for another long walk.

CHAPTER 43

When I finally worked up the courage to call Jesse back, I asked about the funeral arrangements and he gave them to me. It was a quick conversation, full of facts and devoid of emotion. He was going down early Tuesday to help Anna, so I decided to take the train into Manhattan alone.

I hadn't been back to the city since I packed up my apartment and moved to Archers Rest. I was kind of excited by the idea of re-visiting my old hometown, so I went early. Only instead of getting on the subway to Anna's home in Queens, I planned to walk out of Grand Central and head south.

"Well, Nell, isn't it wonderful to see you here." Bob Marshall sat opposite me just as the train pulled out of the Archers Rest station.

"It's a half-empty train," I said. "Maybe you could find another seat."

"No. I'm comfortable here."

I got up, and he grabbed my wrist. "Can you—" I started.

"Sit down, Nell. Talk to me. What can happen to you on a train?"

As a fan of Agatha Christie and Alfred Hitchcock, I knew the answer was "plenty," but I sat anyway. "I know about your criminal history, and I know that you were kicked off the force," I said. "If you're trying to get me to believe you're the good guy and I should be suspicious of Jesse, you're wasting your time."

"Fair enough, but I am a good guy. Maybe not by Jesse's standards, but I'm not interested in causing you any harm."

"What exactly do you want?"

"Your help. I could tell at the shop the other day that you like to help."

"What do you need?"

He narrowed his eyes. "What do you think?"

"I know about the five hundred thousand dollars that went missing from the drug dealer's house. If you're looking for that I can't help you." I watched him. He was studying me, thinking, trying to come up with a way to get me over to his side. It wasn't likely. "If you want my help, I'd like it if you didn't deny that you're involved with the money."

"You're a smart lady, Nell, so I won't insult you by pretending I don't know what you're talking about." He smiled. "But do you mind if I wait two years to say it?"

"What's two years?" The words came out of my mouth as it dawned on me. "Statute of limitations will be up."

He smiled again. This time wider.

"And then, assuming you have the money, you can spend the money as you please without caring if anyone knows or not."

"I believe that's the way it's done."

"But you don't have the money, or else you would never have followed Roger up to Archers Rest."

He looked at me, enjoying his game a little more than made me comfortable. "There were other reasons. The scenery is lovely and I did get my sister a nice gift."

"By the way, how closely did you follow Roger?"

"Not as close as his killer, obviously."

"Was Roger the other officer in the house on the day of the drug bust?" I asked. "The one who backed up your story about no money being found?"

"Roger was the other officer, yes."

"So you stole it together."

He shrugged.

"The third officer, Findlay, swore there was five hundred thousand missing, but the police believed Roger. Why did Roger's word carry so much weight?"

"You never met the man," he said. "Roger was the best cop, the most by-the-book cop I ever knew. If he said something was true, it was true. And he was a nice guy. Unlike me, he had a lot of friends. Friendship can be blinding."

"If he was such a good cop, why did he do it?"

"Assuming that he, or I, did anything, we'll never know. Someone killed Roger, remember?"

"So what's this about? You came up to Archers Rest following Roger, searching for the money that he kept while you went to prison?"

"If your theory is correct, it does seem unfair that I went to prison while Roger enjoyed a few more years on the job, followed by a retirement and healthy city pension." He smiled a little. "Not for long, of course, but at least he died with his reputation intact."

"You went to prison because of your bad temper," I pointed out. "Not because of the money."

"An overreaction on my part. I've since learned you can catch more flies with honey, Nell. All I want is what's mine. I'm not interested in anything, or anyone, else."

Just then the conductor walked into our car. "Tickets, please. All tickets out and ready to show."

Marshall reached into his wallet and took out a twenty-dollar bill. "I was in a hurry to catch the train, so I didn't get a ticket," he told the conductor. "I'm going to Grand Central."

As the conductor made change, I remembered what Greg had told me early on in the investigation. Roger had purchased a ticket with his credit card, then switched to a rental car in Tarrytown.

"You're thinking pretty intently," Marshall said to me.

"Am I?"

"Come on now, Nell. We're all friends here," he said. "You're remembering that Roger took the train from the city, but stopped along the way to switch to a rental car. You can't figure out why."

"He wanted someone to be able to trace his movements. He took a train to Tarrytown because if he just drove his own car, or rented one in New York, he could have disappeared without a trace. He was worried about something, so he was leaving a trail, just in case." The words popped out of my mouth. I knew Marshall was trying to manipulate me at every turn, and I was helping him. He'd found my weakness—the need to show I could solve puzzles.

"Thanks for solving that. Why not take the train all the way to Archers Rest?" he asked.

"I don't know. Maybe he needed a car for some reason. Maybe he had business in Tarrytown before he continued up." I looked into Marshall's eyes. "Or maybe his killer was following him and he just got off the train and changed his plans."

He seemed interested but not intimidated. "Interesting theory. Why do you think Roger was heading up to your town in the first place?"

"I don't know." I did know, but I didn't want to say it.

Marshall answered for me. "Obviously he wanted to see Jesse. And have you ever asked yourself why?"

"If you're going to tell me that Jesse was in on your theft—"

"Alleged theft."

"Whatever you want to call it, if you're going to try to make me believe that Jesse stole that money with you, I won't believe you. Because it's impossible. Not only because he's incapable of that kind of thing, but because he'd left the force by the time of the theft. He was already in Archers Rest, dealing with a dying wife, a young daughter, a new job, and all of the stresses and complications that go along with it."

"Suppose you're right. Jesse is the knight in shining armor; it does bring up an interesting question."

"Which is?"

"Where's the money? It's not in Roger's bank account. It's not in his house in Queens."

"You're saying it's in Jesse's house?" I asked. "You already searched it, didn't you?"

That confused him. "You wouldn't let me in, remember?"

I hated thinking that this awful man might be telling the truth. If he had searched Jesse's house on the night of the murder, why come back when I was there with Allie? He was looking for an opportunity to get into the house, and Jesse's place had an alarm system that rang into the police station. The best way into that house was if someone was there; someone weak and frightened, worried about protecting a child.

Or if you had a key.

I thought for a moment about who had keys to Jesse's house: his mother, me, and there was a set of keys in the front desk at the station in case the alarm ever went off. Anna obviously had a key since she'd let herself in and out while staying at Jesse's house. . . . I couldn't think of anyone else, but I was oddly glad Marshall had forced me to focus less on the big picture—my love life, my future at the shop, and life in Archers Rest—and helped me push my nose close to the puzzle, and into the details that might solve the case.

CHAPTER 44

"I'll see you at the wake," Marshall said as we got off the train.

"You're going?"

"Roger and I worked together for years," he said. "It would be rude not to pay my respects."

"Won't your old colleagues be there? Maybe some of the guys who once cuffed you and led you to jail?"

"Haven't you learned yet that I enjoy making people uncomfortable?"

"I guess I have." Even standing in the midst of Grand Central, with hundreds of people whizzing past with a single-minded focus that only New Yorkers have, I felt uneasy.

But Marshall wasn't letting go. He grabbed my arm as I tried to step away. "I know you think I killed Roger, but before you go sharing this theory with anyone, remember his death has prevented me from finding where he put the money."

I yanked my arm from his grip. "When you came to Jesse's house in search of the money . . . If you could have gotten inside, what would you have done? If you did find the money, would you have killed me to keep me from telling anyone?"

He leaned close to me, putting his mouth an inch from my ear, and whispered, "Interesting question. So if you find yourself in a similar circumstance before this whole unhappy business has finished, you might not want to stand between me and anything that I want."

"Was that Roger's mistake?"

He grinned. "Maybe it was."

I looked him in the eye, hoping I didn't seem as scared as I was. Bob Marshall was, like all good con men, a chameleon. He had been friendly and easygoing when he believed it would earn my trust, and now he was cold and threatening in the hopes of scaring me into helping him find the money. He could have been hinting that he had killed Roger to make his threat all the more intimidating. Or he could actually have killed him.

Marshall walked away, heading toward a kiosk that sold newspapers and cigarettes. In other circumstances, I might have followed a suspect and watched where he went, but with this man all I wanted to do was take the opportunity to escape.

✄

On Twenty-Fifth Street in Manhattan there's a little piece of home, a quilt shop. It was my first stop after I arrived in the city. City Quilter was large, well lit, and well stocked. There was even a gallery for art quilts as part of the shop. While Someday had some of the same fabrics, I still couldn't resist visiting. When I'd lived in New York, I'd passed the store many times but hadn't gone in. I wasn't a quilter then, but now I was, and perhaps even on the verge of being a quilt shop owner.

As I walked around the store, I wondered if this was something I wanted for myself. I pulled at bolts of cottons and silks, checked out the ribbons, the patterns, the books. I looked at the displays, the layout. I talked to the staff. Was this my future? I wondered it over and over again as I shopped.

An hour later, I stuffed my purchases into my already heavy tote bag and walked the streets of a city I once called home. I stopped in a coffee shop in the East Village, the kind that Carrie had modeled Jitters after, and sat drinking a cup of hot coffee and people watching. Did I miss it—the energy and the options that a big city can offer? Did I want to come back? It would mean a life without Jesse and Allie, but it seemed more and more likely that that might be true even if I stayed in Archers Rest. When Jesse thought about the woman he loved, he thought of Lizzie.

"A green tea." I overheard a man at the counter ordering. "And a cookie. Are those chocolate chip cookies gluten free?"

A green tea and gluten-free cookie. Roger's order on the night he was murdered. It had always bothered me that a man so intent on healthy meal choices would be smoking, but people have far worse contradictions in character.

Now something else bothered me more. Greg had said the car was clean when we found Roger, except for a notebook and the business card that Jesse had pocketed. But if that were true, something was missing.

I dialed Greg's cell. "Hey, Nell. Everything okay?" He sounded almost panicked when he answered. "You need help?"

"I'm fine. Sorry if I scared you."

"No, not you. I'm meeting Kennette's plane. I guess I'm getting a little nervous about seeing her again after all this time."

"You'll be fine."

Greg was an awkward but smart guy. He spent a lot of time studying and worrying, and trying to do the right thing, while Oliver's granddaughter, Kennette, was a free spirit who simply went where she felt most at home, which was pretty much anywhere. They made a great, if unusual, pairing.

"I have a question for you," I said, "if you don't mind answering something about the case."

"At this point anything that keeps me from feeling like an idiot would be great."

"You said Roger's rental car was totally clean."

"Yeah."

On the day of the murder I'd glanced inside the car, and what Greg was saying fit my memory of it, too, which is why something about it had stuck with me. "So where were the cigarette butts? I saw smoke coming out of the car, but if the car was clean, then where were they?"

He paused. "Maybe he threw the butts out the window."

"But if that's the case, wouldn't you have found at least one on the ground when you guys did a sweep of the crime scene? He was smoking when I saw him. Where is the butt of that cigarette?"

Greg didn't answer. There was noise and mumbling. "Sorry, Nell. There's Kennette. I have to go. We'll talk later." He hung up.

I knew Greg wasn't exactly smooth around the ladies, but he sounded so nervous I was afraid he'd pass out. Kennette's easy personality would soon relax him. At least I hoped so, for both their sakes.

As I finished my coffee I thought back to the night I walked past Roger's car. There was definitely smoke, but had I been wrong? Was the smoke coming from behind the driver's seat? I tried to picture the scene—the dark street, the open window, the wisps of smoke . . . Maybe they hadn't been from Roger after all, but from a killer sitting behind him. That would explain the missing cigarette butts. They weren't in the ashtray because they weren't Roger's. The killer was smart enough not to leave them, or any incriminating DNA evidence, behind. And there was, as far as I could tell, only one person in the group of suspects who smoked.

CHAPTER 45

The funeral home was crowded when I arrived just after six o'clock. Officers in uniform and plainclothes detectives from what appeared to be every precinct in the city were wandering in and out of the building. Men and women in dress clothing, bundled up against the cold, headed into the place just as I arrived. I took off my coat, and smoothed the pair of black dress pants I was wearing with a gray wool sweater. Though my outfit made me blend in perfectly with the crowd, I still felt quite out of place.

I wandered through the room full of strangers searching for Jesse. When I finally saw him, he was standing at the casket, looking into the waxen face of his friend. Anna was by his side, holding his hand. I almost turned and left. But I didn't. I walked up to him and lightly touched his back.

When he saw me, he let go of Anna's hand and hugged me tightly. "I was worried you wouldn't come," he said.

"I told you I would."

"I know, but you're upset."

"I think this is more important than my hurt feelings."

"Which I didn't mean to hurt."

"I know. And it's not a discussion we need to have tonight."

Jesse seemed relieved.

Anna stayed exactly where she had been while Jesse and I chatted. I turned toward her and smiled sadly. "This must be such a difficult night for you, Anna," I said. "If there's anything you need. . . ."

She was in a simple black dress, with pearls and pumps. The sort of thing a Hollywood costume designer would choose for a grieving widow. She held a tissue in her hand, but she didn't look like she'd been crying. Maybe I was being unfair. Maybe I just wanted to hate her.

"I'm just so glad you could make it, Nell," she said, without actually looking at me. And then she saw old friends over my shoulder and went to greet them.

Jesse held tightly to my hand and took me around the room, introducing me to a dozen or more people he'd known from his New York days. They all talked about straight-laced Jesse and anything-for-a-joke Roger.

"They were mismatched in every way," one man said. "Except as cops. They were both great cops."

"Jesse told me that Roger was a stickler for the rules," I said.

The man laughed. "The worst. That guy used to bust chops if anyone stepped a toe over the line."

This led to a group of officers telling stories about Roger going to almost absurd lengths to follow the law, even letting a thief go when he felt a fellow officer had been too rough. But this was the same man, I reminded myself, who had apparently conspired with Bob Marshall to steal five hundred thousand dollars in drug money, and then kept the whole amount for himself.

Marshall didn't show. Maybe he didn't want to put on a show for his former colleagues after all. But I wasn't interested in that. I was watching a different drama. I was watching Anna and Ken.

Over and over, Anna pulled Jesse away from me, needing him for advice or help, or a shoulder to cry on. And while it annoyed me, it was clear it infuriated Ken. When Anna had Jesse's ear, Ken would circle near them, watching but pretending not to. I didn't bother pretending, I just stared.

A woman in civilian clothes came over and introduced herself as the wife of someone Jesse had known in the police academy. She saw that I was watching the three of them, and seemed just as riveted by it. "Interesting, isn't it?"

"They are a couple, right?" I asked. "Ken and Anna, I mean."

"Yeah, that's what I heard, too. I just don't get it. She's pretty and everything, but I don't see why the men in her life turn into such puppies."

"I heard Roger didn't want the divorce."

"He would have done anything to make her happy. And now Ken. It's just sad," she said. "On the other hand, a burned-out cop and a broken-down ex-lawyer are not exactly great catches."

"Especially for an attractive woman with a successful interior design business."

"What fairy tale has she been feeding you?"

"It's not successful?"

She raised an eyebrow. "I'm not even sure it exists."

Before I had a chance to ask more questions, her husband pulled her away. Anna and Ken might have used her business as cover for an affair, or maybe Anna was just a lousy businesswoman. Either way, she was a liar.

Ken came walking toward me, and for a moment I thought he was going to attack, but he brushed past, whispered an obscenity under his breath, and kept moving. More out of instinct than any plan, I followed him.

When he grabbed his coat, I grabbed mine and together we walked outside into what had to be the coldest night of the winter yet.

"You smoke, too?" He looked at me with confusion.

"No. I just needed a break from Anna."

He snickered. "She's all over your boyfriend. I'd do something about that if I were you."

"It looked to me like she was trying to make you jealous."

"Really?" He sounded optimistic, which made me feel slightly sorry for him. "She knows how to play a guy."

"What do you mean?"

"She's just . . ." He shrugged. "She's a good woman underneath all that. She just likes attention. She used to wrap Roger around her finger, I'll tell you that."

"He would have done anything for her," I said, repeating what the cop's wife had told me.

"So would I." It was an unexpected admission, almost as if Ken was in competition with the dead man, and determined to win.

"You invested in her business," I said. "I'm sure Roger wouldn't do that."

"The guy was a fool."

"Because he didn't help her? Couldn't help her start the interior design firm?"

He took a drag of his cigarette. "Because he's in a casket with a hole in his head."

He looked about to head back inside, but I wasn't done yet. "Can I ask you something?"

He stiffened. "What?"

"Jesse's daughter is into magic. And you mentioned that you are, too."

At that his posture relaxed. "A good hobby for a kid. What do you need?"

"She was telling me about how you get the audience to look one way when you're doing a trick."

"Misdirection."

"Right. Misdirection. She was telling me that real magicians can set off pops or flashes that will make people look away. And in that second or two that their eyes are elsewhere, he does his trick. Is there something I can buy for her to help her do that, even from a distance?"

He blinked, and blinked again. And then he stared at me. I felt sure he knew why I was asking, but his voice was steady. "It's a professional's thing, to do that from a distance, to make a pop. But, you know, a mirror, the right angle, and, say, a flashlight. It would do in a pinch." He threw his cigarette on the ground and stared at me again. "Glad to hear Jesse's kid is into magic. It's a great hobby," he repeated.

Then he opened the door to the funeral home and gestured for me to go in first.

"I guess we should see if we're still in relationships," he said with an edge.

Jesse was still standing where I'd last seen him. And to his credit he seemed completely unaware that he was in a lover's triangle. While Anna leaned on his shoulder or put her arm around his waist, he stood almost motionless, staring into Roger's casket. It broke my heart to see him so sad.

"Hey," I whispered to him. "Come with me for a second."

Anna let her arm drop to her side. "I'm monopolizing him. I'm sorry."

"Don't be. I can't imagine what you must be feeling tonight."

Jesse followed me from the room into a large hallway. We sat at a bench and held hands. "Are you going back tonight?" he asked.

"I can stay, if you want me to."

He let out a long breath. "I want you to. This is harder than I thought. Seeing everyone and remembering Roger. He made mistakes, but he was a good man. He deserved this," he said, motioning toward the large group that was mingling at the funeral home. "He would have liked to know that all these people showed up for him, to honor his service. He was a great cop. Best on the force."

This wasn't the time to contradict that, I told myself. "I'm here, whatever you need."

Jesse rested his head against mine. "Promise me you won't leave my side."

"I promise."

Then my phone rang. As I listened to the frantic voice on the other end, I knew I would break that promise.

"Jesse," I said. "I have to go. Now."

CHAPTER 46

Jesse lent me his car so I didn't have to figure out a train schedule or wait for a car service. He wanted to come with me, but Roger was his friend. He needed to be at the wake and funeral. He needed the support of his old police buddies as they remembered the Roger they wanted him to be, instead of the Roger he seemed to have become.

When Jesse and I sat on that bench and talked, I realized that he knew. That he had known all along. He saw that Roger was a corrupt cop, or had become one. That was the reason for the fight after Lizzie's death, the reason they hadn't spoken. Like everyone else, Jesse must have suspected that Marshall had taken the money, even if it couldn't be proven. And that Roger—the cop who'd backed Marshall's story—had been his partner in the crime. It was only Roger's reputation as a stand-up guy that had kept the suspicion off him. And while Jesse hadn't brought his doubts to anyone, he severed ties with Roger.

In the end, though, friendship was stronger than disappointment. When Jesse saw the card for C. G. Kruger, he kept it out of evidence for one simple reason—to protect the reputation of an old friend and give him the send-off he deserved. Would he now go full force after his killer, or would he rather Roger's memory be intact and his killer free? That I didn't know.

And I also didn't know why Roger was at Jesse's house that night, or what the payments from Jesse's account meant. But those were questions for another time.

✂

I was lucky that the highway wasn't crowded as I made my way north. I was trying to stay within the speed limit, trying to stay calm, but my mother's voice kept replaying in my mind.

"Oliver's at the emergency room. Looks like a heart attack. Come quickly."

"I'm almost there," I said to myself as I reached the exit for Archers Rest.

I found my parents in the waiting room, looking tense. The quilt group was there, as were Kennette and Greg, and Oliver's daughter, Jane.

"Hey, Nell." Kennette hugged me. She had her usual mix-match of plaids and stripes, polka dots and flowers. I realized quickly how much I had missed her.

"I wish we were seeing each other somewhere else."

"He'll be okay," she said. "I know it."

I nodded, holding back tears. "Where's Grandma?"

"Talking to the doctor," my dad said. "Oliver was at the house. We were all having some wine and getting to know his family. Everything was fine. And then Oliver said he had a pain in his chest."

My mother jumped in. "He said it had been there on and off throughout the day, but he hadn't wanted to worry anyone." Like me, she was doing her best not to cry. "Poor Mom. If something happens to him . . ."

"It won't." Maggie had the same certainty as Kennette.

"It's my fault," I admitted. "Oliver wasn't well Saturday and he didn't want Eleanor to know. He said it was his stomach, but I didn't . . ." I felt stupid and careless. I'd wanted to believe that everything was fine. It was selfish of me. "I promised I wouldn't say anything."

I sat down next to my mom, who put her arm around me. "You're not in charge of anyone else's choices, Nell. If Oliver felt sick then he should have done something himself. If he said it was his stomach, then how could you know it was his heart?"

She was letting me off the hook, but it seemed like a cop-out. I felt suddenly like a child who couldn't be trusted with adult things. I wanted to burst into tears, but that felt selfish, too, so I sat there and prayed he'd be okay.

Eleanor came walking down the hall toward us, looking frail for the first time in my entire life. "They've admitted him. They're doing tests. The doctor said it doesn't look like he's had a heart attack, that it could be something else. He won't tell me."

"Maybe he doesn't know," I suggested.

She nodded. "I have a list of things I need from the house. Who can get them for me?"

Greg jumped up. He took the list and Grandma's house keys and headed out. Carrie and Natalie went to get something better than hospital food for the group. The rest of us just waited.

><

Within a half hour, Greg returned with a large brown paper bag filled with the items Eleanor had asked for. Carrie and Natalie had gotten sandwiches, pastries, and coffee from Jitters, and we all began to eat to distract ourselves from the worry.

Eleanor ignored the food, but she clung to the paper bag. When the doctor said it was okay for her to see Oliver, she got up and held the bag close. "Come with me, Nell," she said. Her voice was weak and scared.

We walked down the hall together in silence. When we got to Oliver's room, she paused, took a deep breath, and went inside.

"Hey, there," she said, trying to sound upbeat. "I'd say my chicken dinner was ruined."

He smiled but seemed too tired to laugh. Pain medication, Eleanor told me. She put the bag on the floor and took out one item: a large quilt of squares and half-square triangles. It was colorful and bright, made entirely of scraps left over from other projects. She covered Oliver's bed in the quilt, tucking him in as she went.

"I started this quilt after I met you," she said. "And I can look at the blocks and remember the day I sewed this one or that. There are lots of memories of you in it."

"That's lovely," he said weakly.

"I'll bet you didn't know that when you lay under a quilt, especially when you're sick, you feel the love of the person who made it, wrapping around you and keeping you safe."

He nodded. "I'm going to marry you on Saturday, Eleanor."

Her eyes were watery, but she held her voice firm. "Yes, you are."

Oliver closed his eyes and drifted off to sleep. Eleanor took out the other items—a change of clothes, a toothbrush, and one of the encyclopedias he had brought to her house—and left them on the chair.

"You need to go home, have a cup of tea, and get some rest," I said.

"Maybe I'll stay just a little while longer."

"Then I'll stay, too."

We all stayed. We sat in the waiting room with my parents, Oliver's family, and the quilt group. We assured each other about his condition and caught up on Kennette's adventures in London.

When the conversation lulled and it was clear that Eleanor had begun to let her mind drift back to her worries, Susanne found a new topic. "Did you hear that there's a new method for dyeing your fabrics?"

"Really?" Carrie said. "Where did you hear that?"

"From Mary Shipman. She's started dying fabrics now and making her own clothes."

My mother's ears perked up. "Isn't she the lady who lives in that hideous brown house?"

"She is," I confirmed. "But the house isn't brown anymore. She's painted it to look tie-dyed in shades of blue and orange."

My mother laughed. And then everyone jumped in, eating cookies, talking about fabrics, and sharing news about the folks in town. Even Eleanor stuck her two cents in about all the new embellishments out there, and the ways they could be used on clothes and furniture. And when she was done talking, she ate her sandwich.

After so many failed attempts to get together as a group, we were having a quilt meeting. It was in a hospital, and we had lots of first timers, but it was a quilt meeting, and it felt comforting and familiar to be there.

CHAPTER 47

Eleanor had left for the hospital before I woke up. I lingered in bed thinking. Everything that had been important yesterday—finding Roger's killer, deciding on whether to keep Someday, even what would happen with Jesse and me—paled in comparison to making sure that Oliver and Eleanor walked down the aisle in three days . . . and then had years together as husband and wife.

My dad was out walking Barney when I finally got up, but my mom was on the couch reading the paper, with Patch snuggled on her lap.

"Any word?" I asked.

"Not yet," she said. "Are you going back to Queens for the funeral?"

I shook my head. "I wouldn't get there in time, and Jesse said he'd come back right after."

"Is everything okay with you two?"

"Now you care?"

She looked at me. "I just want you to be happy. I want you and Grandma to be with the men you love." She sighed. "I feel like I've missed a lot this last year. You two have gotten so close and I've been so far away, so unavailable to you."

"That's my fault, too. I've been protecting you from my extracurricular activities."

"How's that going . . . finding the killer?"

"Frankly, it could be one of several people. They're all kind of awful, and Roger himself turned out not to be a great guy. If the killer hadn't also shot up Main Street, I might actually be tempted to just let it go."

"So what do you do now?"

"After everything settles down, I'll tell Jesse what I've learned and hopefully he'll put it together with what he's learned and maybe we'll get the killer."

"Everything will settle down." My mother patted my hand. "When Oliver's out of the hospital and he and Mom have started their life together, you can start making decisions about your future; about Jesse and Allie, the shop, and your pattern company; and about staying in Archers Rest."

I took a deep breath. "I love Jesse. And I love Allie. I don't want to lose either of them from my life. I just think maybe I'll always be in second place. I don't want to wipe out Lizzie's memory. I just don't want to have to compete with it."

"And the shop?"

"I've been a part-time employee. Grandma has run the place. I help and I've had lots of ideas that she's implemented, but doing it by myself? I don't know," I said. "Natalie has a baby and a toddler. Plus she's now got that longarm quilting business that she runs out of the shop when we're slow. I don't see how she can work any more hours than she already does."

"And there's no one else to help?"

"Not unless you and Dad want to give up Malaysia."

She smiled. "I was a terrible employee the first time I worked at Someday. I doubt I'd be much good now. Barney would make a better worker than I would."

We laughed, and woke up the cat.

"So you have no idea what you're going to do?" she asked.

"I'm going to see Oliver." It was the only plan that made sense.

✄

"You can go upstairs to Room 413," the woman at the front desk told me. "He's been transferred there."

I took the elevator to the fourth floor. I hadn't heard from Eleanor, and of course the woman at the help desk didn't have any information on his condition. When I got to the right room, I crossed my fingers, said a quick prayer, and entered.

"Hey there, Granddaughter!" Oliver was sitting up, reading the encyclopedia Greg had brought the night before. Eleanor sat by his bed, working on some hand piecing. "Just in time to see me finish the letter *Z*. It's quite an accomplishment. I said I couldn't die until I did it."

"Oliver!" my grandmother exclaimed.

"It doesn't mean I have to die right away." He laughed.

I came into the room and gave him a kiss on the cheek. "You're in good spirits."

"I'm in more than that. I'm in good health. It was indigestion, just like I thought," he said.

"A little more than that," Eleanor jumped in.

"The doctor gave it a fancy name. The pain that felt like it was coming from my heart was actually coming from my esophagus. Nothing to worry about apparently. Just some medicine, a bit of a change in diet, and I'm right as rain."

"So why are you still in the hospital?"

He rolled his eyes. "Honestly, an old man with chest pains gets almost as much attention from doctors as a pretty young girl gets from, well, everyone." He smiled. "I'll be out this afternoon. I got lucky, Nell. I've got more precious time with my love. And I don't intend to waste a minute of it."

"So the wedding is on for Saturday?"

"Just as planned."

"Then I have work to do," I said. "I'll see you later, Grandma . . . and Grandpa."

"I do like the sound of that," he said.

As I walked out of the room, I nearly bumped into another visitor, a man with a big bouquet of balloons and a to-go cup.

"Geez," I said. "I'm not paying attention. I almost spilled your coffee."

"Tea, actually. And my fault. I guess we're both in a hurry."

As he headed off toward one of the rooms, I watched him. Tea. It nagged at me and I didn't know why.

CHAPTER 48

I had scanned all the photos that Maggie had given me on the night I'd stayed at Jesse's, but I'd left them on his computer. I still needed to put them in order, turn it into a slide show, and transfer it to my computer. Plus, I had to confirm that the tables we were renting were going to be delivered on Friday afternoon, check on the flowers, and go over the last-minute details for the bachelorette party. But first, I had to share the good news.

I headed straight to Jitters. Carrie and Bernie were there, drinking coffee and looking worried. But when I walked in, a big smile on my face, I could see them both relax.

"Wedding's back on?" Bernie asked.

"It was never off."

Carrie made phone calls. I grabbed some breakfast and headed out across the street. Natalie was already there, waiting on customers and keeping things in order. She'd brought the baby, future quilter Emma, who was sleeping in a portable crib.

"You don't mind?" she asked.

"Mind? She fits in perfectly."

"I was thinking I could do more hours if Emma can hang out in the office sometimes. Joey is in preschool, and they could keep him a bit longer on days my mom can't babysit."

Obviously word of Eleanor's three options for the shop had reached the group.

Natalie had also finished her work on the gazebo quilt and it looked amazing. After I made the wedding-related calls, I sewed on the binding so that another task could be done. It was a beautiful quilt, and I was excited to be able to give it as a wedding gift.

"You do realize you can't give it to them," Natalie said as if she had read my mind.

"Why not?"

"You want to turn this into a pattern, right? You need to have it around so you can figure out the shapes of each of the pieces, then you need to photograph it. Plus you'll have to hang it in the store as a sampler quilt, so people can see what the finished piece will look like. A lot of local quilters are going to want this pattern because it's Archers Rest."

I looked at it again. I'd made it as a wedding gift. I couldn't keep it, could I? "I'll take lots of photos of it, and make another one," I said. "What's one more quilt on the to-be-made list?"

I wrapped the gift in wedding paper before I had a chance to change my mind.

✄

"Hey, there, old coworkers." Kennette came into the shop with Greg trailing shyly behind. She had brought the gift every quilter could appreciate—fabric. She had found scraps in discount bins in a very fashionable fabric store in London. While we excitedly exchanged ideas about what to do with them, Greg darted out to Jitters.

"I'll just get a quick cup of coffee for the road," he said.

I nodded toward him, and was about to recommend the apple cinnamon muffin to go with it, but something caught in my throat. The thing that had been nagging at me finally became clear, and I felt suddenly sick. "Be right back," I said to the ladies and followed

Greg out the door. I tapped him on the back and he swung around, surprised. "You saw Roger," I said.

"Of course. I was at the crime scene."

"Before that."

"What are you talking about?"

My heart was pounding. I pulled him away from the shop to a space across the street, in front of the empty storefront that had been Clark's Dry Cleaners. I didn't want to be overheard saying what I didn't want to say.

"You said that Roger had a cup of coffee in his hand. A few days ago when we were talking at Jitters."

"So what? You know he was in there before he went to Jesse's house. Carrie can confirm that."

"Carrie said he had tea. Green tea to be exact. Every time I've heard the word *tea* in the last few days it's bugged me and I couldn't figure out why. It's because you said he drank coffee."

"I must have gotten it wrong."

"It's not that. You said that Roger couldn't have been a good friend because he sat in his car drinking coffee and watching Jesse's house. But there wasn't a coffee cup in the car. You told me, twice, that the only things in the car were the notebook and the business card."

"So? Carrie must have told me."

"No. Carrie would have told you he was drinking tea. I know that you saw Roger that night, after he left Jitters with that to-go cup in his hand. You saw him. You assumed it was coffee, Greg. That's where that detail came from. You saw him, and you haven't said anything."

"Nell, stop . . ."

I was shaking. It felt crazy to be thinking what I was thinking, but I also knew that Greg was hiding something. All along my gut had told me something was wrong, but I'd ignored it. It was just like Marshall had said about Jesse and Roger: friendship can be blinding.

"You have access to keys to Jesse's house," I continued, unable to shut off the sudden torrent of suspicions. "He keeps a set at the station. You know how to shoot all kinds of weapons. You were the one who happened by when Dru's car wouldn't start and the one to check the car the next day after the shooting.

"Nell, you're jumping to conclusions. . . ."

"I know, Greg," I said, looking at a friend who had been a guest in Jesse's home countless times in a frightening new light. "I just can't figure out why. So I need you to please tell me the truth."

Greg frowned, but he nodded his head. "Okay, but I think you'll see that I had no choice."

CHAPTER 49

Greg wanted to go back to the police station, so that's where we went, telling Kennette and Natalie that we had wedding business to attend to. Once we were there, we went into the interrogation room and closed the door.

"I think Jesse is the best chief ever," he said once I'd taken a seat. "He's taught me everything I know, and on top of that, he's a good man."

"I know that, Greg." I sensed that he wasn't going to be hurried, even though I desperately wanted to know the truth as quickly as possible, good news or bad. Sitting in that room I felt like I'd been hit with a two-by-four.

"The night that Roger guy was murdered, you're right. He came in here first. He must have come here from Jitters because he had that cup in his hand. And you're right, I'm such a coffee freak, I just assumed it was coffee."

"He was looking for Jesse."

He nodded. "He seemed nervous. At first I thought he wanted to report a crime, so I said he could tell me and I would relay it to the chief, but he said he had personal business with Jesse." He took a deep breath. "There was something in the way he said it that I could tell whatever the business was, it was bad. Jesse's my friend. I only wanted to protect him."

"What did you do?"

"I told him that Jesse wasn't here. He asked me if Jesse still lived in the same house and I told him I couldn't give out that information."

"And then what?"

"And then he left."

"What did you do after that?" I almost didn't want to hear his answer.

"What do you mean? I did some paperwork, filled out an application to a few local colleges. I'm thinking of going back to school for a criminology degree so I can be chief someday." He blushed. "I didn't want to tell you guys in case Jesse thought I was getting ahead of myself, but I'm just thinking about my future."

I almost laughed. The wave of nausea I'd felt a moment ago had started to dissipate. "That's what you've been hiding? That's it?"

He shook his head. "No." He took a long breath. "Then the other guy came in. He told me that Roger had stolen drug money and he was there to retrieve it and arrest him. He told me that Roger was trying to get Jesse in trouble so he wanted to intercept him before the chief got involved. I told him that I thought Roger had gone to the chief's house. I told him where Jesse lived."

"Which guy?"

"The cop. Bob Marshall. I sent that guy to Jesse's house and he murdered his friend." Tears surfaced at the corners of his eyes. "I'm sorry, Nell. I know I'm just a stupid small-town cop. The guy showed me a badge, gave me a good story, and I bought it. I thought I could tell the good guys from the bad. I was trying to protect Jesse and I got his friend killed."

"Why didn't you tell Jesse after it happened?"

"Because . . ." He swallowed hard and wiped away his tears. "I saw how he was. He didn't want to hear anything about the case. He hid that business card. He took the evidence folder with the notebook himself. He wasn't doing things by the book. I didn't get it."

"So you ran your own investigation hoping to come up with the evidence?" It was an inclination that I understood perfectly.

"The day we found Roger's body, Jesse had me ticketing that guy's car. Stupid tickets. So I knew it had something to do with the case, and I started to look into it. I thought maybe if I could prove Marshall was the killer, I could keep my stupidity out of it. And I could protect Jesse from whatever mess he was making with the investigation."

"And Dru's car?"

"What about it? Nell, I make rounds every night, all around town. I give someone a ride home every night of the week—people who've had too much to drink, people who don't want to walk the few blocks home in the cold, and folks whose cars won't start. Geez, I've given you and Barney rides. Is that suspicious now?"

I patted his hand, relieved in a dozen different ways. "Kennette will be wondering where you are," I said.

"What are you going to do?"

"Go back to New York and tell Jesse we know who the killer is."

CHAPTER 50

This time I drove to New York. I had Jesse's car, and besides that, the romance of a train ride was spoiled, at least temporarily, by the memory of having spent my last ride sitting with Roger's killer. I made it to Queens in far less time than the normal three hours. I must have sped the whole way without even noticing.

I pulled up in front of Roger and Anna's old house just as mourners were arriving for the post-funeral luncheon. I hadn't bothered to change before heading south, so dark jeans and a navy sweater were going to have to do.

I entered the house, a nice but ordinary brick bungalow, and looked for Jesse. Ken was there, seemingly annoyed, so I followed his sight line. Sure enough, Anna was hovering near Jesse as he chatted with some of Roger's friends.

"Hey, there," I said, tapping Jesse's arm.

He spun around, surprised. "Nell, how's Oliver?"

"Good, thankfully." I looked around. There were too many people around for me to shout out that I knew the identity of Roger's killer. "I just wanted to be here for you, and since Oliver's okay, I figured I'd come down."

He kissed my forehead. "I'm glad you're here."

"Can I talk to you for a minute? Alone?"

"Absolutely. Just go straight back. It's the master bedroom. I'm right behind you."

I walked toward the room, down a long narrow hallway, but I soon realized Jesse wasn't behind me. When I turned, I saw why. Anna had grabbed his arm and burst out crying. Jesse looked helpless as he turned away from me to comfort her. I was about to go back when something stopped me.

"We meet again." Bob Marshall stood between me and a living room that was filling up with mourners. But there was a long empty hallway between where I was standing and where I could get help.

"Get out of my way." I didn't wait for him to listen, I tried to go around him.

He stopped me. As he did, he lifted his suit coat slightly to reveal a gun. "I'm a very fast draw." Then he lifted his hand to my throat. "And I don't have anything to lose."

He pushed me toward the door to the master bedroom.

For some reason I was more angry than scared. I was tired of this man's games. "I'll scream if you push me again," I said.

"Wonderful. Your knight in shining armor will come running back and I'll shoot him. Then I'll shoot you."

I stepped over the threshold into the room. Marshall followed me, then closed the door behind him. We were in Roger and Anna's old bedroom. It was tastefully decorated, like something copied from a magazine, but void of personality or warmth. Much like Anna herself, I thought. There were a few coats on the bed, and purses and gloves scattered around. I tripped on Anna's handbag and almost fell on the bed. I stood against a dresser, trying to steady myself and stay calm.

"What do you want?" I asked.

"The money, Nell. I want the money."

"We've been over this. I don't know where the money is."

"I don't believe you. You have been running around looking into this case every minute since Roger died. People will talk to you but won't talk to me. Jesse talks to you. He's told you where it is."

"There is no money in Jesse's house."

"But there is something in Jesse's house. Some clue, some indication of where Roger hid it."

"Why Jesse? He hadn't even spoken to him in three years."

Marshall shook his head and sighed. "Oh, Nell, I thought you were a better gumshoe than that. Roger gave some of the money, some of my money, to your holier-than-thou boyfriend."

The door to the bedroom opened. Jesse was standing there. Marshall didn't reach for his gun, didn't run, didn't do anything. He just stood there. Jesse came in and grabbed me, putting himself between Marshall and me.

"Get out of here," he said to me. "Go."

"Jesse," I said. "Marshall came into the police station on the night Roger died. Greg told him where you lived and he went there and killed Roger."

Marshall laughed. "Now that's an interesting theory. Here's another: maybe Jesse did it so he could keep the money Roger gave him."

Jesse moved toward Marshall. "I paid back the money he lent me. And as far as I know, he got it exactly where he said he got it: from cashing in some stocks he had."

"You didn't believe him then."

"And I don't believe you now," Jesse said. "Nell, get out of here." As he spoke, Marshall grabbed his gun. Jesse lunged at him, shouting for backup as he did. In seconds two dozen members of the New York police force were in the room, cuffing the disgraced detective and reading him his rights.

As they led him from the room, Marshall looked at me. "They have me on a parole violation for carrying a weapon. Maybe unlawful imprisonment, though that's a stretch. But they won't get me for murder. Because I didn't kill Roger. I wanted the money. And with

Roger dead, I'll never find it." His voice was calm, but the look in his eyes seemed desperate, scared. I didn't want to, but I believed he was telling the truth.

✂

When the room had emptied out, Jesse sat with me on the bed and put his arm around me. We sat quietly for a long time. "After Lizzie died," Jesse said finally, "Roger was at the house all the time. He pretty much lived with me for the first few months. He even took time off to help me. He could see the stress I was under, the medical bills, the mortgage on the new house. I felt like I was going under financially, emotionally. Every which way."

"One day, I sent a check in to the hospital to make a payment on what I owed, and they told me the bill was paid," Jesse continued. "And a bunch of other bills were paid. Nearly fifteen thousand dollars' worth. Roger told me he'd cashed in some stocks he'd inherited from his dad years before. He knew if he'd given the money directly to me, I wouldn't have taken it. And it wasn't like I could just write him a check for the full amount. When I confronted him about it, he told me he wanted to help. He said he didn't need or want the money back."

"But you paid him anyway."

"I've been paying him, or I was. A little bit at a time," he said. "Around the same time, I was hearing rumors about Marshall, about the money. Roger had backed him up. He told me to my face that there was no money at that dealer's place. And I believed him. Then Marshall went to prison and a few months later, Anna opened this business. They put a ton of money into it. She said Roger just came up with the money from some investment he'd made. Suddenly Roger was magically coming up with money from all kinds of places. It didn't sit right. I felt like he'd made me party to his corruption and it ended our friendship. I couldn't prove he had done anything. I'm not sure I wanted to, but I knew it in my gut and I felt betrayed."

"I thought Ken invested in Anna's business."

"That story came later. And maybe he did, but not initially. I asked Roger about it. He wouldn't say. He didn't tell me that he was in on the theft, but I could see it in his eyes."

"But why? He was supposed to be this great cop."

"I don't know. . . ." He looked at a photo of Roger and Anna on the dresser, one taken in much happier times. "He told me once that seeing the hell I went through when I lost Lizzie made him certain he could never lose Anna. I think he did it for her."

"And she left him anyway," I pointed out. I looked down at Anna's purse on the floor by my foot. I picked it up on a hunch, dumping it on the bed until I found what I was looking for. "I don't think she just left him," I said. "I think she killed him."

CHAPTER 51

"That's ridiculous. They just arrested my husband's killer not ten minutes ago." Anna sat at her kitchen table. Ken stood by her, but he didn't seem all that surprised by my accusation.

It was difficult to explain my theory in front of a room full of police officers and friends of the widow, but once I told Jesse what I believed had happened, he wanted to confront her there and then.

"Marshall wanted the money. He's right. He had no motive to kill Roger until he got it, or at least what's left of it," I said. "Ken had no motive either. You're using him the way you used Roger. They were only in competition for who was the bigger fool. That leaves you."

"If I hadn't been so caught up in protecting Roger's reputation, I would have seen it," Jesse agreed.

I took his hand. "That was the point. That was the reason for the shooting in the street. It was misdirection. Who is the first person you look at when a person is killed? Their spouse. Especially when they're in the middle of a divorce."

The officers and Anna's friends nodded in agreement.

"So Anna had to misdirect. She shot up Main Street so that we'd be looking for a professional. Someone like a fellow cop. Someone like Bob Marshall. She had Ken here give her the means to set up a flash, a way to send Jesse looking down the street instead of looking up."

Ken cleared his throat. "For the record, I didn't know that's what I was doing. I thought she was just getting into magic. It was only after I talked to you last night at the wake that I realized why she had been so interested."

I nodded. I could see by the anger in his eyes, he had been fooled, too. "She also needed to misdirect me," I said, looking at Jesse as I spoke. "So she whispered in my ear about Lizzie. She kept me off balance so that instead of thinking about who killed Roger, all I could think about was how much you loved Lizzie. How you loved her more than me."

"That isn't true, Nell," Jesse said softly.

I squeezed his hand.

Anna rolled her eyes. "That's charming. It still doesn't prove I killed Roger."

"But this does." I put her purse on the table, and dumped its contents. A wallet, lipstick, tissues . . . a pack of cigarettes, and two sets of house keys.

"Those are from my house," Jesse said as he picked up one of the sets of keys. "But you gave me back the set I lent you."

"She did," I said. "These are Roger's keys. The ones he'd had ever since staying with you after Lizzie died. She took them from him after she killed him. She needed to get into your house."

"I didn't go into the house that night." Anna started to say something else but stopped herself.

"Because my car pulled up," I pointed out. "You were nervous. You had just shot your husband. He was already dead, wasn't he?"

Anna didn't answer. She just stared at me.

"You saw me get out of the car. Maybe you thought I saw you. You certainly knew I saw the cigarette smoke."

"That's what you've got on me? Cigarettes and magic tricks? I mean, it's literally smoke and mirrors." She laughed.

"I have one more thing," I said. I looked at Ken. "You know that

Anna would dump you in a heartbeat for someone with more money, don't you?"

He nodded.

"Where did Anna get the money for her design company?"

He looked at her. "From the money Roger stole. About fifty or sixty thousand dollars. Up in smoke as far as I can tell, and then she came after me. I gave her what I could, but I have problems of my own. So she went back to Roger. That's what it's like with her. Roger said he'd give her more money, but she'd have to stay with him. Anna doesn't like being told what to do."

"You jerk," she yelled at Ken, then calmed herself. "I told Roger being married to a cop is nothing but heartbreak."

I smiled. That's why he said it to Carrie. He wasn't warning me of anything, just reliving his own pain.

"So where's the money?" Jesse asked her.

"Don't ask me," she spat. "Roger gave me money in drips. Making sure I'd always need him. He even blamed me for stealing it, can you believe it? Said his love for me had made him weak." She rolled her eyes. "I was sick of it. Sick of him. I tried to find the money, but he found out. Roger was still a good detective, and he was always watching me. Then suddenly, he told me that he couldn't do it anymore; he was going to get the money and give it to me. All of it."

"So why kill him?" Jesse asked.

"I knew Roger better than anyone, and there was something about the way he said it that made me sure he was lying. So I followed him. I figured he was going to grab the money and head off to Mexico or somewhere. But I found him right in front of Jesse's house. And I found out what he was really going to do. He told me he was going to turn himself in to some old buddy of his in vice, John Toomey. Roger said he'd put the money in a safe place, and he was going to tell the police everything. Try to right the wrong, he said. He told me I might be charged as an accessory after the fact.

He said he was sorry about that, but maybe it was better for both of us to get this burden off our chests." She took a long breath. "I wasn't going to prison because of Roger."

Jesse blinked back a few tears, then borrowed a pair of handcuffs from one of the officers. "Yes, Anna, you are," he said.

CHAPTER 52

The bachelor and bachelorette parties were postponed until after the honeymoon so Oliver could rest. Instead, on Thursday night I worked on the double wedding ring quilt for Jesse. I was alone in the shop, and at peace.

I hadn't formally decided to keep it open, and to run it as my own, but I knew that I would. Someday Quilts was my home and my sanctuary. There would be time enough, I told myself, to figure out how I could do it.

I put the last stitch in the quilt just after midnight, left a note for Natalie to quilt it ASAP, and then I locked up. This time I was careful to remember my keys. There would be no more grandma there to rescue me. Eleanor and Oliver were leaving for the new house a week after their honeymoon. They had gotten a scare, and it reminded all of us that life is too short to waste.

I drove to Jesse's house, where he had made dinner. A little over a week had passed since I'd done the same thing. This time the streetlamp was working and there were no unfamiliar cars parked out front.

We still didn't know why Roger had come to Jesse's that night, or where the missing money was—by some estimates more than four hundred thousand of the original sum was unaccounted for—but there were some mysteries that were not mine to solve.

Instead I enjoyed dinner with Jesse and Allie, then went to his computer to work on the slide show of photos for the wedding.

"How do I get these from your desktop to my laptop?" I asked. "It's too big a file to e-mail."

"Use the zip drive you left here when you brought the photos over," he said.

"I didn't leave a zip drive."

Jesse grabbed a blue zip drive from the desk. "This isn't mine," he said.

"It isn't mine, either."

He went white. "You don't think?"

"It must be. Where else could it have came from?"

"He was here," Jesse said. "And he wasn't looking for something. He was leaving me something, just in case. It's been here the whole time. But why wouldn't he leave it somewhere I'd notice it? It could have been here for months. . . ."

"It was right on the keyboard, but I knocked it over," I admitted. "I guess Roger didn't account for my being clumsy."

We opened the zip drive, and just as we suspected it contained one file. "For Jesse." When I tried to open it, I was stopped. "It's asking for a password."

"I don't know what it could be."

We sat and thought, when the words Roger had said to Jesse on the night before his wedding came back to me. "Your secret code," I said.

"Vigiles keep vigil."

I typed it in, my fingers clumsy and nervous. When I clicked "enter," the file opened. On it was a letter.

Jesse. I made a mistake. A bad one. I don't know a more honest cop than you, or a truer friend. I'm going to the police with some information. I talked to a lawyer about all of this and he says I'm probably going to prison for a long time. But in case I don't make it, in case something happens, I want to explain two things.

The money I gave you for Lizzie's hospital bills really was from some stocks I sold. On my honor, if that means anything to you. Check my safe-deposit box for the papers that prove it. I've left the money you've paid me back in a trust for Allie. It's honest money and it shouldn't be mixed up with the rest of my mess.

The other thing is that I've learned true love brings out the best in people, not the worst. You had that kind of love once and I hope you will again. It was my mistake not to see this earlier. I don't know if you'll ever speak to me again, but I want you to know that I've missed you. Roger.

Beneath it was the information for a safe-deposit box and the number of a bank account in the Cayman Islands. As Jesse read the words, tears rolled down his face. Just when he thought he'd lost his friend, he'd found him again.

" I wish—" Jesse started one of those sentences that doesn't need to be finished.

"You found his killer," I told him. "Vigiles keep vigil."

"*You* found his killer," Jesse said.

"We're a great team."

"Jesse kissed my forehead. "Yes, we are, Nell Fitzgerald, in every way."

CHAPTER 53

"Do you, Eleanor, take Oliver to be your lawfully wedded husband as long as you both shall live?" the minister asked.

"I do."

"And do you, Oliver, take Eleanor to be your lawfully wedded wife for as long as you both shall live?"

"I do," he said. "And I intend to be here for a long while."

We all laughed.

"Then I now pronounce you husband and wife. You may kiss your bride."

As Eleanor and Oliver kissed, I looked over at Jesse and felt, for the first time in a long time, sure that I was on the right path with my life. In my career, in the town I chose as my home, and in the man I loved.

✄

At the reception, Greg and Kennette danced, and while he was terrible at it, she didn't seem to care. Dru and Charlie held hands even when it made drinking coffee a little complicated, and my parents snuggled in a corner. Even Barney and Patch stuck together, working on ways to get scraps from the table to the floor and their waiting mouths. But the bride and groom took center stage, laughing and talking, and looking every bit like young lovers about to embark on a wonderful adventure.

There was a lot of talk about the case, of course. Jesse had turned over the zip drive to the New York City police, who found the remaining four hundred thousand. In Roger's safe-deposit box was his will, the papers that proved he had sold stocks when Lizzie was ill, and a digital tape recorder. Shortly after the theft, Roger had taped a conversation he and Marshall had had about the money. It was the second "insurance" policy Anna had mentioned to me that day in the shop. The recording gave police everything they needed to charge Marshall. He was barely out of prison, and he'd be going back for a long time. That fact helped me breathe a little easier.

✄

I wandered into the kitchen and saw Patch and Barney playing together with a ball of tinfoil, batting it back and forth. When Barney would trap it between his paws, Patch would jump to retrieve it and be momentarily trapped there, too. But she didn't mind. She rubbed her body against Barney's fur, and he rubbed his snout against hers. I called Barney's name, but he didn't hear me. Patch did, though. She looked up at me, then swatted Barney. The poor, almost-deaf dog looked over, surprised but happy to see me.

"She's going to be his ears," Eleanor said, sneaking up behind me.

"They do seem inseparable. Which begs the question, are you taking them with you to South Carolina?"

"It would be a lot to ask of old Barney, to adjust to all those new smells and sights. He might be happier here, with you and the town he knows. I don't think he'll miss me too much with you around."

As if he knew what she was saying, Barney got up and buried his face in Eleanor's dress.

"I think he's decided he'd rather move than be without you for half the year."

She kissed his head. "Me too, dear one."

Patch followed Barney to Eleanor's leg, and rubbed against it. It looked like all three of my roommates were heading south for the winter.

✄

After the cake, Eleanor and Oliver got ready to leave for their train trip to Montreal. Susanne, Bernie, Maggie, Natalie, Carrie, and I grabbed the bride and took her upstairs to the sewing room, for the last quilt group meeting that would include all of us—at least until summer.

"We didn't have a chance to give this to you before, because of all the excitement," Maggie said. "So here."

We piled quilt after quilt on her lap. Each of us had chosen a special one from the quilts in our own personal stash, and Eleanor oohed and aahed at each. When she got to my blue and white bow tie, she laughed. "I was going to steal this from you, Nell. And now I don't have to."

Though Eleanor was now nearly covered in quilts, we had one more. On top of the pile, we placed the group quilt we had made.

Eleanor looked at it with amazement, then tears rolled down her face. "I can't pretend I didn't know you were doing something," she said. "I almost peeked a few times under that muslin Natalie had on the frame but . . ." The tears overwhelmed her. "I just had no idea it would be anything as beautiful as this."

Finally I gave her my gazebo quilt. "The first pattern of the new company," she said. "I feel I've inspired an empire."

"A one-woman empire," Natalie noted.

"Funny you should say that." I turned to Susanne. "Susanne, you design your own quilts, don't you?"

"You know I do, Nell."

"Ever thought of making patterns?"

Susanne looked at me, puzzled. "I thought you were going to do that?"

"I don't want to be a one-woman empire."

She looked stunned, then hugged me. "I'd be thrilled. And I was thinking, if I help out at the shop a few days a week, maybe I could get in a few lessons from Natalie on how to use that longarm machine."

Natalie laughed. "You'll have to let me be in charge, Mom."

"I'll help, too," said Maggie. "I'm there nearly every day anyway. Might as well be of some use."

"Carrie and I have a lot of businesses experience," Bernie said, "so we can show you whatever you need. Anytime."

"And Greg told me Kennette's thinking of staying in Archers Rest, now that they've become our latest town romance," Natalie said. "I wonder if she'd like her old job back?"

We talked about what Someday was and what it was turning into. "Just like quilting," Eleanor said. "It builds on tradition, but it keeps up with the times."

We were all about to break into tears when Oliver found us and told Eleanor it was time to go.

I walked them down to the car. My parents had volunteered to drive them to the station just a couple of minutes away. I hugged Oliver tightly.

"See you next week," I said, a tear rolling down my face.

He wiped it away. "We'll have a few days here before the move to South Carolina, so we'll have plenty of time for that. Let us know if you solve any murders while we're gone."

I smiled. "I'll keep you posted." Then it was Eleanor's turn. "You're a married lady again," I said.

"It's funny that it doesn't seem strange," she said. "Seems the most natural thing in the world. But I suppose when something's right . . ."

"I know what you mean." This time I couldn't stop the tears, and neither could she.

"I love you, Nell."

"I love you, too, Grandma."

"Don't mess up the shop while I'm gone."

I laughed. "No promises."

As they drove away, I thought about the day I came to Archers Rest, tired, sad, and feeling very much alone. And now I had a house full of friends, a business to run, a man I loved—and one more quilt to give away.

I went back into the living room and watched the festivities. People were laughing, dancing, helping themselves to a second slice of cake, and sharing a wonderful day. Carrie was doing her best to pile used plates and bring them to the kitchen, but I stopped her.

"I can do that. It's your day off," I said.

"Nonsense. It's what friends do." She looked around and whispered. "Did you hear that Glad Warren's husband went to New York on business Thursday and hasn't been seen or heard from since? I was thinking we could look into it for her, kind of informally. Since it's not really a police investigation at this point, I don't think Jesse would mind."

I laughed. Knowing Glad, her husband had probably just taken a few days to himself for peace and quiet, but on the other hand . . . "Maybe we can get the group together tomorrow to talk over what we know," I said. Eleanor always said it was good to have a hobby. And now that quilting was becoming my profession, I guessed amateur sleuth could move up to become my favorite pastime.

✂

After a while, I snuck into Eleanor's bedroom, where I'd kept the double wedding ring quilt hidden, rolled it up tightly and held it behind my back. I went back downstairs into the reception looking for its new owner.

"Where've you been?" Jesse found me as I was looking for him.

"Looking around, saying good-bye to Eleanor."

"Five days," he said. "It's only five days."

"And then almost five months," I pointed out. "Eleanor's been my only family in town since I moved here."

"We should change that."

I kissed him. "Wait right here."

I left a perplexed Jesse and went searching again. This time for Allie. I found her dancing with my mom and dad.

"Come with me," I said to the little girl.

We went back to her dad, and the three of us stood in a circle, holding hands.

"What's this about?" Jesse wanted to know.

"There's a quilting superstition, or a tradition, I don't remember which. Anyway, if you wrap a newly made quilt around the one you want to marry, you'll be hitched within a year." As I spoke, I unfolded the quilt and wrapped it around Jesse and Allie.

Jesse looked at me, tears in his eyes. "You're really sure?"

"It's a double wedding ring quilt. If that isn't a hint, I don't know what to tell you." I laughed.

"Are you going to marry us?" Allie asked.

"If that's what you want."

Jesse put his arm around my waist and drew me close. "It's the only thing I want," he said.

As Allie ran off to yell the news of our engagement to the crowd, Jesse and I wrapped ourselves tightly in the quilt. For a moment anyway, we were completely alone. Until I heard Maggie say something about designing a wedding quilt for me, and my mom mention a honeymoon in Europe. Everyone came rushing toward us offering congratulations, hugs, and kisses.

Maybe you don't need a quilt to feel surrounded by love.

But it helps.

For more quilting and mystery in Archers Rest, check out
Clare O'Donohue's Someday Quilts Mysteries.

978-0-452-28979-6

978-0-452-29558-2

978-0-452-29642-8

978-0-452-29737-1

And exclusively for your e-reader...

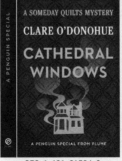

978-1-101-61584-3

PLUME

<u>STREAK OF LIGHTNING</u> – On Sale 7/30
978-1-101-61585-0

Also by Clare O'Donohue:
Kate Conway Mysteries

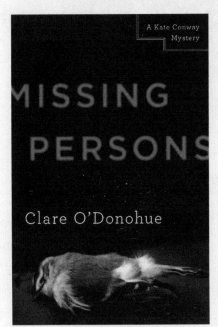

A Kate Conway Mystery

Clare O'Donohue

978-0-452-29782-1

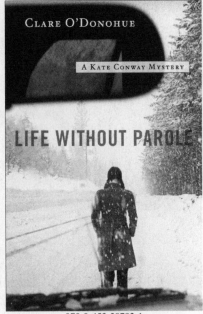

CLARE O'DONOHUE

A KATE CONWAY MYSTERY

LIFE WITHOUT PAROLE

978-0-452-29782-1

"Fascinating characters, multifaceted story lines, and plenty of action."
—*Midwest Book Review*

Available wherever books are sold.

www.clareodonohue.com

PLUME